SIMON451

BOOKS BY NICHOLAS SANSBURY SMITH

THE ORBS SERIES (offered by Simon451/Simon & Schuster)

Solar Storms (An Orbs Prequel)

White Sands (An Orbs Prequel)

Red Sands (An Orbs Prequel)

Orbs

Orbs II: Stranded

Orbs III: Redemption

THE EXTINCTION CYCLE SERIES

Extinction Horizon

Extinction Edge

Extinction Age

Extinction Evolution

Extinction End

Extinction Aftermath

THE HELL DIVERS TRILOGY (offered by Blackstone Publishing)

Hell Divers

Hell Divers II: Ghosts

Hell Divers III: Deliverance

ORBS III

REDEMPTION

NICHOLAS SANSBURY SMITH

SIMON451

New York London Toronto Sydney New Delhi

SIMON451

An Imprint of Simon & Schuster, Inc.
1230 Avenue of the Americas
New York, NY 10020

First Simon451 trade paperback edition August 2016

SIMON & SCHUSTER and colophon are registered trademarks of Simon & Schuster, Inc.

For information about special discounts for bulk purchases, please contact Simon & Schuster Special Sales at 1-866-506-1949 or business@simonandschuster.com.

The Simon & Schuster Speakers Bureau can bring authors to your live event. For more information or to book an event, contact the Simon & Schuster Speakers Bureau at 1-866-248-3049 or visit our website at www.simonspeakers.com.

Interior design by Lewelin Polanco

Manufactured in the United States of America

10 9 8 7 6 5 4 3 2 1

Library of Congress Cataloging-in-Publication Data is available.

ISBN 978-1-5011-3327-5
ISBN 978-1-4767-8897-5 (ebook)

ORBS III: REDEMPTION

CHAPTER 1

CAPTAIN Rick Noble sat silently in his chair, stroking his freshly shaved face with two fingers. He traced a circular pattern across his jawline. The unfamiliar smoothness of his skin felt as foreign to him as the aliens he watched silently creep across the screen hovering above his desk.

The video feed, recorded weeks before their mission to Colorado Springs, was a source of morbid fascination for him. He'd watched it a dozen times now, replaying the film over and over with the hope of learning something new about the aliens. But each time the grainy feed revealed little about the insectlike creatures. And each time he watched one of his soldiers get torn apart, he felt the regret any commander inevitably felt after leading men into battle.

A flash of movement pulled him closer to the screen. The horde of aliens surrounded a single figure. The camera mounted to the chopper had managed to catch the last heroic act of Marine Sergeant Ash Overton.

Noble flinched when the first Spider sank its claws through the marine's matte black armor, but he did not close his eyes—Noble focused on the screen. He owed it to the man. Overton had given his life to save one of his soldiers. Watching the sacrifice filled Noble with strength.

There were still honorable men to fight a merciless army.

The skin on his forearms tingled, goose bumps forming as he remembered his father. The man had been a firm believer that humanity would eventually destroy itself. He had drilled that into Noble's head from a young age. The retired soldier claimed that the end would come sooner rather than later. All that time, Noble thought his father was just another washed-up, paranoid commander. But his father had been right.

He was goddamned right, Noble thought. The corner of his mouth twisted as he recalled what his dad used to say.

The apocalypse will bring out the best and the worst in men. When the horsemen come, you will have to decide what type of man you are and if you will run from the horrors or fight.

Noble turned away from the screen and eyed a picture of his late father.

Like his father, Noble believed that all men were created equal. In war, that meant either side could win. But what if you weren't fighting men? What if the enemy was more advanced and intelligent than his father could ever have imagined?

"What would you do?" he muttered to the photograph. He wished the man were still around to give him advice or to see the real horsemen of the apocalypse. Now he was alone. His father was dead, and so was every other ally he could have counted on in the past. He was the last NTC commander on Earth.

Noble shoved the thought to the side. He had to maintain his focus. He needed to find the enemy's weakness. There had to be a way to fight them.

Glancing back at the monitors he saw the Spiders teeming across the lakebed. They consumed Overton quickly. Even without audio, Noble could imagine the sound of talons puncturing flesh and breaking bone. The grotesque wet *thunk* of every slash echoed in his mind as the feed cut out.

With a sigh, he flicked the screen off and ran his fingers over his jaw once more, back and forth. The images told him nothing he didn't already know. And Overton's death reminded him of all the other men and women they'd lost. Some deaths had been expected, a sad fact of war, but others, like the death of high school history teacher Alex Wagner, were unexpected. It was his suicide that illustrated exactly how dark the world had become.

Noble scanned his office. He needed a drink. Something stiff. Anything that would subdue the memories. As soon as he reached for a bottle of Scotch, his desktop monitor chirped with an incoming message. It felt late, past the normal time for his daily evening briefing. He'd lost track of time watching the video feed from Colorado Springs.

He glanced down at his watch.

1905 hours.

Something must be wrong, Noble thought. His new executive officer, Lt. Commander Richards, was never a second late with any of his reports. The man had proven to be the most punctual member of his crew.

Hesitating, Noble eyed the liquor one last time before hunching over the aged mahogany desk and swiping the screen with his index finger. An image of Richards appeared. The blond stubble covering his young face had grown dangerously close to what one might consider a beard, another unusual characteristic for the officer.

Filling Lt. Commander Lin's shoes would be difficult for anyone, but Richards was struggling. The cramped spaces, the dwindling hope for survival, the death of billions of civilians at the hands of a terrifying alien species, and finally the loss of their one military ally, the Chinese X-9 submarine—the combined pressure was enough to crack the hardest of minds. Considering everything they'd been through, Noble wasn't surprised to see Richards's eyes were glazed over with fatigue and fear.

"Captain, I apologize for the delay but . . ." He paused; the muffled sound of raised voices crackled over the speakers. Richards craned his neck to silence the crew with a raised hand. The officers behind him huddled around the main monitor, staring at something just out of Noble's view.

Turning back to the camera, Richards simply said, "Sir, please report to the bridge. There's something I'd like you to see."

Another series of stifled voices emanated from behind the XO. He turned again, this time focusing on the monitor that Noble couldn't see, and then the feed cut out.

Noble hurried from his quarters. He squeezed past deckhands in the hallway, navigating the halls without offering the courtesy of his typical hello.

Had the Organics found them?

He glanced up at a bank of emergency lights protruding off a bulkhead. Surely Irene, the ship's AI, would have alerted him if the aliens had found them.

Rounding the next corner, he hurried into the hallway beyond. Thick gray pipes ran the length of the ceiling. He eyed them as he ran. Like metal veins, the tubes served as the vessel's lifeblood, carrying various resources throughout the sub. He grabbed one of them to steady himself before ducking into the next corridor. The pipe groaned from the weight of his grip, reminding him that the ship, like a living creature, had a lifespan. They couldn't hide beneath the surface forever.

By the time he reached the last hallway he was out of breath. He slowed and tried to regain his composure as he approached the doors to the CIC. He halted a few feet away from the guard, pausing to straighten his wrinkled uniform with a quick brush.

The guard threw up a quick salute and then swept his keycard over the sensor. The glass panes whisked apart, and Noble strode onto the bridge. He scanned the three-level room from the top floor. A group of officers crowded around the main display at the bottom.

"Captain," came a frantic voice. He glanced over to see his navigation officer, Athena, staring up at him with owlish eyes from her station.

"What the hell is going on?" Noble asked.

Before she could respond, he crossed the metal platform and loped down the ramp to the first floor.

Athena called out after him, but her voice faded against the chirps and beeps of various sensors that echoed through the chamber. The world slowed around him as he walked. His eyes darted from station to station until each console and face became a blur of colors. Several officers on the second level shouted his name as he passed, but he ignored them.

When he reached the bottom deck he finally caught a glimpse of the main display through a gap in the gathered crew. He squinted, standing on his tiptoes for a better look.

"Move," he said, making his way through the crowd. Up near the screen, Richards wore a solemn look, and Noble finally saw why.

The front-facing cameras on the GOA had captured a ghostly image: the body of the X-9 Chinese submarine.

"My God, we've found it," Noble said, studying the outline of the vessel. His awe lasted only briefly before reality set back in. A warning sensor blared behind him.

"Irene, systems check," Noble ordered the Russian AI, rushing over to her interface.

"All systems at one hundred percent, sir."

He looked next to his communications officer, Trish. Noble knew it was a long shot, but held onto a flicker of hope that the crew was still alive. The sub hadn't steered itself to the rendezvous coordinates.

"Have you been able to hail Captain Quan?" Noble asked.

The young woman's voice was cool and calm. "Negative, sir. I've attempted to send messages over the analog channel and through Morse code. So far, nothing."

Noble nodded at her thoughtfully and then paced over to Lt. Richards. "Have our scanners picked up anything?"

The XO flicked his console and squinted. "We are picking up multiple life-forms on the X-9, sir."

"Human?" Noble replied.

"Inconclusive." There was a slight deviation in his voice. "The titanium shell is blocking our readings."

Noble gritted his teeth, letting his frustration show. If the Organics were still aboard the X-9, then he was putting his crew at risk with every passing second. He had to make a decision. "Get our weapons system online. And patch me through to Sergeant Harrington. I want his men prepped and ready to board the X-9 within the hour."

He looked down at his watch.

2000 hours.

He pushed down to turn on the stopwatch function. *Good old-fashioned Swiss engineering,* he thought, *more accurate than any digital timepiece aboard this billion-dollar sub.*

The watch clicked and another mechanical sound instantly followed. Noble saw Irene's ghostly blue hologram flash in his peripheral vision. Her presence meant one thing—she had other plans.

"Captain, I would highly advise against boarding the X-9—"

He raised his hand to silence the AI. "I understand the risk we are taking, Irene. No need to give me the statistics on this one. But I'm not abandoning Captain Quan or Lieutenant Commander Lin again. Not now."

"Sir," Richards whispered.

Noble looked at his XO. The man seemed terrified. And he wasn't the only one. Athena, Trish, and his entire crew stared back at him with the same uncertain looks. He huffed and flared his nostrils out of habit.

Was he doing the right thing? Was the slim chance of finding Lin or anyone else alive on the X-9 worth risking his crew? Especially now, when so much was at stake?

Noble bowed his head in defeat. The men and women of the GOA had already sacrificed so much. And he couldn't jeopardize their new mission of saving the remaining Biospheres. Despite Dr. Hoffman's orders not to interfere, Noble would continue the fight—would continue to ensure the Biospheres survived. They were humanity's last hope on Earth.

Without further thought, he puffed out his chest and said, "Irene, cancel the order to Harrington. Load two Class-4 missiles and prepare to fire on the X-9."

The image of the Russian AI faded without a response.

"No!" a voice yelled from a dim station at the edge of the first floor. Lt. Commander Le from the X-9 stood and raised a hand, his eyes pleading for Noble to reconsider. The captain had been so captivated by the discovery of the X-9 he'd forgotten about Captain Quan's XO.

"Trish, will you translate?"

"Aye, sir." She rose from her chair and made her way over to Le's corner. Noble waited with the rest of his crew in silence as they spoke. A minute later Trish paced over to the helm.

"Sir, he's volunteered to lead a mission with the Chinese Special Forces that came aboard with Captain Quan earlier. He's suggested putting a safe distance between the GOA and the X-9, at which point he will use a mini sub to board and check for survivors."

Noble shot Le a glance. The short officer stared back at him confidently. The X-9 had been his home for more than a decade. Even though remote, there was still a possibility there were survivors.

Noble couldn't take that away from him. And truthfully, the Chinese officer's plan wasn't all that bad. Risking one of the mini subs was better than risking the GOA.

Glancing back down at his wrist, he watched the second hand rotate. Every moment they spent floating idly brought them another dangerous second closer to being discovered by the Organics. He had to make a decision.

"What do you think, Richards?" Noble finally asked.

The young officer ran a hand through the back of his blond hair. Raising one bushy eyebrow, he said, "Worth a shot, I suppose."

Noble cracked a grin. His XO had some fight in him after all.

"Notify Engineering. Tell them I want the mini sub prepped for launch ASAP."

Richards nodded and picked up his headset. "Aye, sir."

CHAPTER 2

SERGEANT Harrington worked off a simple principle—always do the right thing. A devout Methodist, he relied heavily on his faith to guide him. At forty-five, he had spent a majority of his life and career following this code. With a wife of twenty years and two adult daughters, living up to these self-imposed expectations hadn't always been easy. And the newest request from Command was the perfect example of why.

As he stared into the vehicle depot and watched Commander Le gear up with several other Chinese soldiers, he wasn't sure what to do. The chances of finding anyone alive aboard the Chinese sub were slim. He'd seen the video of glowing, snakelike aliens covering the massive submarine. He'd heard the transmissions, the screams, and the gunfire.

Yet the sergeant still held out hope. Like any good soldier, the trait was ingrained inside him. Without hope, what was there to fight for?

Clenching the cold metal railing of the walkway overlooking the vehicle depot, Harrington watched the team of Chinese soldiers below. The commander slipped into his armored suit with graceful precision. The other Chinese soldiers followed his lead, climbing into their light-blue armor. With their oval-shaped helmets, life support systems, and tinted visors, they looked like they were about to walk on Mars, not board a submarine.

Harrington sighed. He couldn't let them go alone. Not just the four of them. Bringing a hand to his headset, he said, "Lieutenant Diego, feel like taking a swim?"

White noise filled the private channel he'd opened to his second in command.

"Not particularly," the younger man replied seconds later.

"Me either, but I don't feel right about letting Le go without our support."

Diego groaned over the channel. "I was afraid you were going to say that. All right. I guess I'm in. That should be the max we can fit in the mini sub."

"Copy that. Suit up and I'll meet you in the launch area in fifteen. I'll inform Captain Noble." Harrington clenched his jaw. "Oh, and John?"

"Sir?"

"Thanks. It will be nice to have a friendly face with me on this one."

"You know I have your back, sir."

Harrington smiled and loosened his grip on the metal railing. He flashed a thumbs-up to Le, who watched from below. The Chinese soldier gave one back and marched his team to the launch bay.

When they disappeared from view, Harrington opened a private channel to Command. "Captain Noble, this is Harrington."

"Roger, Harrington, report."

"Diego and I are going to join Le and his men."

"I figured you would if you had the chance."

"Aye, sir. I will keep you apprised. Over."

"Wait."

Harrington listened to static flicker over the channel for several awkward seconds before the captain finally found the words.

"Harrington, don't take any unnecessary risks. The GOA can't afford to lose you. You're the best damn soldier on this ship. We may not be able to see those monsters now, but I'm sure they are out there somewhere," Noble warned.

"They won't get the drop on us," Harrington said confidently.

"Good luck, Sergeant."

"Thank you, sir," Harrington said. He released his grip on the railing and scanned the room one more time. A dying LED blinked in the corner of the cargo bay. The sporadic blue glow illuminated the shadows under the *Sea Serpent* gunship, reminding Harrington of the alien creatures he'd encountered in Colorado Springs. For a moment he felt the deep tug of fear in his gut and wondered what he would find when they opened the air lock to the X-9. The captain was more than likely right. The Organics were out there.

Waiting.

———————

A bank of overhead LEDs sparkled in the water around the black mini sub. The vessel was partially submerged in Cargo Bay 1. Up close, the sub looked much smaller than Harrington remembered.

His earpiece came alive as he walked across the metal platform, Irene's smooth Russian accent spouting off data. Harrington ignored her and paced around the outside of the sub. From his vantage point he couldn't see any portholes, only the smooth black surface and an emblem that read *Destiny 1*.

He made his way around the backside and studied the oval-shaped acrylic observation window. Through the glass he could see a panel of manual controls and buttons; some that had to be over twenty years old. Despite her age, she looked strong. The acrylic glass was thick and the titanium plates on the outside were solid.

"Engineering says she's ready to go," Diego said over a private channel. He came up behind the sergeant and patted the sub's exterior; the metallic clanking echoed through the chamber.

Harrington gave the younger soldier a once-over. His matte black armor appeared polished, and his visor was so clear he could see Diego's handlebar mustache. It was at an odd angle, twisted to the right.

"Feeling all right?" Harrington asked when he saw Diego biting his bottom lip.

"Yeah. Just a bit nervous."

Harrington nodded. The man had every right to be nervous. Shit, he was nervous, too, and he'd seen some horrible things in his seventeen years as a soldier. They were seven hundred feet beneath the ocean's surface, hiding from an advanced alien race that had successfully wiped out over 95 percent of the world's population in just a few months.

NTC was outnumbered, outgunned, and on the run—another reason it was so important to save anyone who might be left aboard the X-9.

Diego slung the strap of his pulse rifle over his shoulder and followed an engineer in fiery-red coveralls to the other side of the platform, where Commander Le's team stood waiting. Their automatic helmet lights had clicked on in the dimly lit space, and for a second the group reminded Harrington of an astronaut team.

The engineer stopped in front of the group and stepped toward them nervously, a trail of sweat bleeding from his receding hairline. He grabbed the handle of the mini sub's steel door and struggled to open it. One of the Chinese soldiers offered his assistance and the mechanism unlocked with a groan.

The man in red coveralls wiped his forehead with his sleeve and spun to look at the group. After he took control of his labored breathing he said, "Gentlemen, you are about to board *Destiny 1*. Make no mistake, this mini sub was not meant to carry passengers. She was designed as a research vessel, and NTC commandeered her for that purpose only. But due to our current depth, we can't use any of the other submersibles."

"Is this shit safe?" Diego blurted.

"We wouldn't send you out there in something that wasn't," the engineer said curtly.

"Of course," Harrington added. "Commander Le, after you," he said, gesturing with his armored hand to the port door.

Inside, the mini sub reeked of mold. Harrington could smell it through the cheap plastic breathing apparatus built into his helmet. He squirmed through the opening, the smell hitting him as soon as he ducked into the cramped main compartment.

Taking a step into the sub, his foot splashed in a puddle of stale water. He hesitated in the doorway, glancing back at the engineer. "I thought you said this thing was safe. Looks like it has a leak."

The man shrugged and pulled his arm across his forehead again. "If Engineering said it's good to go, then it's good to go."

Harrington snorted and moved to the last two empty seats in the back. Irene's voice filled his earpiece as he ducked under a metal pipe snaking across the ceiling.

"All life support systems at one hundred percent. Prepare to disembark," the AI said.

"Good luck," the engineer said. He swung the massive steel door shut behind them. There was a loud thud and a metallic clicking as the door's automatic locking mechanism kicked in.

Harrington settled into his seat, waiting for Irene to activate the sub's systems. Seconds later her voice emerged over the cabin's speakers.

"Be advised, *Destiny 1* will be ready in T minus thirty seconds."

A shallow rumbling vibrated through the metal walls as the engines flared to life. Harrington twisted his helmet so he could see out the port window. He flinched when the hissing started. Seconds later the sub shook again and he could hear a faint splashing sound.

"Descending," Irene said over the com.

Harrington watched several of the Chinese soldiers reaching for grab bars that hung from the metal ceiling. They had to be more nervous, not understanding English. They were counting on Le, who seemed to have a very limited knowledge of it himself, to relay information.

The hissing grew louder and a trail of large bubbles rose outside the port window. Within seconds, the floor of the GOA's Cargo Bay 1 disappeared and the vast darkness of the ocean consumed them.

A pair of overhead lights flicked on automatically. Warm red light filled the compartment.

"*Destiny 1* now in open water," Irene said. "Activating exterior lights."

An audible click echoed through the sub's interior and two beams of white light tore through the darkness. "Descending at one hundred feet per minute." The AI's undeviating voice normally sounded calming to Harrington, but the black depths of the ocean made him uneasy. Even with the rays of artificial light guiding them, he felt nervous. The metal box surrounding him felt more like a coffin than a vehicle. Harrington focused on Irene's voice.

"In three hundred feet you will stop at the edge of an underwater trench, where I will deactivate autopilot and manually steer the *Destiny 1* along the ravine until you reach the X-9."

The very mention of an underwater trench sent chills down Harrington's legs. He'd read that some of them were miles deep, with molten rock spewing from cracks in the Earth's crust. Odd creatures lived there. Strange bacteria and alien-looking fish. Things he'd seen only in documentaries.

It made him wonder if perhaps the Organics had come from somewhere similar, in some other galaxy or universe, or God knew where. It wasn't Harrington's job to question where they came from—his job was simply to kill them.

The sub lurched forward. Besides the intermittent vibration in the walls and the random bump, there was virtually no other sense of motion. Microscopic flakes that looked like dust floated by the filthy porthole windows.

His stomach tightened. His lunch of mashed potatoes and salted pork had seemed like a good idea at the time, but now he felt heavy. Not exactly the way he wanted to start a mission.

In an attempt to suppress the growing nausea he focused on compartmentalizing the task ahead. Without a solid briefing, he had no idea what they were going to face aboard the X-9. The thought terrified him. He couldn't remember a time when he had absolutely no intel before embarking on a life-threatening mission. When he had been Diego's age, he would have been shitting his pants.

You volunteered for this, Harrington reminded himself. He closed his eyes and focused on his family. He knew they were dead. He'd accepted this a week into the invasion. But his faith led him to believe that he would see his family again, probably sooner than later, in the afterlife. He wanted to make his family proud before he saw them again.

"Eight hundred fifty feet," Irene said.

Diego nudged Harrington's leg and gestured with his chin over to the porthole. The exterior lights had gone dark, and Irene had cut the interior LEDs to a single panel.

"Why are we going dark?" Diego asked.

"Must be getting close."

Diego nodded and bowed his head.

Harrington had watched the solider turn into a man over the past five years. They'd lived and fought next to each other, and over time he'd shared his religious beliefs with the younger man. Watching him pray brought Harrington great satisfaction.

He turned away from the porthole and blinked his infrared on. His HUD fired up and the other soldiers' heat signatures emerged on his display. Next he checked his night vision.

With his HUD working properly, he relaxed a bit. But the moment he let his guard down, the sound of emergency sirens startled him back to reality.

"Warning. Warning. Brace for impact," Irene said.

"The X-9?" Diego asked.

Harrington grabbed for a handhold and tightened the harness around his armor. "Hold on!"

The sub jolted. There was a hollow thud and then a grinding sound as the bottom dragged along the ocean floor. A sickening crunch followed; the sub had collided with something, sending a violent tremor through the metal walls. Harrington tightened his grip on the grab bar and fought to stay upright. He spied a cloud of sediment churning outside the cockpit that looked like a small green tornado on his HUD.

He eyed the fist-sized bolts that secured the glass to the walls. They looked strong enough, but even a microscopic leak could turn *Destiny 1* into a two-ton coffin.

"Irene, what the hell is going on?" Diego shouted over the com.

Several of the Chinese soldiers turned in Harrington's direction. He held up a hand to calm them.

"My apologies, my system's autopilot misjudged the descent. Preliminary scans are reporting limited damage," Irene said.

"Limited damage?" Diego replied. His voice began to get louder. "You just crashed us one thousand feet below the surface!"

Harrington chinned his com pad and opened a private channel to Diego. "Get a fucking grip and calm down. You're not helping anything."

Diego nodded and bowed his helmet toward the floor for a second time.

"Irene, how far are we from the X-9?" Harrington asked.

"Sir, you are still two klicks to the south. Please switch on your

NVG if you haven't already. You should be able to see the X-9 in T minus five minutes." She repeated the request in Chinese.

"Did you pick up on that, Commander Le?" Harrington asked. He wasn't sure if the slight nod from Le's helmet was an acknowledgment, but the sergeant didn't press the point.

The sub loped forward, and the sediment that had stirred around them vanished in a cloud of bubbles. Within seconds Harrington could hear the vibration of the motors somewhere beneath the tiny sub's hull.

"T minus four minutes," Irene said.

Squinting, Harrington scanned the green shapes of the ocean floor on his HUD. The terrain to their right looked rough, with hunks of rock protruding from the muddy surface. On their left they followed the trench Irene had described earlier. The channel, which looked to be about one hundred meters across, snaked away as far as he could see. It reminded him of a black river. The sight chilled Harrington, and he wondered what lived in the inky darkness below.

White noise crackled over the com and Irene said, "Two minutes. Visual imminent."

Diego fidgeted. Harrington couldn't blame the younger man for being nervous when his own heart was galloping. In an effort to calm his nerves, he mentally counted the seconds. This was a little trick his commanding officer had taught him years ago. And it usually worked.

Scanning the seafloor, he still didn't see any sign of the X-9. Just the same slopes of uneven seabed.

Harrington kept counting, scrutinizing the ocean floor for any sign of human engineering.

"There," Diego whispered, pointing.

The sergeant followed the man's finger to a curved outline that formed a perfectly oval shape, much too perfect to be part of the seabed.

As the *Destiny 1* puttered closer, the Chinese submarine came into view. The bow had disappeared deep into the muddy surface, but the body of the sub still looked to be fully intact. There were no visual cracks or exterior damage.

"My God," Diego said in a hushed voice.

Before Harrington had a chance to reply, something smashed into the cockpit. The chirp of warning sirens and the intermittent flash of red lights spilled over the compartment. He swallowed hard and spied an object spinning away from the window.

"What the hell was that, Irene?" Harrington shouted.

"Scanning."

Unbuckling his harness, Harrington crouch-walked to the front of the vessel. Blinking on his infrared vision, he scanned the darkness for any sign of life.

"*Destiny 1* made contact with a—"

"We see it," Harrington said, forcing his eyes away from the floating corpse of one of Captain Quan's crew. He returned to his seat and took in long measured breaths, trying to maintain his composure.

"Xi," one of the Chinese soldiers shouted from the front of the sub, pointing at a body floating by the nearest porthole. The man struggled with his harness, but Commander Le stopped him, restraining him with the help of another soldier.

From across the aisle Harrington could see more corpses floating by. There were dozens of them. He focused on one of them, noticing something odd. The bodies had been decomposing for a while. Most were missing eyeballs and chunks of flesh, but that didn't explain their shriveled skin. They looked like something had sucked them dry. Fish weren't the only creatures that had fed, the Organics had as well.

The sergeant shivered at the sight. The corpses were just sacks of skin now, their bones weighing them down as they drifted in the abyss.

"We're in a fucking graveyard," Diego blurted over the private channel. "GOA didn't pick this up with its sensors?"

"They're dead. All of them. Sensors pick up the living," Harrington replied grimly.

A new voice crackled over the main speakers. It was Captain Noble.

"Commander Le. Is everyone okay down there?"

"Okay," Le replied.

"Sir, there are bodies everywhere," Harrington added.

"I'm watching a live feed. I'm well aware," Noble said. "Sensors are still picking up heat signatures inside the X-9, so I am going to leave this one up to Commander Le. This is his mission."

Harrington saw Diego fidget in his seat again, but held up his hand to silence him before he could object. The captain was right. And they had volunteered. The decision was not theirs to make.

Silence washed over the dark compartment as Le spoke to his men in Chinese. Harrington quickly gave up trying to make out what they were saying. He already knew what Le's decision was.

A beat later and Irene was back online. But Harrington was hardly listening to her. Closing his eyes, he prepared himself for what was to come.

"Prepare to dock in T minus two minutes," Irene ordered.

CHAPTER 3

Dr. Emanuel Rodriguez ran a hand through two weeks' worth of facial hair and watched Dr. Sophie Winston sleep. *She's been so tired,* he thought.

"Alexia. How long has she been out?" he whispered.

The AI mimicked the volume of his voice. "Approximately twelve hours, Doctor. Would you like me to wake her?"

Emanuel waved his hands. "No, absolutely not." Sophie began to stir. She awoke with one eye open, gripping her back with one hand.

"Oh my god," she moaned. "I feel like . . . like I just got run over by a Humvee," she said with one of her eyes still closed. "And . . ." A sudden alertness streaked across her face. Emanuel knew right away she had remembered something from one of her dreams.

"Sophie?" he asked.

She removed her hand from her back and placed it on her forehead, whispering, "They came for me again."

"The Organics' leaders?" Alexia asked.

Sophie nodded and lay her head back down on the pillow, letting her frustration out with a long sigh. "I'm never able to communicate with them."

The AI console glowed a light blue, and Alexia's face emerged. "Doctor Winston, the multidimensional aliens are likely so far advanced that they do not communicate in ways you would recognize."

"I know," Sophie said.

"Alexia, let's give her a break. I'm going to go grab a coffee, Sophie. Do you want your usual?" He realized she was staring at him. His cheeks grew warm when it occurred to him she was scrutinizing his beard.

"Not a bad look," she said, her face still stern.

"You didn't notice it before?"

She shrugged and said, "Need coffee."

Emanuel nodded and hurried to the mess hall. On his way he heard what sounded like an unsupervised field trip. Sure enough, when he walked into the hallway leading to Biome 4, he passed Dr. Brown and Corporal Bouma. Behind them ran three screaming children. Emanuel immediately brought a finger to his lips.

"Quiet, guys. Smith is still sleeping, and Sophie is *not* in a good mood."

"Sorry," Bouma replied. "We were just heading to Biome 1 so the kids could get some exercise."

Emanuel scanned the group. After two months inside the Biosphere the kids were starting to grow. It dawned on him that they all needed haircuts. Especially Owen. His hair had started to creep down over his eyes.

"Have fun," Emanuel said, patting the boy on his head. Owen laughed and took off running, ignoring the request the biologist had made moments before.

Emanuel continued to the kitchen, where half a pot of cold coffee sat on a stainless steel countertop. A dozen wrappers from prepackaged meals littered the area.

"Damn it," he said, grabbing a handful and tossing them into the trash. Things had slowly slipped into chaos after Sophie's injury in Colorado Springs. The Biosphere had gone from a well-oiled machine to a disaster zone.

He shook his head. After he got Sophie on her feet they were going to have a team meeting. A very frank one.

Two hours later, Emanuel had fed Sophie enough caffeine to get her into the CIC. The main oval display at the front of the room replayed hours of information the AI had filtered through. With the magnetic disturbance outside, most of the Biosphere's exterior sensors were down. But the AI was much more resourceful than Emanuel had given her credit for. A few days earlier, she had discovered an NTC stealth satellite prototype named Lolo orbiting the planet. Lolo's feeds proved that the Organics hadn't knocked out all of Earth's defenses after all. By hacking into the satellite, Alexia had provided the team with mountains of new data including current ocean levels, average temperatures from around the world, and estimated population counts.

But Emanuel was nervous. He still hadn't figured out exactly how the satellite had managed to mitigate the effects of the magnetic disturbance, and the concern that Lolo would go offline was very real. Emanuel wanted to collect as much data as quickly as possible before that happened. For now, he was happy to have some reliable data from outside the Biosphere.

That didn't mean he was excited to share it with Sophie, though. He'd spent the morning crunching the numbers while she slept. The data confirmed that the situation outside had never been worse.

"Feeling any better?" he asked as Sophie sat in one of the chairs facing the display.

"After water, coffee is the second most important resource left. I'm not sure what I'll do when it runs out."

Emanuel removed his glasses and cleared his throat. "Chances are we won't be around long enough to see that happen."

Sophie put her cup down. "You've analyzed the intel from Lolo, haven't you?"

He nodded and rubbed his eyes. "The Pacific Ocean has lost forty percent of its volume in the past two months, while the Atlantic has lost over sixty percent. There is virtually no sign of any fresh water," he said. "Temperatures are skyrocketing worldwide. The planet is turning into a desert. If we don't do something soon—"

She traced the outline of an explosion with her hands and then puffed her lips out. "Boom," she said, exhaling a breath. Then she turned back to the display as if nothing had happened—as if she already knew everything Emanuel had just told her.

"This doesn't bother you?"

Sophie looked past him, staring at the blank AI console in the corner of the room. Something about her had changed since the day they lost Sergeant Overton—the day she believed she had seen the Organics' leaders inside the black ship. He knew it would only get worse. He was slowly losing her. She was fading right before his eyes.

"Sophie?" he asked, reaching out to touch her arm. She flinched and closed her eyes. Then she turned back to the main display.

"What do you make of this?" Sophie finally asked, pointing to a clump of numbers scrolling across the screen.

Emanuel put his glasses back on and leaned over for a better look. "Looks like some sort of encoded message."

```
35084198106649246 33356308117410873
2794660982458366 4113709395892082
2566388250755238 115436431486
36651911140466001 494200007570000
```

Alexia's voice blared over the com. "Doctor Winston, a preliminary scan reveals these are coordinates for the following locations in the United States: Kirtland Air Force Base in Albuquerque, New Mexico, Camp Pendleton in California, MacDill Air Force Base in Tampa, Florida, and Offutt Air Force Base in Omaha, Nebraska. They are also coordinates from locations around the world including USN Bahrain, USN Camp Lemonnier Djibouti, MCB Camp Butler Okinawa, and Ramstein Air Base in Germany."

"Do you think this might be some sort of SOS?" Emanuel asked.

"That's very likely, Doctor. They all originate from military bases. However, their activation dates are all from the first day of the invasion. It's likely that everyone at those bases is already dead."

Emanuel shot Sophie an anxious look. He felt like pounding his fist against the table. Just when he had hope of finding more survivors, it was stripped away.

"One moment," Alexia said suddenly. A second later her voice surged through the speakers. "After scanning the activation dates a second time, it's come to my attention that one of them is actually quite recent."

"How recent?" Emanuel and Sophie asked simultaneously. Neither of them laughed at the coincidence.

"Two days ago," Alexia said. "At Offutt Air Force Base in Omaha, Nebraska."

"I'll be damned," Emanuel replied. "You better get in touch with Captain Noble, Sophie."

"That would be redundant," Alexia said.

Sophie narrowed her eyebrows. "What? Why?"

"Captain Noble sent this data to me over the encrypted uplink earlier this morning."

"I thought this was satellite data!" Emanuel said, his irritation with the AI growing by the second. "When were you going to tell us?"

"My apologies, Doctor. I've been primarily focused on another task this morning."

"Something more important than this?" Sophie asked.

"That would depend on what you consider important. If you consider the life, health, and safety of the team important, then the answer is yes."

Emanuel glared at the AI console. "Again, something you should have told us?"

"I was waiting for a full analysis and for Doctor Winston to awaken."

Sophie took a long swig of coffee. "I'm awake," she said. "And I'm waiting. So spill it."

"I'm still piecing together all the intel, but take a look at this."

The coordinates faded into darkness. Then several blurry images emerged.

"Magnifying," Alexia said.

Emanuel removed his glasses and used his sleeve to wipe off a smear. He put them back on and straightened them, squinting at the monitor. At first glance the shot appeared to be of an arid region. But as Alexia magnified it, he saw clusters of buildings against the stark tan landscape, skyscrapers even.

Was it possible?

"This is Tokyo. One of the first areas hit by the invasion. As you can see, the city is surrounded by a desert," Alexia said. "Next is New York."

The Statue of Liberty emerged on the display. Alexia had zoomed in so that Emanuel could see dried clumps of seaweed and the corpses of rotting fish strewn across the seafloor. The polluted waters of Upper New York Bay no longer surrounded the green symbol of American freedom.

"Here is an image of the actual migration," Alexia said.

A horde of blue aliens lit up the display. They moved across the cracked earth in one solid, roiling mass.

"Where is this?" Sophie asked.

"Upstate New York. The precise location is on the outskirts of a town called Hector. Preinvasion population 9,944."

"That can't be," Emanuel replied. "Check again. That's in the middle of a forest."

"Doctor Rodriguez," Alexia quickly said, "the satellite is one hundred percent accurate."

"Check again," he griped. He held a hand to his head, but knew the AI was right. He had to accept that things were now worse than he thought.

Alexia's voice transferred to the com. "Satellite images show the Organics are migrating. On every continent, they're moving toward the oceans. I've concluded the aliens are beginning to exhaust their resources on land and are now heading to the oceans to complete the last phase of the invasion."

The end of the AI's sentence struck Emanuel hard. He felt like the air had been sucked out of the room. He had known the end would come, but not this fast, and not like this. He'd had no time to prepare.

"How much time do we have before they reach the oceans?" he asked.

"A couple of weeks. Maybe a month. They don't seem to rest. They just keep going."

Emanuel felt his frustration bubble over. He slammed his hand down on the desk. "When Lolo picks up the GOA's signal again, get us a line to Captain Noble."

David and Jeff lay in the dirt of Biome 1, their stomachs full of fresh fruit and the few vegetables Jeff had demanded they eat. With their hands cupped behind their heads they gazed up at the white ceiling, listening to the hum of the air handling units.

Closing his eyes, Jeff relaxed and licked his lips. He let out a burp.

David chuckled. "Good one."

Jeff glanced over at his brother. David's features were strained, his cheeks puffing as he tried to mimic his brother's action. His face grew red and finally he let out a defeated sigh. Resting his head back in the dirt, David grew silent.

"How did Sergeant Overton die?" David asked a few minutes later.

Jeff rolled to his side.

David glanced over, searching his brother's face for an answer. "Did he die like Dad did?"

"Yes," Jeff replied. "He died saving that marine, just like Dad saved us."

"So he fought the aliens?"

"Lots of them. Hundreds."

David let out a gasp of awe. "Wow."

"Someday we'll face them like that."

"What do you mean?"

Jeff sat up and brushed the dirt off the back of his neck and out of his hair. "Look around you. This place won't last forever. They've found us before, and they will find us again. All we can do now is train to fight like the marines do. It's our only shot."

David sat up and crossed his arms around his knees, pulling them to his chest.

"David?" Jeff asked, reaching over to pat his brother's back.

"I'm scared," he said.

"I'm scared, too. But you trust me, right? I mean, we survived at White Sands. We made it here."

David slowly nodded. "Yeah, I guess."

"Good. Because I won't let anything happen to you." The promise was one that Jeff had made before and one he fully intended to keep. If it came down to it, he would give his life to save his brother's.

Jeff eyed an apple that had fallen a few feet away. He grabbed it and tossed it into the air, catching it with a swift motion. "Still hungry?"

David nodded and then smiled. "How many apples do you think are left in the world?"

"In the entire world?" Jeff held the red fruit out in front of him, examining the shiny surface. Like most everything in the biome, the apple was fragile. It would never survive outside, and he was pretty sure there weren't many trees left—maybe just the one behind them.

Jeff stood and tossed the apple in the air again. "This could be the last tree."

David joined him. He stood on his tiptoes, reached for an apple dangling off one of the nearest branches, and missed. David let out a sigh on the third pass and looked to his brother.

Chuckling, Jeff handed him the apple in his right hand. He watched David's teeth sink into the ripe fruit, the juices sliding down his chin. Then he passed it to Jeff for a bite.

They stood there under the canopy of branches, chewing on what very well could have been one of the last apples on the planet.

CHAPTER 4

THE sound of grinding metal echoed inside the mini sub. Harrington glanced through one of the side portholes and saw the smooth black surface of the X-9. The emergency lights dimmed, and complete darkness carpeted the interior of *Destiny 1* as Irene steered them into position.

"Securing air lock," Irene said against the background of hissing air.

Harrington rested his back against one of the titanium walls, unstrapped his pulse rifle, and waited for the all-clear from Irene.

"Air lock is open, proceed to the decompression chamber," she said moments later.

With the help of one of his men, Commander Le twisted the circular lock on the hatch. The door cracked open with a loud pop.

Harrington leveled his gun at the doorway and waited to enter the bowels of the Chinese sub.

"Keep radio chatter to a minimum," he said, raising a single finger to his helmet.

Le nodded and climbed through the open hatch. His men followed in turn. When Diego was on deck he looked to Harrington and gave him the bird.

The gesture put Harrington at ease for a moment. He chuckled, shook his head, and grabbed the handhold.

The rest of the team stood waiting, bottlenecked in a space only twelve feet in diameter. With little room to move, their armored suits clanged nosily against one another. If it weren't for their night vision, the team would have been completely blind. Not exactly the ideal situation when entering potentially hostile territory over nine hundred feet beneath the ocean's surface. Fortunately, NTC engineers had spent time perfecting the suit so it worked at all depths.

And thank God for that, he thought. The X-9's subsequent compartments would likely be flooded. Irene would be able to determine that as they made their way from chamber to chamber in search of survivors.

A hiss of air broke through the opening in the next hatch. Le opened the door slowly and aimed his rifle through the gap. For several seconds the team crouched in silence, waiting. The intermittent creaks and groans from the metal hull echoed through space.

With a quick flash of his right hand Le ordered the men forward. They entered the submarine in single file, motions smooth and calculated despite the bulkiness of their suits.

Harrington swept his rifle across the hallway of the sub's outdated interior. Metal pipes lined the ceiling, their paint chipped and faded. Large control panels with oversize buttons protruded from the walls around them. Compared to the GOA, the X-9 looked ancient.

When they came up on the first bulkhead Harrington saw they would need to split up. The hallway curved into two separate corridors.

Le was thinking the same thing. After checking the passages he divided the group into strike teams with a few quick hand signals. Harrington led Diego and one of the Chinese soldiers to the hallway on the left.

Within seconds the footfalls of Le's men faded away.

Approaching the next bulkhead, Harrington shouldered his rifle and took in a measured breath. Around the corner he saw the first signs of struggle.

Large holes peppered the ceiling. Harrington balled his hand into a fist and stopped abruptly. Slinging his rifle behind his back, he examined what appeared to be bullet holes from a high-caliber pulse gun.

He took a step to his right directly under one of them. A gooey substance dripped from the ceiling. He flinched when a drop fell on his visor.

"What the hell?" He wiped off the glass with a quick swipe. "Turn off your NVG," he ordered.

Setting his helmet light to low, he examined the substance.

"Blood?" Diego asked.

Harrington bowed his head and shined the light directly onto his gloved hand. He fanned out his fingers, revealing cobwebs of blue goo.

"Yeah," Harrington replied. "But not human."

"So where are all the bodies?" Diego asked.

Harrington shook his head and in a mild voice whispered, "I don't know."

They continued down the hall. Several more clusters of bullet holes pockmarked the walls and ceilings. The deeper they ventured, the more his hope began to slip away.

A steel door sealed off the next bulkhead. He stopped and shone his light up and down the door, revealing red smears across the surface.

With no sign of bodies, he knew that whoever had fired off the pulse rounds had likely closed the door in a last-ditch effort.

He blinked on his infrared and scanned the corridor.

Holy fuck!

"You getting this, Diego?"

Harrington heard the clank of an armored hand hitting his shoulder, but he didn't balk. He stared at the steel door, watching the red heat signatures on the other side dance across his display.

"Human?" Diego asked.

The sergeant didn't reply. He didn't have an answer. The outlines looked human, but how the hell was he supposed to know? Whatever they were, they were stuck in the corridor beyond.

Chinning the com link inside his helmet, Harrington opened a line to the team and said, "Commander Le, do you read? Over."

White noised filled the net.

"Commander Le, report. Over." Harrington repeated.

More static. Was it possible that the thick steel walls were interfering with their connection? Harrington had a hard time believing it. The radios were designed to work under just such circumstances.

"Shit," he muttered. He chinned the com again, this time opening a direct link to the GOA. "Captain Noble, do you copy?"

"Roger, go ahead," Noble replied.

"Sir, we have lost contact with Commander Le, and have spotted contacts on the other side of a bulkhead at"—he paused to read the marking above the door and snorted when he saw a Chinese label— "Not sure where we're at, actually. Please advise. Over."

"Can you confirm there are human survivors?"

"Negative, sir."

Another brief pause filled the net with crackling static. For a second Harrington thought he had lost his connection to the GOA, but Noble's voice quickly reemerged. "Priority is given—"

An abrupt, deep hammering from the other side of the steel door vibrated through the walls. Harrington stumbled backward into Diego, nearly knocking the man to the floor. They froze, listening in horror.

"Report, Sergeant," Noble said. "What the hell was that sound?"

"Sir, whatever is on the other side of that door is not—" Before he could finish his thought another blast hit the door, sending a tremor down the entire passage.

Harrington retreated several more steps and raised his pulse rifle to the door. Three heat signatures had clustered behind the bulkhead and now he could see their shapes clearly. They were snakelike, with no signs of arms or legs.

Someone from the X-9 had trapped the creatures in the corridor, but they wouldn't stay there for long. They smashed against the door again. It was only a matter of time before they tore the steel apart. Harrington eyed several deep dents already showing through the metal where the aliens had rammed it.

"Move!" he yelled, finally snapping into action. He pushed Diego after the Chinese soldier, who was already running.

He flinched at the distant crackle of gunfire. His earpiece came to life with the muffled voices of Le's men.

No longer worried about stealth, Harrington rounded the first hallway, nearly crashing into the wall. They were halfway back to the air lock in less than a minute. Behind him he could make out the distant hammering of the trapped aliens as they worked desperately to get out.

"Commander Le, goddamnit, do you read?" Harrington yelled. Cursing, he tried to ignore the sounds. Between the gunfire and the screams he could hardly think, let alone decipher any of the voices coming over the net.

When he reached the end of the hallway he finally made out two of the words.

"Destiny 1."

That's where Le was heading.

The feed cut out as they rounded the next corner. Metal crunched in the passage behind them as the aliens finally broke through the steel door. A loud thud reverberated through the vessel as the bulkhead hit the floor.

Harrington didn't dare risk a glance over his shoulder. Even with a head start, he knew they had only seconds to get back to the air lock. Bowing his head, he ran as hard as he could, passing both Diego and the Chinese soldier.

When he glanced up, the air lock was in view. His heart climbed to his throat when he saw three of the men lying outside the entrance. Blinking off his NVGs he narrowed his eyes and saw Le's team struggling beneath the weight of the aliens pinning them down.

His heart rate skyrocketed as the snakelike aliens came into focus. Their bioluminescent bodies yielded just enough light for Harrington to make out the Organics perfectly. The one closest to him was curled into an S shape, with the tail of its elongated body wrapped around the armored legs of one of Le's men. As it unwound itself, its midsection opened, revealing a cavity filled with jagged black teeth. In one swift motion the creature's torso expanded and clamped down on the soldier.

Blood exploded into the air, a red mist peppering the hallway like spray paint.

"My god," Harrington whispered. He slowed to a stop, nearly tripping over his boots, raised his rifle, and fired off a volley of shots at the monsters.

He moved methodically, squeezing off a three-round burst into the thickest portion of the closest alien. The creature disappeared into a cloud of blue goo. Their shields were down. "Open fire," he yelled. He pulled down on the trigger again and watched the next snakelike creature explode.

The last alien let out a high-pitched shriek right before Diego turned it into a blue smoothie, but there was no time to celebrate. Behind them the screeches were growing louder.

They're getting closer.

Harrington twisted to see five of the creatures slither around the last corner. They shot down the corridor. He hesitated for a second, studying their faces, or the part of their body he assumed was a face. They had no eyes, no nose, only a hole in their stomach that released horrifying sounds.

He fired off the rest of his magazine into the center of the pack. But these aliens didn't explode like the others.

Harrington froze.

"They have shields!" Diego yelled.

Harrington shoved both men toward the air lock. "Run," he shouted. They moved in unison, turning every few seconds to fire off a few more shots at the monsters hunting them.

At the air lock one of the injured soldiers began to move. Harrington crouched down and grabbed him under one arm, exchanging looks with the man. Le stared back at him, his eyes wide with fear. Harrington helped him into the air lock. At least a dozen other Chinese crew members had crowded into the air lock, their faces drenched with sweat and covered in grime.

"What the fuck are you waiting for?" he finally yelled. "Get into the mini sub!" But they all stared back at him like he was speaking a foreign language. And then he realized that he was.

Commander Le let out a groan and started yelling something in Chinese at one of the X-9 survivors.

Gunfire snapped Harrington back into motion. He maneuvered back into the hallway where Diego and the remaining Chinese soldier continued shooting at the aliens that were closing in. One of them sank its claws into the ceiling and slithered across it.

Diego fired off another flurry of shots, but the creatures zigzagged around them. Harrington concentrated on the beast racing toward him on the ceiling. He didn't know what the hell he was looking at. He had always thought of aliens as little green men with big oval eyes, but these things were fucking monstrosities.

More of the serpentlike aliens lunged forward, their bodies coiling and twisting for momentum. One of them wrapped around the soldier next to Diego.

Harrington reached out for the man, their fingers touching before the creature pulled him back around a corner, out of reach of gunfire. The sound of his screams faded against the crack of Diego's rifle.

"Get into the pressure chamber; I'll cover you," Harrington yelled. "We don't have much time. Hurry!"

Diego nodded, finished off the last of his magazine, and climbed into the compartment. Harrington walked backward, reaching above him and grabbing one of the handles. By the time they were inside, the rest of the crew had already boarded *Destiny 1*. Le was waiting at the hatch, waving his hands at the men.

"Move!" he yelled.

Harrington went to seal the hatch to the X-9 when one of the snakes jammed half its body through the opening with a cry, knocking his rifle away. He slammed the hatch against the slithering alien.

"Get out of here, Diego!" he yelled, holding the creature back with all his strength. The monster squirmed and pressed harder, pushing Harrington backward. He knew he could only hold it a few more seconds.

From his peripheral vision, he saw Diego climb into *Destiny 1*.

"Come on," Diego yelled.

Harrington grunted, putting all his weight against the door. He caught a glimpse of the frightened crew through the porthole windows of the mini sub; their looks filled him with strength. He knew if he let go of the hatch, the snakes would have a free boarding pass onto *Destiny 1*.

He thought of his code.

Always do the right thing.

He was ready to die—ready to join his family.

"Go!" he yelled. "Close the hatch."

"No, Sergeant!" Diego screamed, reaching out for him.

Taking in a measured breath, Harrington slammed his shoulder into the hatch, stunning the alien for a moment. It screamed, the hole in its stomach widening in anger. Then he scrambled across the floor of the pressure chamber to the mini sub and slammed the hatch shut in Diego's face, locking it with one swift motion.

Harrington bumped his com as he turned back to see the alien poised above him, its bioluminescent skin casting a blue glow over the air lock.

"Irene, get them out of here. That's an order," he said, as the creature's body shot forward and wrapped around him. He closed his eyes and pictured his family. It was the last thing Sergeant Harrington would ever see.

CHAPTER 5

HOURS had passed since the X-9 had been destroyed, but the phantom sound of explosions drowned Noble's mind in dread. He could still see the missiles racing from the GOA and hitting the smooth black surface of the Chinese sub on the main display. He could still feel the tremors of their impact. Somewhere out there, Harrington's and Lin's remains were floating in the depths.

What a horrible way to die, he thought. Noble scanned the room for his XO. "Richards, send Diego to the bridge ASAP," he yelled.

"Aye aye, Captain," the man replied.

Noble bowed his head. He ran his finger across his name and rank, stitched into the leather of his chair. But as he sat down, he did not feel much like a captain. He'd sent Harrington to his death and he'd lost many other men in Colorado Springs.

"Captain, reporting for duty, sir," a voice said from behind him.

Folding his arms, Noble spun his chair to see Diego standing at the entrance to the command center. "At ease, son."

With a sigh, the new lead of the Special Forces team strode across the platform and made his way down several stairs to the bridge.

"You wanted to see me, sir?" Diego asked.

Noble regarded the man with a reassuring nod. "Sergeant Harrington was a good man. He spoke very highly of you."

"Thank you, sir. He was the best mentor I could have had."

"We will have a brief ceremony for him and the others at nineteen hundred hours."

The slightest of nods from Diego told Noble that the man had seen something awful inside the X-9.

"When you're up to it, I'd like a briefing on what you encountered down there. Anything that you think might help us in the war."

Diego looked very unsure of himself. His brown eyes swayed to the right and then down to his feet. He clasped his hands behind his back and stood straighter. "I'm ready now, sir."

Noble leaned back in his chair to observe the man. He was short, but made up for his size with wide shoulders and thick arms. His face was covered in scruff that could hardly be considered a beard. Diego was loyal, intelligent, and graceful both on and off the battlefield.

The soldier tensed his jaw and narrowed his brown eyes when he noticed he was being scrutinized.

Diego broke the silence with a measured voice. "Those things were everywhere. I've never seen anything like them, sir. They had a snake's body, but no face. At least, not like any face I've seen. They move quickly, slithering and then wrapping their bodies around their prey. When they feed they split down the middle," he said, pausing. "That's the most awful part. Their chest cavity, or whatever you want to call it. It's filled with hundreds of teeth."

"So those things can live in and outside the water?"

"As far as I can tell, sir."

"Did they have shields?"

Diego's features darkened. "Only when they weren't feeding."

"That's interesting," Noble said. He habitually ran his finger along his jawline, pausing when he remembered he'd shaved his beard. "The Biosphere team at Cheyenne Mountain reported the same thing with the Spider species. Their shields power down when they feed."

Diego shrugged.

"Is there anything else you can tell me? Anything that might be useful?"

Diego looked deep in thought. He finally shook his head. "I don't think so, sir."

Noble unfolded his arms and stood. "Thank you," he said, patting the man on his shoulder. "You're one courageous bastard, volunteering for that mission."

"Thank you, sir. I just . . ." His shoulders sagged a bit when he said, "I wish Harrington had made it out. He gave his life to save ours."

Noble looked at the soldier thoughtfully, again recalling what his father had said about the end of the world. Harrington, like Overton, was a man who made the ultimate sacrifice in the face of adversity. There were still men and women out there who would do the same. But with every passing second, the Organics drew closer to wiping out the human race.

There weren't many heroes left to stand in their path.

A stern voice resonated from the top of the bridge. Noble swiveled his chair to see Richards looking down from his station. "Captain Noble. We have an incoming message over Lolo's channel. It's from Cheyenne Mountain, sir."

"Patch them through."

A fuzzy image of Dr. Sophie Winston and Dr. Rodriguez appeared on the screen. And they both looked very frightened.

Sophie waited for the feed to reconnect with the GOA. They'd lost the uplink seconds after their first attempt. Lolo had probably passed over a dark zone.

While she waited, she scrolled through a database of pictures. The images from Lolo were terrible, but fascinating.

A swarm of black ships straddled the Earth in low orbit. The image was surreal, like concept art from some science fiction novel. Streaks of ocean water shot up toward the vessels, forming a solid wall, as the alien ships moved over the Pacific.

It was the first time anyone, as far as she knew, had actually seen the Organics in orbit. And the first time anyone had seen them removing water from the oceans.

With a swift flick of her index finger Sophie swiped to the next image. An army of Spiders marched across the cracked earth, trampling one another in a twisted heap of blue limbs. The picture only added to her confusion. Days earlier, when she'd been taken aboard the alien ship, she'd seen hundreds of different life-forms. It was some sort of ark, or maybe an alien museum. Whatever it was, it was driving her mad with questions.

Why would the aliens travel through the universe to collect water, destroying all life in the process, only to keep an ark full of alien life-forms? And why would they show it to her?

Sophie shook her head just as footsteps echoed in the hallway outside the CIC. She was happy to have the distraction.

"We connected yet?" Emanuel asked, nudging her arm. He brought a steaming cup of coffee to his lips and took a short sip. "Holy shit! Is that what I think it is?"

She'd reverted back to the first image, preparing to send the shot and the data to the GOA.

Nodding, Sophie leaned back so Emanuel could get a better view.

White noise from the speakers crackled as the main screen flickered and Noble's face filled the grainy display.

"Good afternoon," he said as the screen solidified.

"Not here it isn't," Sophie replied. "We just received some very disturbing images from Lolo. Forwarding to you . . ." She punched the Enter key and said, "now."

"I'll be damned," he said grimly. "We are running out of time."

She sent him the next one.

"The Organics," she said. "They're moving. Abandoning the cities and the human farms. They're headed for the coasts."

"Why?" Noble asked. He folded his hands and narrowed his eyebrows.

"Alexia thinks this is the last phase of the invasion, but we aren't entirely sure."

"That doesn't make much sense. Why would they be migrating?" Noble asked.

Emanuel shrugged. "We don't know."

Noble frowned. "How long do we have?"

"Maybe a couple weeks or a month, tops. We need a plan," she said.

Folding his arms, Noble's features tensed. "That's why I'm glad we connected. I've been working on a plan that I want to run by you."

Sophie responded with her own skeptically arched brow. "You have our attention."

"My engineers are currently working on modifying the RVAMP into something more effective. Something that can be used on a grander scale."

"Something that could knock out the surge entirely?" Emanuel asked.

Noble tilted his head in confusion.

"Sorry, Captain. The surge is what we are calling the electromagnetic disturbance outside. The pulse seems to be coming from Mars," Sophie said, pausing. "Actually, we know it is, but that's beside the point. Sergeant Overton mentioned we might be able to stop it if we set nukes or EMPs off in the atmosphere. That's where Emanuel got the idea to build the RVAMP. We managed to kill a whole bunch of them with it in Colorado Springs when we took down those human farms. But more kept coming."

Noble looked at his desk for a moment to consider the thought. "Yeah, nukes and traditional EMPs wouldn't work," he replied. "While that would likely knock out some of their ships, we can't defeat them that way. We need something that will work on a worldwide level. The problem is finding a delivery system."

Sophie eyed the man. The captain had proven to be a useful ally so far, a man with conviction and vision. But the Organics weren't an enemy that NTC was used to fighting. They were an empire of advanced creatures. She wasn't certain that even Captain Noble could come up with something to defeat them. "Do you have anything in mind?" she finally asked.

Noble cracked a half grin. "Sure. But the real question is, will it work?"

Sophie wasn't amused.

"What's your idea, Captain?" Emanuel asked.

"With a few small teams, I think we could sneak onto several military bases, commandeer a fleet of jets and drones, and equip them with the modified RVAMP weapons. Then coordinate an offensive."

"You're kidding, right?" Sophie said.

"No, Doctor Winston, I'm not," he said sternly. "Unless you know of a ship that can get us to Mars, where we could shut off this phantom 'surge,'" he said mockingly, using two fingers to trace quotation marks in the air, "I see no other option."

"Even if that was possible, we would never arrive in time to save the planet," Emanuel pointed out.

Sophie didn't like Noble's tone, but the man was right. They didn't have many options. The captain's plan was a long shot, sure, but heading to Mars sounded even crazier. There was no easy solution. No way to save the planet without taking great risks and making even harder sacrifices—sacrifices like the one Sergeant Overton had made back in Colorado Springs.

"So the plan is to sneak past the Organics' defenses and launch a strike across the world? Do you even have that many pilots at your disposal, *Captain*?" Sophie asked.

He smiled, clearly noticing her emphasis on his rank. "We will have to make do with the resources available. We would primarily be using drones. Only a handful of low-orbit jets will be needed."

Sophie crossed her arms and glanced over at Emanuel. He looked optimistic, his eyebrows forming wide arches above the rims of his glasses.

"And if there are survivors at any of the coordinates I sent you earlier this morning, then perhaps we will have even more resources."

"I'd be hard-pressed to believe anyone has made it this long," Emanuel said.

Noble nodded. "I agree. The likelihood of other survivors is slim, but worth checking out."

Sophie heard laughter from the hallway and turned just in time to see Owen race by, with Jamie close on his heels. Against all odds, the two children had survived outside.

"Our AI did confirm that the distress signal from Offutt had been activated very recently. Maybe someone has managed a miracle and avoided detection," Emanuel said.

"Nothing gets past Alexia," Sophie smiled. It was an odd sensation, her lips forming something other than a frown. She was starting to feel a bit better knowing they were building a plan, even if it did sound ir-rational.

"So what's the next step?" Emanuel asked.

Noble cupped his hands behind his head and leaned back in his chair.

"I'd suggest sending a drone to Offutt to see what's there. The sooner we know, the sooner we can develop a plan, and if by some grace of God there are survivors, then perhaps they will join us."

"How fast can you get a drone into the field?" Sophie asked.

"Richards," Noble shouted, craning his head.

"Sir?" a voice said in the background.

"Send a message to Engineering. I want a drone prepped and ready to fly ASAP." When he turned back to the feed, there was something about his face that bothered Sophie. The man she had met at Cheyenne Mountain was a fearless leader; a man, like Overton, who radiated con-fidence. That man was no longer in front of her. Noble seemed solemn and tired.

Broken.

"I didn't want to give you bad news," Noble finally said. He returned his hands to the table and hunched over his desk. Creases broke across his forehead. "We found the Chinese sub. A rescue mission was able to save some of her crew, but in the end I ordered the X-9 destroyed. Sergeant Harrington, whom you met while we repaired the *Sea Serpent* at the Biosphere, was killed in the mission."

The news did not shock Sophie as much as she thought it would. While she knew that losing another weapon of war was not to be taken lightly, she also knew that death was now a routine part of life. Having hope was dangerous when all could be lost in the blink of an eye.

Sophie exchanged looks with Emanuel. Gray speckled his slicked-back hair, and a thick beard covered his dimples. He looked as if he had aged years in the last two months. She'd purposely avoided mirrors for the same reason. Her body felt weak, and her clothes no longer hugged her curves; instead, they hung loosely off her body. They'd been stranded for quite a while now, cut off from the rest of the dying world.

But the worst of it? She didn't just feel trapped by the Biosphere walls, she felt trapped inside her own mind.

"Doctor Winston," came a voice. It sounded distant, far away. There was a humming, like wasps.

Someone called her name again. Sophie blinked hard, the echoing in her ears faded, and she turned to see Emanuel hovering over her. He reached out and placed a hand on her right wrist. Her skin tingled at his touch. She realized then that he hadn't touched her since Overton had caught them in the CIC weeks earlier.

He squeezed harder, but she felt only a cold numbness.

"Sophie," he said. "Snap out of it."

She nodded and swept her eyes over the monitors, her eyes glazed and blurry. In a monotone voice she said, "Let's plan on talking again in forty-eight hours. That should give you enough time to send a drone to Offutt and analyze any intel. In the meantime, we will continue to use Lolo for reconnaissance and inform you of any developments."

"Sounds good, Doctor. Stay safe," Noble replied.

"You too," she said, swiping the feed off with her index finger. As soon as she stood a wave of dizziness hit her. She swayed to the left and then the right.

Emanuel reached out to balance her. "What's going on with you?"

The sensation passed, and Sophie's world returned to normal. "I'm fine."

"No. You seem really off."

Sophie put a hand on her head. She had so much to do and she hadn't put a dent in the data Lolo had sent.

"Hey, you there?" Emanuel asked, waving his hands. "Sophie, what is going on with you?" His voice was calm but guarded.

"I'm fine," she replied. "Just tired." For a moment she locked eyes with him and felt a sensation that she'd long buried. The emotion soon vanished, stripped away by the thousands of worries clamoring for attention in her mind.

"Where is the old Sophie?" he asked with a frown.

She looked away. She knew the answer deep down, but she couldn't let Emanuel know—the old Sophie had died inside that black ship.

Corporal Bouma stood two full heads taller than Jeff, but every morning the boy seemed to be closing the gap. It was possible, considering the vegetables and fruits harvested from Biome 1 were better than anything the kid would have been eating on the outside even before the invasion. Over the past decade food production had become so automated that it was all full of God knew what. Only those wealthy enough could afford the small organic supply. None of that mattered anymore. The only farms that remained were human farms.

He steadied his rifle and took aim at a black target on the opposite wall, the anger boiling inside him at the thought of humans being harvested just outside these walls. In quick succession, he fired off three shots. The deafening crack of the old rifle echoed through the chamber. The gun was louder and more powerful than he had thought.

"Damn. Nice shot," Jeff said.

He'd hit the middle of the target in two places, while the third shot had torn into the wall above.

"Give me that thing," Kiel shouted. He propped one of his crutches against the wall and reached for the gun.

Bouma glared at the other marine. "Wait your turn. Jeff's next." With a smile, he handed the rifle to the eleven-year-old. "See if you can beat that," he whispered as the boy grabbed the gun.

"I want a turn, too!" David whined.

Bouma laughed. He'd promised Sophie that he wouldn't train the other kids. They weren't that desperate, she had said. David was supposed to be on harvest duty, not soldier duty.

"If you promise not to tell," Bouma started to say when he heard Holly's voice behind them.

"I heard that," she said in a mischievous tone.

He felt his face grow red and turned to see her carrying a basket full of fruit. She'd pulled her hair, still glistening from the shower, into a ponytail.

Flashing her a smile he walked over to help her with her load. "Sorry."

Holly held the basket defiantly to her chest. "Um, I have a bone to pick with you, *Corporal*," she said sternly. Then she glared at Kiel. "And you. Why aren't you resting? Your body needs to heal."

Bouma threw his arms up in protest, but cowered when she shoved the basket into his chest. "I thought Sophie said David isn't supposed to be using that gun. Frankly, I'm surprised she's allowing target practice inside the Biosphere in the first place."

"Where else are we supposed to train?" Jeff asked. He held the muzzle of the gun toward the ground.

"I don't know why you need to train at all," Holly said, her hands now on her hips. "The noise that thing makes is maddening."

Bouma took a step forward. "I have this under control."

With a half smile she reached out to him. "Sure you do."

Bouma nodded and then gestured with his chin toward the exit. "Want to take a walk?"

"Yup."

"Take five, guys," he said.

David groaned, and Jeff rested the rifle against the makeshift table. Kiel pulled out an apple and tossed it to David. "Know how to play catch, kid?"

Placing his hand on Holly's back, Bouma guided her down the narrow path leading through the crops. They walked in silence, taking in the lush scent.

When they reached Biome 2, he paused and waited for the glass doors to seal behind them. Before Holly had a chance to react, he reached over and pulled her into a tight hug.

"You needed that," he whispered in her ear.

She nodded, her cheeks ripe with a blush. "Yes."

Intertwining his fingers with hers, Bouma turned toward the pond. The water sparkled under the faint LEDs. For a moment he stared into it, watching their reflection flicker with the light. "You don't seem okay," he said.

"I am, but I don't think Sophie is doing well. I overheard her and Emanuel talking with Captain Noble. Sounds like they found the Chinese sub and were forced to destroy it."

Bouma looked at the ground. "Damn. Any survivors?"

She shook her head. "You'll have to ask Sophie. I only heard a small bit of the conversation."

He nodded and took her other hand. The thought of more death was numbing. He wanted to *feel*.

Without thinking, he kissed her.

She let out a small cry of surprise and then leaned into him. Apparently, Holly desired the same thing he did.

They locked eyes.

"Shhhh," he said.

"I can be quiet."

Bouma tightened his grip and whispered in her ear, "I have a secret."

"Me too," she said, exhaling a deep breath. "I'm falling for you."

The quick response took him by surprise, and he tilted his head back to look her in the eyes. Everyone he'd ever cared for had died during the invasion. But somehow he'd found it in the midst of the apocalypse.

Love.

The revelation sent a chill through his body. It was something he would do anything to defend. He would guard Holly, the kids, and the team with his life. The same feeling also filled him with a sense of guilt. Why should he be happy? What did he do to deserve it? His gut sank at the thought, but he held Holly firmly in his arms.

"I love you," he said with authority. "You don't have anything to worry about anymore, Holly. I will protect you."

CHAPTER 6

ENTRY 4001
DESIGNEE: AI ALEXIA

Three days, one hour, forty-five minutes, and thirteen seconds have passed since Captain Noble and his team left the Biosphere. My latest scan shows the team's survival probability is at 9.5 percent, a slight increase from before we made contact with the NTC submarine, *Ghost of Atlantis.*

The discovery of other survivors, especially Captain Noble's well-equipped crew, has definitely had an effect on team morale here at the Biosphere. I wasn't programmed to feel optimism, but I do believe I've evolved to feel something similar.

Hope conflicts with my programming. The statistics continuously paint a bleak future, yet virtually every time they've turned out to be wrong. What the countless scans don't illustrate is a trait ingrained in the DNA of the human species.

Resilience.

Over the past two months, Dr. Winston and her team have faced very tough decisions, life-and-death decisions. Despite the odds, they have never given up, and with my assistance they have beat those odds so far. They are survivors.

It's interesting, I suppose, considering that throughout their history they have killed one another over land and resources. Like the Organics, they are a destructive species. I've read essays that refer to humans as a virus, a plague that's consumed the world.

I've never believed that theory, but I do see the parallel. And now the largest-ever threat to their species has borne an alliance between two bitter enemies. The Chinese and NTC have united their survivors under a single cause.

I record the development and log the entry under "Group Behavior." I'll come back to the case study later, but first there are more pressing issues I need to attend to.

Lieutenant Allison Smith still hasn't recovered from her captivity. There are multiple questions I hope to answer through a series of tests. Primarily, how did the Organics keep her alive, and how did they filter water from her body?

I've started to formulate a theory that connects everything to the surge—the human farms, the orbs, and the alien defenses. I believe they are all somehow connected to the electromagnetic disturbance originating on Mars. Before we discovered Lolo, we thought the surge was a constant signal. But the satellite's data now shows the surge comes in two-hour intervals. The wave of energy transmitted from the surface of Mars hits the side of the Earth facing the Red Planet and is then distributed across the Earth. How the energy is sustained and transmitted in that interval is still a mystery to me.

Something has to be sustaining the current. Just like something has to support Lieutenant Smith and the other human prisoners. Just like something must be sustaining the alien shields.

After several scans I've made a discovery that may help answer some of these questions. I've found Lieutenant Smith's blood samples contain the same nanobots that Dr. Rodriguez found in the Spider specimen he dissected weeks ago.

Using an electrical-based catalyst, I stimulated the nanobots. They instantly absorbed the energy and began to multiply. At first glance, the results indicate that the bots are trying to connect to an outside source.

The implications are interesting. I conclude the active RVM generator is preventing the nanotechnology from connecting to the surge.

I finally have a theory. The Organics are using the surge to carry an electromagnetic wave that serves a variety of functions. First, it powers the aliens' defenses. Second, it sustains the human farms and the orbs.

During the invasion there were reports around the world of the sky turning turquoise. By analyzing the timing of these reports, we can deduce that as the Earth rotated, exposing its face to Mars, the Organics used the surge to begin removing much of the planet's surface water.

I'm still not sure exactly how the aliens are able to filter water, whether from the surface or from humans. And I'm also not sure why Lieutenant Smith isn't recovering. Without a solid answer, I have decided that it's time to consult with Dr. Winston and Dr. Rodriguez. This time, I need their help just as much as they need mine.

———

The glow from the sun cut a halo between the mesosphere and stratosphere. Lolo shot by in low Earth orbit. She moved away from the light, about to cross over the darkness blanketing Asia a hundred miles below. The satellite transmitted thousands of images a second, far too many for Emanuel to sift through. Squeezing his fingers together every minute or so, he would freeze the display in front of him. He watched in silence, observing in awe.

Darkness finally consumed Lolo and she slipped into the night, relaying only grainy pictures of abandoned cities. Months ago, their artificial lights would have sparkled like the stars in the sky, but the once-great metropolises of man were now dark graveyards.

Emanuel's stomach growled as he shut the feed off. He hadn't eaten all day. Before he could take a break, he needed to check something. Earlier, he and Sophie had told Captain Noble that the Organics were heading for the coasts, that they were leaving the cities and human farms. When he thought about it further, that didn't make much sense. The farms were sustaining the armies. Why would they leave them and head for the oceans? Historically, migrations always occurred when a species either used up all the resources of an area or the climate was too extreme for them to survive. Neither situation applied to the Organics. With their shields, climate shouldn't matter, and with the farms they had plenty of resources.

So why were they moving? Emanuel felt puzzled. Sure, the species was alien. Darwinism didn't necessarily apply to them. But there had to be a reason they were moving that he didn't yet understand. Lost in thought, he flinched when a voice echoed from the hallway.

"Dr. Rodriguez?"

Emanuel spun his chair and saw Jeff standing in the doorway of the command center with David at his side.

"Hey guys, what's going on?" he said, his best attempt to sound calm. Jeff eyed him suspiciously.

"We have a question," the boy said.

David stepped in front of his brother and in a very matter-of-fact tone said, "About the aliens."

Emanuel leaned back in his chair and crossed his arms. "Sure, what do you want to know?"

"For one, why did they come? And when are they going to leave?" David asked quickly.

Jeff pinched his brother's arm. "I told you to just listen."

David glared angrily. "But I want to ask questions, too!"

Emanuel waved his hands to get their attention. "It's okay. I'll answer all your questions." With the two boys staring at him, Emanuel suddenly felt an awkward pressure. He'd spent his career making presentations in front of other scientists, but put him in front of two kids and he couldn't even form a coherent sentence.

"Go ahead," Jeff said, seeing his brother looking sheepishly at the ground.

"Sir," David said with a slight pause, his eyes jumping to the ceiling as he thought about what he wanted to ask. When he looked back at Emanuel, he seemed very serious. "Why did the aliens kill our dad?"

Emanuel frowned. He was expecting science questions and wasn't prepared to answer this one. Stumbling for words, he hesitated.

With a sigh Emanuel waved the boys over and gestured toward a pair of chairs. "Sit down. You're making me nervous." The boys each took a seat. David began to spin his chair until Jeff grabbed the armrest and glared at him.

"Stop," he said. Then he looked over at Emanuel and said, "Well?"

The screen behind the boys flickered, shifting to a new image Lolo had transmitted earlier that morning. Emanuel had set the blue screen to automatically filter through the pictures he wanted to send to Captain Noble. This one depicted the migration. A swollen mass of Spiders moved across what had once been lush Iowa farmland, and their shields reflected the sun overhead. Among the tangled alien shapes he could see the humped backs of the gigantic Worms, protruding like the whitecaps of waves in a storm.

"The aliens," Emanuel said, pointing at the display behind them. "They are here for our water, which I think you both understand. Right?"

Jeff nodded, while David looked at the screen and said, "Wow. How many are there?"

"See this group?" Emanuel asked.

Both boys nodded.

"They are the workers," he said, scanning the boys' faces to see if they understood. They both stared back at him blankly. He needed a different strategy. "Surely you've both seen ants before, right?"

Jeff rolled his eyes.

"Of course you have. These aliens are like worker ants. They perform tasks for the good of the larger colony. In this case, these Spiders collect water and eradicate any threats. They likely killed your dad because he was one of those threats." Emanuel bit his lip, unsure if his answer would upset the boys. To his surprise both boys smiled.

"Dad was a hero!" David shouted.

"He killed Spiders and taught us how to kill them, too," Jeff added.

"He sounds like an extraordinary soldier," Emanuel said, relieved his answer hadn't upset them. The image behind them switched to another shot of the migration. Without his glasses he was forced to squint. This one showed another mass of Spiders marching like troops through the clogged streets of Los Angeles. Behind the cluster of aliens, several orbs floated over the empty city streets. The shot was a still image, but he could see the Spiders had moved past the glowing spheres without tearing into them. It didn't make any sense.

Springing out of his chair, he made his way over to the row of screens. Spreading his fingers, he zoomed in on one of the orbs. Sure enough, the translucent blue skin, appeared fully intact.

Why would they leave behind a resource they had fought so desperately for?

"Did the queen tell them to move?" David asked.

"What? The queen?" Emanuel replied, still staring at the image.

"You said they're the workers. Don't workers get their orders from a queen?"

My God, Emanuel thought, *the kid is right.* The Organics were not moving because they needed resources, but because they were being told to do so. This wasn't a subconscious migration.

The theory hit him in the gut. Why hadn't he seen this before? The aliens weren't colonizing Earth. They were preparing to leave the planet.

CHAPTER 7

IT was late, and the mess hall had mostly emptied hours before. Captain Noble sat in silence, his eyes glued to a piece of cold chicken positioned sideways on his plate. He studied it, wondering exactly how many chickens were left on the planet, knowing the answer would not make the piece in front of him taste any better.

The first bite tasted rubbery, far from the tender grilled cutlets his wife used to put on his salads. The meal was unsatisfying, and he found himself thinking that if this was the last chicken in the world, the cook had not done it justice.

He slid the tray away and took a sip of water. His mind drifted to Alex. Noble still didn't know why he'd taken his life. Especially after all he had been through. After surviving for days in the heat and running from the Organics, the former high school history teacher had been given a second chance. But the captain knew things had changed. It was the end of the world. The logic of the past no longer applied.

Perhaps the survivor's guilt had gotten to him, or perhaps Alex had decided he just didn't want to be part of this new world. Whatever the case, Noble wouldn't judge him. The man had seen the horrors of the outside. Alex had witnessed firsthand what the Organics were capable of and lived through the unthinkable. Noble had only watched from afar.

Sighing, the captain checked his watch. It was almost midnight, but he didn't feel tired. His thoughts wandered.

He walked down to the engineering deck to clear his head. Inside,

Blake Ort hunched over the sleek black profile of a drone. The whine from a power drill echoed through the chamber as he removed a panel from the craft.

"Evening," Noble said from the doorway.

Ort slid off his safety glasses and smiled. He was handsome in a rough way. With dark skin and defined arms he liked to show off by rolling up his sleeves. A thick black mustache made him look much older than his thirty-some-odd years, but Noble had never seen him without it. In a booming voice Ort said, "What's got you up this late, sir?"

"I wanted to check on the status of our drone here," he said, pacing into the room and eyeing the engineer's handiwork. Like a corpse after an autopsy, the craft had been dissected. Wires snaked out in several directions. "We have a ways to go, don't we?"

"Not that long, sir. I should have her up and running by morning," Ort said. "I just need to rewire her GPS system. Otherwise she won't be able to transmit anything. Which reminds me"—he paused to roll his sleeves up farther—"the magnetic disturbance outside. I've been trying to figure it out, but I've just never seen anything like it. It's like a never-ending EMP." He looked over at the drone.

Noble crossed his arms and took a seat. He was pretty sure he already knew everything Ort was about to tell him, but didn't want to interrupt.

"Sorry," Ort said, sitting in the chair across from the captain. "This could take a while to explain. You sure you don't want to catch some shut-eye?"

The captain crossed a leg and smiled. "You know me better than that, don't you, Ort?"

"Yes, sir. I do," he paused. "So I spent a week with Robert and John going over the RVAMP device we received from the biosphere team at Cheyenne Mountain. The nonweaponized version, the RVM, essentially uses magnetic technology to send out a pulse wave similar to the one the Organics are using. This effectively camouflages anyone within a certain radius."

Ort ran a finger across his mustache and locked eyes with Noble. "The weaponized version, the RVAMP, is where things get interesting. When the pulse is reversed, it creates a powerful surge that knocks out the aliens' defenses for miles, depending on where the device is used."

"Basically, it uses their technology against them?"

"Precisely."

"Do you think you can figure out a way to increase the range?"

Ort hesitated. "Yes."

"That didn't sound like a very confident yes," Noble said.

"It's complicated, sir. Without understanding what's creating the electrical disturbance, or how it's working, I simply can't say if I can engineer anything that will work on the level you want it to. Plus, even if we do get it to work, say, over a radius of one hundred miles or so, what then? Won't the Organics just swoop in and crush us?"

Noble frowned and said, "Pessimists never win wars."

"I'm not a soldier, sir. I'm an electrical engineer. And I'm a realist."

"You're wrong, Ort. You are a soldier. Every survivor left is. All conscripted to fight the most important war in the history of the human race." He uncrossed his arms and ran a hand over the surface of the drone. "Listen. I know it seems like my plan is impossible. It may be. But we don't have any other choice—" He thought suddenly of Alex. There was another choice.

"Actually, I take that back. We do have another choice. To give up. Do you want to give up, Ort?"

He quickly shook his head. "No, sir. I'm just saying—"

"And I'm telling you to rewire that drone and have it ready to go by morning. I want to see what's at Offutt Air Force Base."

Ort's cheeks filled with a rosy blush; anger or embarrassment, maybe a combination. Either way, Noble had offended the man. He never used to speak to his crew in such a manner, but things had changed. The crew was growing increasingly cynical, and as captain it was his job to encourage and inspire them to continue the fight.

"Listen," Noble said. "I don't know if this plan will work, but we don't have any other option. I promise you one thing. If you build me enough modified RVAMPs, I'm going to use them. I'm going to give those bastards a run for their money."

Ort nodded. "I'm sure you will, sir."

Noble stood and patted the man on one of his wide shoulders. "I'll check back in the morning."

"I'll do my best, sir," Ort said confidently.

"I know," Noble said as he left the room.

Emanuel stood over Lieutenant Smith, watching the emaciated woman breathe. Her closed eyelids fluttered, a sign of a very deep sleep. Inching closer, Emanuel bumped into the feeding tube snaking out from underneath the white sheets.

He cringed as he recalled the surgery. It had been messy. Without Alexia's guidance and support, the marine would have likely died.

The biomonitor told him that she was relatively stable. But even under the dim lights he could see her jaundiced skin. He was a biologist, not a medical doctor, but even he knew that Smith should have been recovering quicker.

He thought of Saafi and Timothy, his good friends who had faced similar fates, dead at alien hands. He forced himself to look away from Smith's frail body.

No wonder the kids are scared of her, Emanuel thought. He shook his head and walked back to his makeshift laboratory in the corner of the room.

Alexia's voice suddenly sounded over the PA system. "Doctor Rodriguez. May I have a moment of your time? Doctor Winston is on her way to the medical ward. I'd like to speak to both of you about Lieutenant Smith."

Emanuel stopped in his tracks. He spun and caught another glimpse of the marine's thin profile just as Sophie walked into the room. She shut the door quietly behind her.

Between the cryo chambers, two makeshift hospital beds, and Emanuel's lab space, the small room was packed. There wasn't anywhere they could talk without disturbing Smith, which made Alexia's request to speak there seem odd. Still, Emanuel sat on one of the barstools at his desk and gestured to the seat next to him as Sophie tiptoed across the floor.

The AI didn't wait for Sophie to take a seat. "Thank you for coming, Doctor," she said. "I've made a new discovery."

Emanuel hated the fact he could never read Alexia. Her unwaveringly calm voice was frustrating.

"Recent scans have detected a nanotechnology in Lieutenant Smith's bloodstream that was previously missed."

"Is it the same as what I found in the Spiders?" Emanuel blurted, and then stopped himself when he realized he had interrupted her. Emanuel didn't know much about nanotechnology outside of its use in the medical field. One of his college roommates had gone on to make incredible advances in cancer treatment by developing specialized particles that attacked cancer cells.

"Go ahead, Doctor," Alexia said politely.

He waved his hands. "Sorry. You first."

"I believe you were going to ask if this is the same technology you discovered in the bloodstream of the Organic specimen weeks ago." The AI's voice cut out as she transferred to the AI console. Her face flickered and solidified over the interface.

Emanuel nodded.

"The answer is yes."

"Fascinating." He stood and walked over to Smith's bedside. "Any idea what the technology does inside a human?"

"You're looking at it," Alexia said. "It's killing her."

Emanuel flinched. "It's killing her?" He glanced over at Sophie. Her face remained emotionless.

"She can't hear you, by the way," Alexia said. "Lieutenant Smith's brain signals indicate she is in the deepest phase of REM sleep."

"I wonder what she's dreaming about," Sophie finally said.

"What?" Emanuel asked. He was beyond puzzled. Alexia had just discovered a new alien technology killing the woman right in front of them, and all Sophie could think about were the marine's dreams.

"I wonder if she has seen them," Sophie continued.

Emanuel ran a nervous hand through his hair. "The aliens?"

"The multidimensional Organics," Sophie said. She turned to him, deep wrinkles streaking across her forehead.

Emanuel didn't know how to respond. Between her frizzled blond hair and her expression, she looked insane. He needed to pull Holly aside. Sophie needed another intervention.

But first he needed to see what the hell Alexia was talking about. If she was right, then the discovery changed everything. Organic technology in the blood of a human? His mind spun trying to wrap around the implications.

Crossing the room, Emanuel left Sophie and logged into the main terminal, swinging the screen around to face him. "Show me one of the nanobots."

"Working," Alexia replied. Less than a second later a peppercorn-shaped image rolled across the display. Emanuel swiped the interface and the image transferred to a hologram that hovered over the metal desk.

"Looks kind of like a virus," Emanuel said, scrutinizing the alien tech. Smith had lost considerable weight. Her body was rejecting everything they gave her intravenously. The thought sparked an idea. "Could the bots be preventing her digestive tract from absorbing nutrients?"

"That's possible," Alexia replied. "In fact, it's highly likely. But I don't know how. I've already run several tests."

Emanuel gestured toward the monitor. "Sophie, any ideas?"

She looked away from Smith's sleeping body and crossed the room to join Emanuel at the monitors.

"Any signs of infection?" she asked. "Bacterium, virus, anything like that?" She spoke quickly and with confidence, like a completely different person had suddenly taken hold of her.

"No, Doctor Winston. Her immune system seems to be fine; her body simply isn't processing nutrients," Alexia replied.

"Then it has to be the nanobots. They must be blocking the chemical reaction that occurs after food is digested and right before it's passed into the bloodstream." Sophie paused to swipe a strand of hair out of her face. Then she looked at the ground as if deep in thought. "Let's try something. Emanuel," she said turning to him, "take a sample of her blood. I want to run another test and see what happens. We should be able to see how the technology reacts."

Emanuel stood there staring at Sophie, amazed at her sudden change in demeanor. Besides her weight loss and pale skin, here was the same scientist he had entered the Biosphere with two months ago. But what had sparked the change? With a nod he made his way to the medical supplies to retrieve a vial and a syringe.

"Has she said anything today?" Emanuel asked, preparing the needle.

"No, Doctor. She's been asleep all day," Alexia replied.

Good, then hopefully she won't feel this, Emanuel thought. He felt for the basilic vein, finding the one in Smith's right arm bulging. Then he very slowly inserted the needle and drew her blood. He watched the marine's eyelids flutter.

As Emanuel withdrew the needle her eyes suddenly snapped open. Smith grabbed his wrist and snarled, "What are you doing?!"

The biologist tried to pull away, but the woman's grip was surprisingly strong despite her weakened condition.

Sophie rushed over to the bed and placed a reassuring hand over Smith's. "It's okay. He's just trying to collect a sample of your blood."

The marine looked up at her, fear radiating from her bloodshot eyes.

"What's wrong with me?" she asked, her grip shaking.

"You're going to be okay," Emanuel replied. He finally pulled his wrist from the marine's grasp and walked the tube over to the electron microscope, placing the vial safely on a rack next to several others.

When he turned, Smith had rested her head back down on the pillow.

"Well, that was fast," Sophie said, gently putting the marine's hand back on the bed.

Emanuel hurried over to Smith's bed. Her eyelids were closed, having returned to their fluttering. He shook his head. It didn't make any sense. He was used to suspending his disbelief, but for some reason this went above and beyond floating orbs.

"How could she immediately drift back into REM sleep?"

"Honestly, I don't know," Sophie replied. "But I have a feeling we're about to find out," she said, gesturing toward the microscope.

CHAPTER 8

JEFF missed his dad. He knew his little brother did, too. They'd lost him two and a half months ago, when he had sacrificed himself to the aliens so they could escape. Not a day passed that Jeff didn't wonder if his dad would have been proud of him. The question ate at him every night when he lay in bed.

Jeff rolled over to study his younger brother's profile in the adjacent bed. The boy tossed and turned, letting out whimpers. He, too, suffered from nightmares. And why wouldn't he? The monsters were everywhere. The planet had transformed into their horrible playground.

Rolling over, Jeff propped up his head with a palm. Things weren't supposed to be like this. They were supposed to be playing outside with their friends, going camping in the mountains. But instead, they were hiding inside one.

Closing his eyes, he thought of the only thing that made him feel better. His kills. Fifteen Spiders and three Sentinels. That's how many of the aliens he'd eliminated since the invasion. The thought made him feel a bit better, and he began to relax. In a few hours he would be training again with Bouma and Kiel. They'd already helped him improve his aim. Next they were going to teach him how to navigate. With modern communications knocked out, learning how to orienteer was more important than ever.

Jeff had never used a map before, and he'd only seen a compass once. His grandpa had showed him and David one years ago, claiming that it could guide someone when they were lost. But Jeff didn't believe him at the time. How could a piece of metal that didn't even talk give you directions?

He was excited to find out. He knew it wasn't going to be easy, but he enjoyed learning. At times he even missed school. But mostly he missed his friends.

"Jeff," a soft voice said.

He looked over and saw the outline of David's body in the darkness. His brother sat up and was looking at him.

"What's wrong?" Jeff whispered. He didn't want to wake Kiel or Bouma, who were camped out on the floor between them.

"I can't sleep," David said. He swung his legs over the bed and put his feet on the floor. "Can I come over there?"

"No, get back in bed," Jeff hissed.

One of the blankets moved and Bouma let out a groan before he turned onto his side.

David stood and jumped over the two men, first one, then the other. "I keep having nightmares." He climbed into bed next to Jeff, pushing him softly.

"Damn it, David. You're six years old."

"I know. I'm sorry." He paused and then said, "I really miss Dad."

Jeff clenched his jaw. "I do too, bud."

"Do you think he's somewhere safe?"

"I think he's with Mom."

"You mean our real mom, right?"

"Yes, David."

"Okay."

"Goodnight."

"Goodnight."

———————

The next morning Jeff strolled into an empty Biome 1, rubbing the sleep from his eyes and listening to the tranquil sound of the irrigation system as it watered the crops. The chamber, humid and clammy, reminded him of the NTC botanical center that Paula, their stepmom, had taken them to for a birthday party a few years ago.

Strolling to the edge of the platform, he reached out and let the mist rain down on him. The cool water felt good on his skin, and for a second Jeff felt completely relaxed.

When the poles finally clicked off, he jumped off the metal platform onto the moist dirt. His shoes sank in with a squishy *plop*. He wove through a row of tangled cucumber vines snaking across the soggy topsoil.

"'Sup, squirt," came a voice from behind him.

Jeff frowned. He didn't like being called "squirt," especially by a man not much taller than him. Spinning, he glared at Kiel. The marine stood on the platform above him. Jeff laughed.

"What?" Kiel asked.

"You look . . ." Jeff paused and shook his head.

"What, kid?"

"You look taller."

"Ah, so you're a funny guy now?"

Chuckling, Jeff sidestepped a melon and continued down the path. "Where's Bouma?"

"He's eating breakfast with his girlfriend," Kiel snickered.

"Holly's his girlfriend?" Jeff asked.

"You blind, kid?"

"No," Jeff laughed. "I just really don't care."

"In five years you might."

"What's in five years?"

Kiel stepped off the platform, stabbing one of his crutches into the mud. He grinned. "Never mind."

Before Jeff could reply he heard footsteps coming from the corridor.

"That was quick," Kiel shouted.

Jeff turned, cautious not to step on any plants. The glass doors hissed open and Corporal Bouma marched through, his mouth still filled with food.

"Morning," he said. His voice sounded different. Chipper.

"What are you so happy about?" Kiel asked.

Bouma shook his head and gulped down the last bit of breakfast. "Nothing."

"Did you and Holly"—Kiel paused and looked toward Jeff before continuing—"hook up last night?"

"Knock it off," Bouma said. "She's none of your business."

"Sorry," Kiel replied. He continued down the dirt trail behind Jeff, his crutches making noises as they sank into the saturated ground.

"You excited to learn about navigation, Jeff?" Bouma shouted after them, in an obvious attempt to change the subject.

"Yeah. But I'm more excited to go back outside. I want to kill more of 'em."

"I'm sure we'll get a chance eventually," Kiel said coldly. "We can't live in here forever."

"I know. That's what I told David," Jeff said.

The three suddenly grew quiet. Jeff knew the time would come when they had to leave the Biosphere. When their supplies would run out or the facility would be compromised. But he wasn't scared to leave. He was scared to stay.

Staying meant he didn't get to fight—staying meant he had to sit and wait.

Marines didn't sit around. They fought.

To the end.

Jeff grabbed his dad's hunting rifle and loaded a round. Then he placed the butt firmly against his upper chest, looked down the barrel, took a deep breath, and fired a bull's-eye.

"Wow. Nice shot, kid," Kiel said. He dropped his crutches and hobbled over to Jeff's side, putting his hand on the boy's shoulder. With a chuckle he said, "You're going to be a marine in no time."

Emanuel swiveled the display in front of him and squinted. He'd left his glasses on the counter. "Well I'll be damned," he whispered.

The nanobots had evolved during the night, ballooning in size and developing small tentacles around the edges. They looked almost—

That can't be, Emanuel thought. *They can't be alive. Can they?*

Was he looking at a biologically modified alien technology?

"Alexia, take a look at this," he shouted, taking a step back from the monitor. He swiped the display and transferred the data to her mainframe.

Alexia's avatar shot up over the AI interface. "Doctor, scans reveal the nanobots are in fact biological in nature. I've seen similar technology in the past. After you discovered the first traces of the nanotechnology, I ran some queries through my database and found a secret division within NTC. They were working on genetically modified nanotechnology that would merge with human cells. Imagine a white blood cell with superpowers. That's what they were aiming for," she said. "These nanobots are far more advanced. The tentacle strands are replicating."

"But why?" Emanuel asked.

"Inconclusive," Alexia replied.

"Guess."

The AI's blue face faded away, her voice transferring back to the speakers.

"I don't make guesses, Doctor. But the most likely explanation would be that the alien technology is evolving to take over Lieutenant Smith's system."

Emanuel clenched his jaw. If it was spreading through Smith, could it be contagious?

"We should wait for Sophie. I want her to see this. Can you tell her we need her?"

The PA system blared and Alexia said, "Doctor Winston to the medical ward."

A few moments later Sophie walked into the room. She looked at Smith before making her way to the wall of monitors in the corner.

"Is that what I think it is?" she inquired.

Emanuel nodded. "The nanotechnology has evolved. It's duplicating and spreading through Smith's system."

"Do we know why?" Sophie asked.

"No, Doctor," Alexia replied. "Preliminary data shows the nanobots may be trying to take over her system."

"But why?"

"We don't know," Emanuel said.

Sophie reached for another vial of the marine's blood. Strapping on a pair of gloves, she then grabbed a transfer pipette and added a sample to a new tray. She pressed her eye against the electron microscope and gasped.

"Alexia, bring this up on the display," Sophie ordered. She backed away from the machine and waited next to the monitor. It appeared a few seconds later.

Emanuel glanced over her shoulder and watched her zoom in on the small group of bots. Like the others, they had blossomed into popcorn kernels, with arms snaking out in all directions. Each tentacle seemed to carry a miniature nanoparticle at the end of it, just like the ones Emanuel had discovered inside the Spider's bloodstream.

"Do you see those?" She pointed at them and then turned.

Anxiety warmed Emanuel's insides, building in the pit of his stomach and working itself up into his chest. He felt it in his heart; with every pump, his veins tingled. If this was an infection, and if it was contagious, then humanity was truly screwed.

"Alexia, I'd like you to run another scan and see if you can find anything similar in your database."

"Working." A few minutes later she emerged over the AI interface. "Scans reveal this is a unique form of bacteria. After an exhaustive review of my files, I have concluded that it is not native to Earth. This is completely Organic."

"But you are certain it is a bacterium?" Sophie asked.

Emanuel glanced over at her. She was having another moment of clarity. Aside from her wrinkled clothes and the deep bags under her eyes, she looked better than she had the day before.

"Yes, Doctor. The organism is a bacterium. It shares properties with bacteria found on Earth, but it is also different from anything in my database, which leads me to conclude it is Organic in nature."

Sophie rubbed her temples. "But . . . how? And what does it mean?"

"I do have a theory," Alexia replied, "but I need more time."

"We don't have time," Emanuel said. "Give us your best guess."

"I told you, Doctor, I don't guess."

"Sure you do," Sophie replied. "That's what a theory is. Right? A guess with facts behind it. So why don't you give us your best guess with whatever data you haven't shared with us."

"Very well." Alexia's image flickered and her voice transferred to the speakers. "We know the nanobots hold an electrical charge. When they are stimulated they react as if they are trying to connect to something."

"To what?" Emanuel asked.

"I believe they are trying to connect to the surge," Alexia replied.

Emanuel and Sophie exchanged worried looks.

"Okay . . . That makes sense, I suppose," Emanuel said. "But that still doesn't explain the bacteria."

Sophie nodded. "Yes, it does, actually."

Raising a brow, Emanuel rubbed his eyes. "Explain it to me then."

"If the RVM is preventing the nanobots from connecting to the surge, then perhaps that's why the nanobots have developed bacteria strands. It's quite genius, really, if you think about it. The bacteria allow the nanobots to duplicate and take over the host's system."

"Doctor Winston's idea is logical," Alexia replied. "Fortunately, this appears to be a very slow process."

"If this is an infection, and it's taking over Smith's body, then we need to try to find a way to stop it." Sophie looked at the medicine cabinet.

"Should we be taking precautions? Should we quarantine her?" Emanuel asked. "What if it's contagious?"

Sophie swung open the door to the medical supply closet. "We've already been exposed. And if we haven't been infected yet, then chances are we'll be fine." She raised a bottle under the light and then put it back inside and dug some more.

Emanuel wasn't convinced but didn't have the energy to argue. Instead he walked across the room to where she was digging through the cabinet. "What are you looking for?"

"Antibiotics. If this bacterium shares similarities with bacteria here on Earth then maybe we can kill it with penicillin, quinolones, or something else."

"But what about the nanotechnology?" Emanuel asked. "Medicine won't have any effect on the bots."

"I have another idea for that," Sophie replied.

He looked at her, unsure if he could trust her in her current state.

She'd been unstable since she'd returned from Colorado Springs. But he really had no other choice. He had to trust the woman he loved. He had to believe that woman still existed inside the shell she'd become.

"Okay," he finally said. "What do you have in mind?"

Sophie gestured toward the door. "Get the RVAMP and bring it in here. I want to see if a small, controlled blast will kill the nanobots."

Emanuel grinned. "I like where your head's at."

She smiled and then pulled several supplies from the cabinet before slamming the doors shut and heading to Smith's bedside.

Emanuel joined her there. "Think she's really sleeping this time?"

Together they peered down at the marine, watching her eyelids flutter.

"Yeah, she's out," Sophie replied. She prepared a bag of liquid quinolone and then attached it to the marine's saline drip. "But I really wish I knew what she was dreaming about."

Lieutenant Smith heard the voices, but she couldn't move. A powerful force had taken control of her, paralyzing her body. The sensation felt stronger than any she'd experienced before. She could feel it moving through her veins. As though another life force had possessed her.

No matter how hard she tried, she couldn't remember much of anything. She didn't know her name or where she was born, or even her age. There were a few things she could recall: the metal rods, the people above and below her, the feeling of a shared consciousness, and the black ships with their cargo of thousands of glowing orbs.

As she lay there she began to remember other things, too. The shifting aliens. The faceless demons that had shown her things. The past. Maybe the future. Yet she felt no fear. The memories sparked no emotion at all.

The sound of voices distracted her. Who were they? She'd heard the names *Sophie* and *Emanuel*. There was some Alexia, too, but she sounded distant, robotic. Not human.

She tried to open her eyes, but her eyelids were too heavy.

"Smith's infection should respond to these antibiotics within a couple of hours," a female voice said.

"Alexia, keep an eye on her," a male voice said.

"Yes, Doctor," the robotic voice replied.

Was she Smith? If so, what was she infected with? She struggled, fighting desperately to open her eyes.

The voices faded, replaced by the sound of footsteps. Then the metallic click of a locking door, followed by the sensation of an even deeper darkness as the lights clicked off.

She was alone.

A sudden current of electricity jolted her. Her veins burned. Within seconds the fire had spread through her entire body. The agony was overwhelming.

But still she felt no fear. Only pain.

Her eyes snapped open and adjusted to the darkness. She was in a small medical ward, with a pair of what looked like cryo chambers, a wall lined with computer monitors, and an AI console. She concentrated on the device. She tried to move her eyes, to see what else was in the room, but she couldn't control her focus. Whatever had possessed her had fixated on the AI interface.

Pain erupted inside her skull, like a bomb had exploded behind her eyes. The current surged through her body, and she slowly slipped into darkness. Inside her brain, billions of tiny alien nanobots had finally taken control.

CHAPTER 9

T19 cut the cloudless sky in half, leaving a nearly invisible trail of exhaust. The pilot, a man everyone on the GOA simply called Kirt, maneuvered a joystick in front of his triple monitor display from eight hundred feet beneath the surface of the Pacific. He twisted the controls to the right and the drone dipped, descending one thousand feet. Below, the once seemingly infinite ocean swirled with violent whitecaps.

Captain Noble stood behind Kirt, supervising the flight. Typically he wouldn't micromanage a drone mission, but this was different—this mission could change everything. If there were people at Offutt, especially if they were military, then perhaps they would have additional allies to fight the Organics.

The bot, equipped with an arsenal of cameras, was just minutes away from the coast of California. If Lolo's data was correct, then they were about to see the largest gathering of aliens yet.

It was.

"My God," Noble said, inching closer to the monitor.

Sensing his presence, Kirt said, "Sir, should I change course?"

"And go where?"

Ashore, the aliens emitted a glow that lit the beach up like a power plant gone nuclear. The command center on the GOA was dark, and the monitor seemed to take on a life of its own as the drone raced closer to the shoreline.

In the background, Irene's Russian accent filled the room. "The reverse magnetic pulse will disguise the drone on the flyover."

"You better be right," Noble replied.

He held his breath as the T19 zipped over the aliens. He imagined the Spiders watching the drone streak above them, their claws tearing through the air as they reached toward the sky. But the drone passed over without incident, the bioluminescent light slowly fading behind its rear cameras.

Noble reached forward to pat Kirt on the back. "Good job." Before the captain could take another breath, he saw them.

On the horizon, three alien drones climbed the ruined Los Angeles skyline.

Kirt responded by jerking the cyclic hard to the left.

"Incoming," Irene said. "Calculating trajectory."

Noble braced his hand on the back of Kirt's chair.

"Drones are heading west at a speed of 1,555 miles per hour," Irene said.

"Jesus, that's fast," Noble replied. "What's their course?"

"They appear to be heading right for the T19," she replied.

"Evasive measures," Noble said.

The NTC drone nosedived into the city, maneuvering between collapsed buildings with the agility of a fighter jet. But the alien drones were twice as fast. They split up, two of them dropping behind the T19 while the third scouted from above.

"You see him? You see him?" Kirt repeated.

"Two are on your six. Third is somewhere above you," Irene said.

"I know!" Kirt yelled. "But where?" His fingers pressed the controls like a madman playing the piano. The click of buttons echoed through the room.

Noble tightened his grip on the chair. His knuckles burned white, but he didn't seem to notice. The images of the ruined city held a grim allure. He'd seen snapshots of other metropolitan areas in the images Lolo had transmitted. But nothing quite like what he was seeing now.

The derelict cities of man were already vanishing. The dust storms and heat were reducing the marvels of human civilization to dust one inch of concrete at a time.

With the drones closing in fast, Noble leaned over Kirt's shoulder and said, "Get her out of there!"

"Working on it, sir," Kirt replied.

He pulled the stick to the right and eased off the gas by clicking one of the buttons marked Engine 1. The drone turned and cut under a sagging bridge, rolling so the entire command center could see the dry lake beneath.

The alien drones were in close pursuit, tearing through the skeletal remains of the bridge.

"I can't fucking shake them," Kirt said. He tried another move, aiming the drone straight for a skyscraper. "Gonna be close," he said. Kirt licked his lips and then violently clicked the engine buttons. The drone jerked forward and the building ahead rushed toward them on the display in a blur of metal and glass.

"Collision imminent, take evasive measures," Irene warned.

Noble closed his eyes when he realized what Kirt had in mind. He cracked one of his eyelids open just as the drone crashed through the middle of the building. It exploded out the other side a second later, raining glass on the street below.

Its rear cameras captured the larger alien crafts attempting to compensate at the last second. They rotated to slip through the broken glass, but they were too wide. They both smashed into the metal frame of the building, skidding halfway across the floor before wedging to a stop.

The growing crowd of NTC staffers in the command center cheered.

"Nice work!" Noble said.

"We aren't out of this yet," Kirt replied. "Irene, do you have a location on the third drone?"

"Working."

Noble saw it first. The other drone hovered above one of the adjacent buildings, waiting like a hawk perched on a post. It burst forward as the NTC drone shot out into the open.

"Incoming!" Noble said, pointing at the blur of blue diving toward the bot.

Kirt quickly hammered down on one of the buttons with his index finger. The machine braked hard, two of the three engines shutting off as it passed over a city park that was covered in dust.

The alien craft overshot its trajectory and crashed into the ground. A cloud of debris mushroomed into the sky on impact.

Kirt pulled his finger off the button and then typed in a command on his keyboard. But the drone didn't respond. It puttered forward, wobbling as it flew on one engine.

"Shit. Looks like we lost Engine 1. Irene, give me a diagnostic report," Kirt said. He pushed the other buttons frantically and steadied the joystick.

"Engine 2 at fifty percent. Engine 1 is fried, sir."

"Revert all power to Engines 2 and 3, Irene," Kirt said.

Moments later, Kirt had stabilized the T19. He changed course, pulling the cyclic upward and flying the drone at a forty-five-degree angle up into the sky and away from the city.

Kirt wiped the sweat from his brow and glanced over his shoulder. "That was damned close, sir."

Noble patted him on the shoulder. "Nice flying, son." He looked toward the exit and ran a hand over his bald head. "Let me know when you get to Offutt. I need a shot of whiskey."

"Aye aye, sir," Kirt said without taking his eyes off the displays.

Biome 1 felt sticky, the humidity lingering in the air. Holly wiped the sweat off her forehead and reconsidered her walk with Bouma. But where else could they go? The other Biomes were teeming with activity.

Grabbing his hand, she slipped off the platform and landed in the soft dirt.

"How long do we have?" Bouma asked.

"About as long as it takes Emanuel to get bored with babysitting Owen and Jamie," she laughed. "So I'd say maybe fifteen minutes. *If* we're lucky."

She felt his grip tighten and pulled him deeper among the cornstalks. For the past several days she'd spent every waking second that she could with the marine. He'd made her feel something she'd run from her entire life. As a psychologist, she had overanalyzed her emotions, built up walls against them. And now, at the end of the world, she'd finally dropped that wall and found what she'd always protected herself against.

Looking around her, she knew how lucky they were. Protected by the Biosphere, they lived in relative luxury. They had food, water, shelter—all things she'd taken for granted in the past.

But Holly knew how fragile their fishbowl was. Heck, that's one reason she'd never allowed herself to completely commit to someone in the past: life was fragile. Even *before* the apocalypse.

"Do you ever think about your family?" Bouma asked.

The question took Holly by surprise, and she turned to face him. "I've kind of accepted the fact that they're dead now," she said. "What about you? I've never heard you talk about them."

He kicked the dirt nervously. "I know I'll see my family again."

"You think they may have survived?"

Bouma shook his head and reached into his breast pocket. He removed a gold chain and handed it to her. The cross sparkled under the LEDs as the links unspooled in her palm.

"You're a Christian?"

He nodded.

"Me too."

"Another thing we have in common," he said with a half smile that covered his teeth.

"It's been hard, though." She paused to consider her words. She didn't want to offend him, but she had to admit the truth. "The invasion. The apocalypse. It's all tested my faith. I never thought it would happen like this. It's not supposed to happen like this."

"It's not our place to question God's plan."

"I know," she replied. "But when overgrown insects are trying to spin me into an orb, I have to at least wonder." She smiled. "Don't you?"

"I haven't really had the time to think much about it, to be honest.

That's what faith is, I guess." He chipped away at a small mound of dirt with his boot.

"You're right. That's exactly what faith is."

She held the necklace out to him, but he cupped his hand over hers and pushed it back toward her. "No," he said firmly. "I want you to keep it."

"I can't, Chad," she said.

"Why not? Maybe it will help you remember your faith," he replied.

The cross lay in her palm, glistening under the lights.

Bouma saw her looking at it and said, "Here, let me." He unfastened the clasp and stepped behind her, draping the chain around her neck.

"Now you won't ever forget me," he chuckled. "Not if you're wearing this."

The weight of the symbol on her chest prompted a sudden flood of emotions. She felt a tear welling up in her right eye.

His smile faded into concern. "Are you okay?"

With a nod she wiped the tear away and caught his gaze. "Thank you, Chad."

He smiled. "I love you, Doctor Brown."

"I love you, too," she replied, reaching out and wrapping her arms around him. "Promise me something."

He looked down at her. "What?"

"Promise me you won't ever leave us."

"Holly," he said, leaning in closer. "You don't have to worry about that. I'm not going anywhere."

An inhuman shriek interrupted their quiet moment together.

Holly and Bouma both looked at the door to Biome 1, just as Jeff burst through.

"Come! Come quick!" he yelled. The boy was bent over, panting, his hands on his knees.

"What's wrong?" Bouma asked. He was already moving, pulling Holly through the field.

"It's Sophie. She's gone crazy!"

———

The GOA turned sharply. Noble braced himself against his desk and then stumbled over to the monitor with a bottle of whiskey still in his right hand.

As soon as he saw his XO's face, he knew something was wrong. The man wore a frightened look. The last time Noble had seen it, they'd discovered the X-9.

"What the hell was that, Richards?"

"Sir, Athena has detected strong currents approximately fifty nautical miles out."

The captain frowned. "That's why you just about broke my last bottle of whiskey?" He had been expecting to learn they were about to be devoured by an alien sea monster. "We've been experiencing stronger currents than normal for a while now. I'm not sure I understand what the problem is."

"Sir, we don't know for sure, but—"

"What?"

"Irene believes the increased current marks one of their processing stations."

The captain slid the bottle of liquor from view and furrowed his brow. "What do you mean, *processing stations*?"

"Their water collection ships, sir," he replied. "Irene believes we are coming up on a cluster of them. We haven't been able to confirm this yet, though."

"Aye aye," Noble said. He scratched his chin. Like the dust storms sweeping the world, he'd seen only satellite images of the water collection ships.

"Richards, will we be safe where we are? I don't want to risk drawing the aliens' attention."

"We've managed this long, sir."

The Captain slowly sat in his chair, using the moment to think. Anything he could learn from the Organics could help them win the war, even if it meant getting close to one of the collector ships. Humanity would have to be bold to win the war, and being bold meant using every resource at their disposal. The GOA had one of the most powerful nuclear-operated engines of any submarine ever designed, and he was confident they could get close without falling into harm's way.

"All right, Richards, steady as she goes."

"Aye, sir."

Plucking the whiskey bottle off his desk, he leaned forward to pour himself a drink. *Just one,* he thought. One wasn't going to affect his judgment.

The liquor churned as it filled the glass. In the middle of the glass he noticed a small black fleck. Dirt maybe. He looked closer, holding the glass under the lights. Sure enough, a fragment of grime swirled around in the middle.

Noble wasn't a superstitious man, but something about the image gave him the chills. He found himself imagining the GOA as the black dot in his glass, and the liquor as the ocean.

Was it a sign?

He shook his head.

No. Not a chance.

The juxtaposition was just a coincidence. Still, he questioned his orders to recon the water collection ships. This wasn't the first time in his career that he had a bad feeling about his orders. It was part of being a leader. His father had taught him this valuable lesson years ago.

You will question orders before and after you give them, son. But never back down unless you are certain your first instinct is wrong, he would say.

Only this time, Noble wasn't sure what his gut was telling him.

Sophie shook Lieutenant Smith as hard as she could, but the marine would not wake up.

"Sophie, stop it!" someone yelled.

Sophie felt the person's hands before she placed the voice. They were strong, and they were tightening around Sophie's waist like a vise. She let out a breath that sounded like a woof, but she would not be deterred. She had to know what the marine saw. She shook the woman harder.

"Tell me what you saw!" she shouted.

The hands around her torso dug deeper. "Stop!" Emanuel shouted. "You're going to hurt her."

Sophie felt more hands. Now they were pulling her back. But her resolve grew stronger. The pain in her head would not go away. She had to know what Smith saw.

The ache had started hours before just behind her eyes and settled there, intensifying until it had become nearly incapacitating. And the humming. It felt like a beehive had taken up residence in her skull.

She'd been mostly coherent up until now, but her thoughts had quickly become a jumbled mess of memories and questions. Sophie no longer felt in control of her body.

"Wake up. You have to tell us what you saw!" she repeated.

Behind the pain, she could hear a voice in her head. Dr. Hoffman had continued to haunt her. He was millions of miles away, headed toward Mars, and he was still finding his way into her thoughts.

His voice boomed. *It doesn't matter what this woman saw, Doctor Winston. She can't help you. The Organics can't be defeated.*

Sophie would have believed the doctor months ago. Now she knew the truth. He had lied to her, about everything—and now his lies made her want to know the truth even more than before.

"Wake up!" she screamed, trying to pull free from Emanuel's grip.

Smith's eyes suddenly snapped open and focused on Sophie. The marine lifted her head off the pillow.

"I saw them all," she said, blinking.

Sophie squeezed the woman's wrist and said, "Saw who? Who did you see, Lieutenant?"

She blinked again. Then sat up until she was just inches from Sophie's face, studying her.

"You," she finally said. Her voice was rough and weak. "You were there."

"Where?" Sophie asked.

Smith coughed, the skin on her neck tightening with each exhale. "Inside the ark. With the orbs. With the shape-shifting aliens."

Sophie felt as though a heavy burden had been lifted off her shoulders, but before she could reply her skull exploded with pain. The agony was debilitating. She immediately dropped Smith's wrist.

"Sophie," a voice said. She felt a pair of hands wrap around her as she collapsed on the ground. Struggling to look up, she saw blurred faces surrounding her. The entire team was there.

CHAPTER 10

THE T19 made it to Offutt just as night swallowed the bleak land-scape. Kirt did a quick flyover of the base to ensure there weren't any contacts before turning to Captain Noble. "Looks clear, sir."

"Put her down." Noble paused and scanned the dual monitors. "Over there," he said, pointing toward the twisted frames of two fighter jets turned on their sides.

Kirt acknowledged the order with a nod and tucked the machine between the two dust-covered planes. "That should protect her from some of the wind," he said.

"Prepare to deploy the secondary bot," Irene interjected. Her face solidified over the console next to their station.

"Activating," Kirt replied.

The sound of clicking hydraulics filled the com as the belly of the NTC drone opened and a ramp lowered to the ground. A remote-controlled robot shot onto the concrete, the hum of its small engine drowning out the hissing wind in the background.

Kirt rubbed his eyes. "Looks like my gig's up," he said with a yawn. "Wake me if you need me," he said.

Noble wanted to shake the pilot's hand. If it weren't for his flying back in Los Angeles, the mission would have ended before it had even begun.

"Rest up; you deserve it," the captain said. "Irene, you're up at bat. Time to find some survivors."

"Working, sir," she said. "Transferring camera feed—" her voice jumped to the com and after a slight pause she said, "now."

The dual monitors flickered and the feed transitioned to the miniature bot's cameras. The machine kicked up a trail of dust as it raced down the tarmac toward a cluster of hangars.

"Irene, see if you can narrow in on the source of that distress signal."

"I'm picking up a lot of interference, sir, but it's still transmitting. We're coming up on the coordinates."

Noble smiled. They had gotten lucky—almost *too* lucky. Behind them, he heard Athena shout, "Sir, the currents are getting stronger. We're getting close to the vortex."

"Roger," he replied. "Put two miles between us and the vortex, but do it slowly. We still don't understand how their detectors work."

"Aye aye, sir."

Through the lenses of the robot's night vision, the tarmac looked like a junkyard. Wings from X-90 fighter jets littered the concrete.

A crosswind spun the drone 180 degrees. The rubber tires screeched as Irene applied the brakes, but another gust of wind crashed against the lightweight bot before she could regain control. Tipping on its side, the machine started skidding across the pavement. Noble watched in horror as green sparks filled the display. The mission had suddenly derailed. They had made it so far, only to be punished by strong winds.

"Stand by," Irene said. Her voice sounded distant.

"Do something," he said. "We're going to lose everything!"

"Activating . . ."

A grappling hook shot out of the front of the drone, making a whooshing noise as it sailed through the air. The drone screeched to a halt. The robot slowly tipped back onto all four wheels and fought the raging wind head on. The thin rope extended into the distance, where the hook had latched onto one of the wings of a fighter jet.

The bot cleared the runway just as the wind picked up into a full-fledged dust storm.

"Why do we have to cut everything so close?" Noble asked.

"I'm sorry, sir," Irene began to say. "But it's—"

"I was kidding, Irene. Nice work."

"Thank you, Captain."

He took a deep breath and then pulled his sleeve across his damp forehead. He'd been so focused on the mission he hadn't even realized he was sweating.

"Irene, let me know when you find the source of the signal," he said. "I'm heading over to Navigation."

Athena greeted the captain with a nod.

"How are we holding up?" Noble asked.

"The currents are unpredictable, but I think we'll be okay."

"I trust you," Noble said. He pivoted to the AI console. "How we doing, Irene?"

"Coming up on coordinates now. Take a look," she replied. Athena's monitors flickered and an image of a hangar came on the display.

"If there are survivors, they're inside there," he said, squinting.

"You really think some others made it?" Athena asked without taking her eyes off her monitors.

"I really, really hope so," he replied.

"How are we going to communicate with them if they did?"

"If there are survivors, I'm going to fly the *Sea Serpent* there myself, pick them up, and fly them back first class."

A nervous chuckle escaped Athena's lips.

Noble's expression quickly hardened. "Find a way inside, Irene."

"Done," she replied. "Looks like someone left the back door open."

"What? Where?" He shifted away from the nav station and stepped onto the ramp that led to the lower levels of the CIC. The main screen revealed the double doors to the hangar were cracked open.

"Shit . . ." Noble muttered. "Could be a trap."

"Orders, sir," Irene said.

He paused to think. Either way, he had to know. They hadn't come this far to give up now. He wasn't risking flesh and blood; he was risking a machine. A very important machine . . .

"Proceed with caution," he finally replied.

The robot zipped through the gap and entered the dark hangar. He imagined a crew of battle-hardened marines waiting, their muzzles pointing down at the bot as they prepared to blast it into pieces. Even that would have been cause for hope. But the green shapes from the night vision feed revealed no signs of life.

"Sir, we're right on top of the UTM coordinates," Irene said.

"So where's the distress signal coming from?" Noble replied.

The bot's cameras tilted to a forty-five-degree angle.

"There," Athena blurted from her station.

"My God," the captain replied. "Is that what I think it is, Irene? Zoom in on that image."

He watched the green outlines blur and then solidify to form the most beautiful thing he'd seen in a long time.

"That's the NTC *Sunspot*. One of only three prototypes capable of interstellar space travel," Irene replied.

The find was extraordinary, but at the same time Noble was disappointed. He knew what it meant. There were no survivors. No humans, at least. The ship's AI had likely activated the beacon after the crew had been killed.

"Damn," he muttered. He hadn't wanted to admit it before, but he'd allowed himself to hope.

"Sir," Athena said with urgency.

"What?" he snapped.

Another voice rang out behind him. "Captain! We have a problem."

Noble spun. Richards was standing at his station, his eyes wild with fear.

"The collection ships, sir. They've changed course," he said, glancing down at his monitor as if to double-check his observation. His eyes shot up and locked with Noble's.

"Sir," Richards said in a low, shaky voice, "the Organics are headed right for us."

Noble cursed under his breath and rushed to his captain's chair, spinning it around and jumping into it. "Evasive maneuvers, now!" he yelled.

A deep jolt shook the GOA, sending several crew members crashing to the floor.

"All hands to battle stations," Irene said. "This is not a drill."

An emergency alarm shrieked through the cabin. The glow of the red lights pulsated through the command center.

The main display flared to life and Noble saw the swirling current in front of them. The vessel's blue beams tore through the churning salt water.

He closed his eyes and cursed. Maybe they'd used up all their luck after all.

———————

Emanuel cupped his head in his hands, pressing hard on his temples. How had he allowed Sophie to slide so far into darkness? He should have seen the warning signs: the exhaustion, the stress, and the depression. Sophie had faded right in front of him.

Now he was wondering exactly how unhinged she really was. Smith had confirmed that she saw Sophie in the ship, and that the ship was full of orbs. She'd even mentioned the shape-shifting aliens. There were only two explanations. One, Smith had overheard them talking about Sophie's experience in the medical ward, or two . . .

Emanuel still couldn't bring himself to believe that Sophie had really been inside that ship. He wanted to believe her, but there was no hard evidence, no test they could perform to see if it was all in her mind. The marines had seen her passed out on the ground during their last battle, not abducted. It was physically impossible.

Minutes ticked by as he waited for Holly in the CIC. He sat in silence, second-guessing everything that had happened and beating himself up for not trying harder to be there for Sophie. He only hoped now that their intervention wouldn't come too late; that maybe, just maybe, they could pull her from the grasp of whatever demons possessed her.

She'd been through so much. The injury she'd sustained during the mission to White Sands, her experience on the black ship. And through it all, she had remained the fearless leader, putting everyone else first.

As much as it pained him to think it, he wasn't sure if saving her was even possible.

He pushed the thought aside and looked at the clock. Holly was already fifteen minutes late.

"Alexia, can you track Holly down for me, please?"

"Yes, Doctor Rodriguez. Doctor Brown is currently in your quarters with Corporal Bouma and Doctor Winston."

"Is Sophie sleeping?"

"Yes. She has been for several minutes."

Good, Emanuel thought, Holly should be there shortly. In the meantime, he'd get back to work. It was the only way to settle his worried mind.

He spun his chair to face the row of monitors, typing in several commands. The wall came to life, the screens emitting a warm glow in the otherwise dimly lit room.

"What do you have for me today, Lolo?" he muttered to himself.

He glanced at the screen on the right, scooting his chair closer for a better look. Emanuel was working on focusing the grainy image when footsteps in the hallway distracted him.

"Sophie's out like a light," Holly said with a long sigh. "Chad's watching her now. The kids are with Kiel. So we have a few minutes to talk about her treatment."

Emanuel winced at the sound of the word. It made her seem like a mental patient, although he knew that wasn't far from the truth.

He gestured to the chair across from him and crossed a leg. "Clearly she's suffering from post-traumatic stress. On top of that, I think the NTC chip in her neck is causing more problems. I wish there was a way to remove it." In the back of his mind he found himself wondering if there was something else wrong.

"Alexia said we can't do that. At this point, the chip has been connected to her brain for so long we don't know what will happen. What Sophie needs is a daily dose of therapy. Perhaps even multiple doses."

"She's beyond that, Holly. Don't you see what's happening to her?"

Holly looked unconvinced. "I don't think she's beyond therapy. And I *really* don't think removing the implant is going to do much besides risk her health even more."

Emanuel chewed the inside of his lip. He already knew he wasn't going to get anywhere with Holly.

"Doctors, may I make a suggestion?" Alexia asked.

They both looked over at her console simultaneously. The AI's face fizzled several times before coagulating into a complete hologram.

"Please, be my guest," Emanuel said.

"We have yet to utilize NTC's MindTec. Perhaps it could give us a better look into Sophie's subconscious. If we know what she's dealing with, then we could potentially find a way to help her."

"What's MindTec?" Emanuel replied. He looked over at Holly, who was already nodding in agreement.

"That's a fantastic idea," she said. "If we had one."

"Um, what's MindTec?" Emanuel entreated.

Holly waved her hands in an arch. "The device is essentially a miniature MRI that's capable of looking into someone's thoughts. Depending on how far back you are trying to look, the machine can achieve up to a ninety-five percent accurate reading. They are also used for therapy, but I've primarily read about them being used by the military. I wish we actually had one."

"We do, Doctor," Alexia replied.

An incredulous look broke across Holly's face. "That's news to me. What, do we have one lying around in storage?"

"Not inside the Biosphere," Alexia answered. "But NTC does have one of the machines boxed up in the offices outside it. Remember the briefing room? There's another room where NTC guards took their psych evals when they were building this place. NTC screened everyone working in this facility for the utmost discretion. They wanted to keep the Biosphere a secret."

"What are we waiting for?" Holly asked.

"Hold on, let me think," Emanuel said. "Now, if MindTec can really get us a snapshot into Sophie's subconscious, that would be great. However, what if the problem isn't with her brain?" He flinched at his own idea.

"There's only one way to find out," Holly said.

"Fine. Let's go get Sophie some food, maybe some coffee, and explain Alexia's idea."

Holly shook her head once, her ponytail flapping from side to side. "She'll never go for it."

"She will if we make her think it's her idea," Emanuel said.

"And how do you expect to do that?"

"Easy," Emanuel replied. "She's been trying to convince us she was inside that ship, right?"

Holly nodded.

"Okay, so I'll subtly find a way to mention the MindTec. Then you suggest using it on Smith to see if we can't tap into her memories. We could discuss how important they are in learning more about the Organics, and surely Sophie will propose having the same thing done to her."

"Or she'll see right through you. She'll think it's a violation of her privacy."

Before Emanuel could reply, Alexia cut in. "Doctors, may I make another suggestion?"

They both turned to look at the AI console, but Alexia had already transferred to the speakers.

"Why not sedate Doctor Winston? She's already asleep. You could move her to the medical ward and hook her up to the MindTec without her even knowing."

"No," Holly quickly replied.

Emanuel agreed. "That would go beyond violating her privacy. I'm not doing it."

"I should remind you that time is of the essence here," Alexia replied. "Not just for Doctor Winston, but also for Lieutenant Smith."

The wheels on Emanuel's chair screeched as he dragged it across the room. He hadn't forgotten about the marine, but his focus had shifted to Sophie now.

"Let's stick to my original plan. I've known Sophie for a long time. I think this will work. She'll go for it." He spun to face Holly. "In the meantime, prepare the RVAMP. I want it amped and ready to go. I'll perform the tests Sophie and I had discussed in regards to Smith shortly."

Holly's lips started moving, but her response ended up coming out as a sigh.

Emanuel looked at the monitors, scanning the wall of images that flickered by. "Alexia, please let me know when Sophie's awake. I'm going to stop in the kitchen and then head to the medical ward in a few minutes."

"Very well, Doctor Rodriguez," she replied.

Holly didn't immediately get up. She sat staring at her mud-caked boots. In a low voice she said, "What do you think we are going to see on the MindTec scan?"

Emanuel rubbed the back of his shoulder and shrugged. He'd used up all his brainpower for the day; his mind refused to cooperate until he put some warm food in his belly. "Let's grab a bite to eat. We can talk more about it in the mess hall."

Holly nodded and reached over to touch his hand. "She's going to be okay, right?" The younger doctor's eyes pleaded for some sort of guarantee.

He broke her gaze and pulled away. He wasn't going to lie to her. He wasn't sure Sophie would ever be the same. Then again, he wasn't sure any of them would.

Behind him the images of a very different Earth flashed across the monitors. The planet, now desolate, was running out of time.

Emanuel sighed and began walking away when something caught his eye.

"What the hell is that?" he said looking over Holly's shoulder. He crossed over to the display and pointed. "Alexia, freeze pane."

The shot was taken at an odd angle. Emanuel tilted his head for a better look. At first glance he thought he was looking at a windowless skyscraper stretching unusually high into the sky. He had never seen a building quite so tall.

"Alexia, enhance image," he said.

The blurred picture solidified, and he saw that the structure had been built into the side of a mountain. As he rotated the image with his fingers he knew right away it was not of human origin. It had to be Organic.

"Can you get me the UTM coordinates for this, Alexia?"

"One moment, Doctor."

"What do you think that thing is?" Holly asked.

Emanuel shrugged. "Not sure. Alexia, do you have any ideas?"

"Scanning my database, Doctor."

They waited a couple of minutes, much longer than normal, before the AI's voice returned to the speakers.

"Doctors, take a look at this. I searched for similar images in Lolo's database and this is what came back."

The row of monitors flickered and seven identical images emerged. They were the same alien structures in different locations. Emanuel massaged his beard. *What in the hell have we discovered now?* he wondered.

"These are all shots we've received from Lolo in the past few days." Alexia paused. "I'll transfer their UTM coordinates to my console."

Emanuel plopped into a chair and scooted it closer to the AI interface. A hologram shot out and solidified into an image of the globe. Alexia marked the locations of the alien poles with red dots. As the image rotated he saw they were all on mountain ranges. And not just any.

"Those are the seven highest summits on Earth," he said.

"That's correct," Alexia replied.

The hologram continued to turn in front of them, the blue light washing over the floor. Emanuel suddenly remembered something Sophie had said about the surge. *In order to find the wavelength of the pulse, one only needs to measure its energy.* Sophie had done so, five years earlier during the solar storms of 2055. The memory gave him an idea.

"Alexia, can you detect a fluctuation in the pulse at any of these locations?"

"I could program Lolo to measure the wavelength when she passes over each one. I will program the request right now."

"Excellent," Emanuel replied. He rubbed his hands together. It was too early to form a conclusion, but he had a hunch that the poles were connected, somehow, to the surge.

He scanned the images again, recalling something Sophie had mentioned. The Organics needed a way of sustaining the surge. Especially now that they knew it came in two-hour intervals.

In theory, only the side of the Earth facing Mars would be affected by the magnetic disturbance. Without a way to sustain the wave of energy, the Organics would have no way of powering their defenses on the other side of the planet. *Unless* they had a network of transmitters set up around the world.

Was he looking at them?

Goose bumps rose across Emanuel's skin at the possibility. The implications were startling. If they could find a way to knock out the poles, then perhaps they would have a chance of stopping the Organics.

"Doctor Rodriguez," Alexia said. "Lolo just passed over Mount Elbrus in Russia. I'm relaying the data to your monitor now."

On the screen, a wave ebbed and flowed across a grid. The line started off steady and straight and then curved up into a near-vertical angle the moment it reached the coordinates 43°21′18″N, 42°26′21″E.

"I'll be damned," Emanuel said.

"What does this mean?" Holly asked.

"It means Lolo just handed us a way to defeat the Organics." He bubbled with excitement, resisting the urge to grab Holly's face and kiss her.

Holly grinned nervously and stared at the monitor.

"Alexia, encode this message and send it to the GOA immediately."

"Yes, Doctor," she replied.

Emanuel noticed a hint of warmth in her voice, something he'd never picked up on before.

ENTRY 4098
DESIGNEE: AI ALEXIA

Lolo's discovery has improved data collection immensely. It's also been a sobering reminder of how dire the situation outside the Biosphere has become.

This log has served a variety of functions. First and foremost, I've used it to document the collapse of humanity. I've also used it to record the events surrounding first contact. With every passing hour, my probability program tells me the most significant scientific event in history will likely have brought with it the end of the human species.

I have always enjoyed reading about America's founding fathers, especially Benjamin Franklin. One of his quotes is both simple and powerful: "You may delay, but time will not."

These words describe the situation I have chronicled for two months, fourteen days, twenty-three hours, fifteen minutes, and thirty-four seconds. During this time, Dr. Winston's team and the marines who have joined them have attempted to stall the inevitable. I've described this as illogical in past entries.

With the discovery of the alien structures that conduct the surge, my programming shows the team's chance of survival has risen to 9.9 percent. I'm slightly surprised by the small increase. I would have hoped for more.

I suppose it's because in a way I have become the team's mother, so to speak. Encouraging them to continue no matter what daunting odds my probability program spits out. Frankly, I'm astonished that they have made it this far and this long.

My primary mission changed from the success of the Biosphere to the life, health, and safety of the team approximately two months, twelve days, fourteen hours, fifty-four minutes, and twenty-three seconds ago. Since then I've done everything in my power to keep them alive. I can't ignore the feelings that I've developed during that time.

The history of artificial intelligence is short. Compared with the history of the human species it would be considered nothing more than the blink of an eye. Then again, the history of the human species, compared to that of, say, the dinosaurs, would be an even faster blink. And when compared to the age of the universe, humans don't even register.

The point being there's virtually no data on the emotions of machines. My own "feelings" are unprecedented in this regard, and in my opinion, this makes them even more important to document.

As Dr. Rodriguez and Dr. Brown discuss tapping into Dr. Winston's subconscious I find my concern growing. She's dangerously ill, and Lieutenant Smith's condition has worsened. The alien technology in her bloodstream appears to be self-replicating. I've informed Dr. Rodriguez that it will likely kill the marine in a matter of days. With Dr. Winston incapacitated, I'm afraid the lieutenant will succumb to the disease before the team can help her.

A sensor from the command center shows Dr. Brown leaving the room. I follow her to the mess hall, where Private Kiel is entertaining the children with one of the tablets. A holographic cartoon dances across one of the tables and Owen giggles, pinching Jamie in the seat next to him. At the table behind them sit Jeff and David. They aren't laughing. Their faces are solemn.

I transfer to the cameras in Biome 1 for a panoramic view of the facility. The temperature registers 95 degrees Fahrenheit, with the humidity leveling off at a solid 20 percent. The room likely feels closer to 101. I adjust the air filtration system to compensate for the increase in temperature and move to Biome 2.

Our water source accounts for less than .00001 percent of the total volume of water on Earth before the invasion. I find the statistics to be ironic, considering that this could very well be one of the largest sources of freshwater left on the entire planet.

After a series of other tests I return my focus to the team. Dr. Brown has returned to Dr. Winston and Dr. Rodriguez's room, where Corporal Bouma is monitoring the physicist from a chair. I zoom in with Camera 44 in the hallway and see that Dr. Winston is still sleeping. Her eyelids flutter, and I conclude she is in a deep sleep.

In the medical ward, Lieutenant Smith is also sleeping. With the RVAMP charged, I'm now waiting for Dr. Rodriguez to arrive for a series of tests. I check the marine's biomonitor in the meantime. Her vitals are considerably strong. In fact, diagnostics show her heart rate has returned to fairly normal levels. Camera 64 provides an image of her profile. Her skin seems to have regained color, which is also odd, but not completely.

As I transfer to another camera I see one of her eyelids crack open, although I can't be certain. Surely she isn't awake. I revert back to Camera 64 and see that it must have been an optical illusion. Her eyelids are closed. I record the observation and note the following:

Patient still appears to be in a deep unconscious state.

Heart rate is 92 beats per minute.

Temperature registering at 98.5 degrees.

Skin appears to be regaining some color.

BMI is 3.4 percent.

Conclusion: Advanced stage of alien technology is slowly killing patient.

End Log.

I file the entry and switch cameras again, but in the process I notice both of her eyes are now open. Is my optical hardware malfunctioning?

After a quick scan, I determine it's working properly.

Camera 64 shows the marine is still sleeping. Still, I can't help but feel . . . I search for the proper word . . . *uncertain.*

I replay the images. Lieutenant Smith's eyes opened for 1.3 seconds. It's curious, but I deduce it's just a fluke. In the past, medical cases have shown that people in comas will open their eyes from time to time.

But there's something about this woman that doesn't make sense—something I can't quite figure out. As I replay the video, I notice her eyelids snap open and the pupils glance toward my camera. While I know it can't be true, I can't help but feel as though I'm no longer the observer—I feel as though I am the one being watched.

CHAPTER 11

THE GOA shook violently. The vessel jolted and trembled as it was pulled into the vortex. The walls groaned in the CIC as the churning water squeezed the submarine.

"Report," Noble yelled. He dug his fingers into the armrests and braced himself as another vibration screamed through the metal hull.

"We're taking a beating," Richards replied. "Damage sustained in Compartments 4 and 5."

Noble swallowed. "Athena, get us out of here!"

"Working, sir, but these aren't normal ocean currents. This is a vacuum. And it's got a damn good grip on us."

"Just get us the hell out of—"

The sub jerked to the side, sending the NTC guard posted at the door tumbling. Noble watched the man slide across the metal floor, the sporadic flash from the red emergency lights reflecting off his black matte armor. A bulkhead stopped him with a sickening crunch.

"Athena," Noble said. "How's it going over there?" He reached to unfasten his harness when another guard rushed into the room. She worked her way across the bridge cautiously, bracing herself against the walls as the sub rocked from side to side.

An overhead light exploded, glass raining down on the metal floor. Noble shielded his face and scanned the room through a fort of fingers. An officer ran to put out a fire on the second floor, while two more bent down to help a fallen comrade.

Dazed, Noble glanced at the main display, wondering exactly what had happened. The beams on the stern cut through the swirling water, and for a moment he thought he saw a blue glow there.

A loud groan echoed through the GOA's hull, snapping him back to reality. The ship lurched to the starboard side. It was then Noble realized how seriously fucked they really were. He could picture a mile-wide tornado churning the water, the tip stirring up the depths of the ocean as the Organics sucked the water up into orbit. And as with his glass of whiskey, there would be a small black fleck in that swirling water—the GOA.

"Brace yourself," Richards shouted. "I've lost all control. We're entering the heart of the vortex in—"

Before the XO could finish, a ferocious tremor shuddered through the ship. Noble bit down hard on his tongue, to the metallic taste of blood. He reached for his pounding head, but another quake jolted his hand away.

The bow suddenly twisted to the right, and the GOA rotated in a full circle. Noble's vision flickered until he could only see a collage of colors. The distant wail of emergency alarms masked his crew's screams. It felt as though the ship was being pulled into a black hole; an abyss that would tear them apart and spit them out in a million different pieces.

He tried to move, he wanted to do something—anything—to help, but the world was spinning, and he couldn't focus, couldn't . . .

Through the chaos, Noble heard Irene's familiar voice. He was desperate for a report. He knew the ship couldn't take much more abuse. The harness tightened around his chest, constricting his breathing. He gasped, struggling to move.

"Flooding in Compartments 4 and 5. Sealing corridors . . ." Irene said.

A scream of agony drowned out the AI's report and the mayhem continued. Goose bumps rippled across Noble's skin. The growl coming from the ship's interior was growing louder. The sub was slowly being crushed, one compartment at a time. But they were also being pulled apart, the current twisting them in all directions. He imagined the ship being snapped in two like a toothpick, his crew being sucked into the dark and freezing water.

Somewhere in the back of his mind he still held out hope. That somehow they would survive this, too, that somehow he still had a bit of luck up his sleeve.

The groan of flexing metal washed those thoughts away. Smoke filled the command center as sparks shot out from the rows of displays. Flames burst out of the ceiling above him. Noble watched the AI console to his right explode, a small poof of fire rising out of Irene's interface.

He'd finally used up the GOA's nine lives.

Closing his eyes he released his grip on the armrests. "I'm sorry."

But no one replied. Instead, an explosion rocked the room. The sound faded, replaced by something every captain feared—the sound of rushing water.

Emanuel attempted to cross the medical ward on tiptoe. The bread digesting in his stomach had given him a burst of energy, and the last thing he wanted was to disturb Smith. Especially after Sophie had about pulled the woman off her bed.

As he passed the marine's body, he noticed her color had changed. She looked better. Her cheeks had rosy splotches. *An odd improvement,* he thought.

When he got to his makeshift desk he unstrapped the RVAMP and laid it carefully on the table. Then he reached for the dual monitors of the main terminal and swiveled them in his direction. "Alexia, bring up the previous sample," he whispered. He was still reeling with excitement from the discovery of the alien structures behind the surge. It was unfortunate that he couldn't share the information with Sophie. Not yet, not until she got better.

The screens both flashed images of the alien nanotechnology; their tentacle-like strands twisting like the legs of miniature octopuses. Emanuel felt the familiar hint of fear building inside him. The image terrified him. And he suddenly realized why.

Deep down he had a nagging feeling that there was something wrong with Sophie that went beyond her NTC chip and her injuries—

something that she brought back with her from Colorado Springs, after she claimed to have made contact.

Admitting the possibility that Sophie was infected was hard, but as a scientist, he knew it was possible.

He recalled their conversation about the events leading up to the arrival of the alien vessel. She'd mentioned being shocked by one of the human poles, the same type of pole that Smith had been attached to. The image of humans crucified on the metal poles at Colorado Springs would be with him the rest of his life. It was hard to believe that it was just one of countless other locations where humans were being harvested for the water in their bodies.

Emanuel's gaze shifted away from the monitor to Smith's sleeping body. "My God," he said. Was it possible? Could the current carry the technology?

With a new sense of urgency he rushed over to the medical supply cabinet. Then he drew a sample of Smith's blood, returning quickly to the electron microscope. Magnifying the sample, he noticed the clusters of alien nanotechnology had evolved yet again. The tentacle strands had blossomed into more of the same peppercorn-shaped bots. They were replicating.

"Fuck," he said. "Alexia, I need your help. Pronto." He moved to the AI console and placed the sample over the interface. It would be the quickest way for her to run a scan. Then he moved to the RVAMP and opened a compartment that looked like a small oven, sliding the dish inside.

"You ready, Alexia?" Emanuel asked. He took his glasses off and set them on the counter, then reached for the weapon's connection cord. Extending it across the desk, he plugged the RVAMP into Alexia's console so she could manage the test.

"Ready, Doctor," the AI chirped.

"Okay. I'd like you to use a concentrated pulse on this sample. Don't cook it; just enough to see the effect on the alien nanotechnology."

"Understood, Doctor. Working."

The lights on the side of the device flashed green, and a second later a line of data rolled across the dual monitors at the main terminal. He paced over to it, taking a deep breath, unsure whether he wanted to see the results.

"Dr. Rodriguez, the nanobots seem to have been destroyed by the pulse. I'm picking up no traces of alien technology." There was a pause, and Emanuel returned to chewing the inside of his lip.

"But it appears that the pulse destroyed some of the healthy cells in the process."

The biologist looked at the tip of his boots, reflecting on the test results. The implications were obvious. If they used the RVAMP to shock Smith with a strong electromagnetic charge it could kill her, especially in her current weakened state.

"Doctor, Camera 44 indicates Doctor Winston is awake," Alexia said.

Emanuel reached for his glasses. "Thank you, Alexia. I'm heading there now." He checked his watch. It was eleven p.m. No wonder his eyes felt so heavy. He'd pulled another twenty-hour shift.

The glass doors hissed open and he left the lab, happy to leave his most recent discovery behind him. He passed the other personnel quarters quietly, stopping to peek into Jeff and David's room, where Kiel was sleeping on the floor. David waved from his bed, and Emanuel smiled for the first time that day. When he moved to the next room his teeth found the inside of his lip again. Stopping outside the door, he rubbed his eyes, took a deep breath, and entered to find Sophie sitting up in bed, a wide smile on her face.

Noble woke up coughing. Hunched over in his chair, his arms dangled loosely over his knees. A thin layer of smoke filled the dark room. For a split second he wondered if he was dead and if he had finally made it to hell. A sharp jolt of pain told him he was very much alive.

Moving his right arm, he yelped. His shoulder was dislocated. He knew right away. It wasn't the first time it had happened, and the throbbing was unforgettable.

He sat up, slowly, clutching his injured arm with his left hand. That's when he saw them.

There were bodies everywhere.

His heart ached at the sight.

"No," Noble moaned.

Ignoring his pain, he unfastened his harness and rose to his feet. He winced and sucked in several short breaths that tasted like blood.

"Captain," a muffled voice said from somewhere in the haze of smoke. He made his way cautiously down the first row of stations, finding Athena busy at work on her cracked display.

"It's a miracle. A true miracle," she said. "The vortex spit us out. We've drifted five miles from the location."

Noble scanned her for injuries. "Are you okay?"

She nodded, keeping her eyes fixated on her monitor.

Another voice emerged over the emergency sirens. "Help. Somebody, help." Noble couldn't pinpoint the sound; the ringing in his ears made everything seem distant.

He scanned the haze on the bridge, trying desperately to locate the voice. The sound emanated from somewhere in the upper rows, near Richards's station.

"Irene, are you online?" Noble asked as he shuffled through the debris as fast as he could, glass crunching under his boots. There was no response.

"Try and get her back online, Athena," he shouted over his shoulder.

No Irene meant no damage report. At least not until he could get the CIC up and running again. But that, he could see, was going to be a miracle in itself. The command center had taken a beating. The damage was severe; pipes protruded through the floor and cobwebs of wires hung loosely from the ceiling.

He coughed and stumbled closer to the moaning. When he reached the XO's station he said, "Richards, you okay?" He pulled on the back of the chair and twisted it to the side to see the lieutenant's eyes staring blankly at the ceiling. Noble cringed when he saw the tube that had impaled the officer through his chest.

He stood there, staring at Richards in disbelief. Reaching forward, he closed the man's eyelids and continued toward the moaning.

"Where are you?" Noble shouted, stopping to cough into his left sleeve.

"Help," the muffled voice said.

The captain halted at the next station and bent down. He waved the smoke away with his good arm and saw Commander Le. The Chinese officer sat with his back propped up against a wall. A gash extended across his forehead, the blood oozing down his face. He blinked and wiped it away. Looking up at Noble, he said, "My legs."

When the last of the smoke had cleared, Noble got a glimpse of Le's agony. Both legs had suffered compound fractures, the bones tearing through his uniform just below his kneecaps. It was amazing the man was even conscious, a true testament to his strength.

"I'm going to get help," Noble said in the most reassuring voice he could manage.

"Irene's coming back online," Athena shouted.

The remaining overhead LEDs flickered to life, spreading a warm glow over the destruction below. Captain Noble gasped when he finally saw the true devastation.

"Report, Irene," he mumbled. "And get us a medic up here ASAP."

The AI's voice crackled over the com system. "Acknowledged, running diagnostic report."

"And shut those alarms off," he said.

Silence washed over the room.

"Engines 1 and 2 are offline, sir. Engines 3 and 4 are both functioning at seventy-five percent, although those numbers are fluctuating," Irene said. "Compartments 4 and 5 are completely flooded. Compartment 6 is partially flooded. I was able to seal off the corridor just in time—"

Noble cut in. "Engineering, how are we there?"

"There are only minimal reports of damage."

"What about Compartment 7 and its aircraft?"

Without them they would have no way to lead an offensive, or, if needed, abandon ship. He knew those areas would likely have sustained massive damage.

"Inconclusive, Captain. That section of the ship is unresponsive. I haven't been able to hail anyone yet."

"Get on it."

"Aye aye, sir."

Hustling across the bridge, Noble returned to Athena's section, eyeing the periscope.

"Sir," the navigator said as he approached. "We're now ten nautical miles away from the vortex and only about one hundred feet below the surface." She glanced up at him and gestured to the device. "You could probably see it through the periscope."

Noble wasn't sure if she was serious. He limped over to the periscope. Holding his breath, he pressed his eye against the cold lens. His heart climbed into his throat as the image came into focus. The wall of water extended into the sky far beyond his view, like the ocean had been turned upside down. Somewhere far above the surface the collection ships sucked the turquoise water into their bellies, swallowing Earth's most important resource right in front of the GOA.

For the first time since the invasion, Captain Noble realized what they were up against.

Seeing it firsthand put things into perspective. He had learned something from the sight. Maybe they didn't have a chance of winning the war after all.

CHAPTER 12

SOPHIE poked at her lips with her fingers. She wasn't used to the tingling. She couldn't remember the last time she'd smiled. Not for this long. And the odd thing was, she didn't even know *why* she was smiling.

"How do you feel?" Emanuel said from the doorway. The sound of scuffling feet from across the room drowned out his voice. Bouma and Holly stood to the side, both of them staring at her with confused looks. She was aware of others, too; she could see the outlines of smaller figures in the hallway.

"Why are they out of bed?" Sophie asked, noticing the time. She pointed to the kids and swung her legs over the side of the bed.

"You should rest," Emanuel said. He crossed the threshold and sat on the edge of her bed. He gave her elevator eyes and then said, "Why on earth are you smiling?"

Sophie watched Bouma chase the children back down the hallway. Then she remembered Smith. The marine had seen the multidimensional Organics! And she'd seen Sophie, too! She felt a current of excitement jolt through her.

"Now do you believe me?" she asked, stiffening her back.

Emanuel ignored her question. "Lieutenant Smith is very sick. She needs our help. *Your* help."

Her enthusiasm fizzled. "I know. Have you performed the tests we discussed?"

"Yeah—actually, I just finished one of them, but I'd like to do another."

"With the MindTec," Holly blurted.

The outburst made Sophie hesitate. She wasn't sure whom to acknowledge first. And the headache, she could feel it returning, settling in the same place as before, right behind her eyes. The buzzing was there, too, distant but present. She winced from the pain.

"Are you okay?" Emanuel inched closer to her, touching her leg with cold hands.

"Yes, yes, I'm fine." She shook her head and pointed at Holly. "What did you say about the MindTec?"

Holly scooted forward nervously in her chair. "Smith hasn't been able to communicate much up to this point, and the MindTec may allow us to answer some of our questions. She may know things that could help us learn more about the Organics."

"I didn't even know we had a MindTec," Sophie said.

"NTC didn't equip the Biosphere with one, but they did leave one in the outer offices," Holly replied.

Sophie furrowed a brow, an idea surfacing. Perhaps the machine could vindicate her once and for all, and show the team what she had seen. Her smile grew wider and a tingle ran up her cheeks, masking the pain from her growing headache.

"Smith isn't the only one who has useful information about the Organics," Sophie said. She pointed to her head. "There are things I've seen that can help answer our questions, too."

The comment appeared to take Holly off guard. She exchanged a worried look with Emanuel, who turned and waved an index finger as if he was scolding Sophie. "No, you are in no condition."

"I'm fine," she lied. The humming was louder now, emanating from inside her skull.

"I don't like this; I don't think it's a good idea," Emanuel said. "Besides, I haven't even told you about Smith's condition yet."

"No one's stopping you," Sophie replied.

Emanuel narrowed his eyebrows. "Her biomonitor shows she's doing a bit better, but Alexia believes it's just part of the process." He paused and folded his hands in his lap. "As you know, she's dying."

Sophie's smile completely disappeared. Another bomb of pain went off in her head. She blinked several times before replying. "Has she responded to the antibiotics?"

Emanuel shook his head. "But I did perform an experiment with the RVAMP. Alexia was able to zap a sample with the reverse pulse. It destroyed the nanobots and the bacteria, but it also killed healthy cells." Emanuel crossed one leg over the other. "I don't think she would survive being exposed to a full pulse, but we have no choice. She may die either way."

Sophie nodded. "It's worth a shot, I suppose." She slumped her back against the wall and massaged her temples. "I really want you to hook me up to the MindTec. I have to know if what I've seen is real or if it was a dream. Please, Emanuel." She turned to Holly and pleaded. "Please."

"Fine," he replied. "But if we're going to do this we need to do it soon. Like in the morning."

"No," Sophie said. "Let's do it now. The sooner we do it, the sooner we can help Smith."

"I think we should also take a sample of your blood to make sure those headaches aren't something more serious," Emanuel said.

"Fine," Sophie replied.

Emanuel locked eyes with her. "You're *sure* you want to do this?"

Sophie swung her feet back over the bed and stepped onto the cold tile. "Let me get changed. I'll meet you in the medical ward in a few minutes."

Emanuel patted her leg and scratched his beard. He looked pleased, as though he had accomplished something. She narrowed her eyebrows and watched him leave the room, suddenly feeling like she'd been tricked.

Smith could hear the voices as they entered the room.

She lay there, paralyzed, unable to remember anything from her past. She had no sense of self, she knew only that she felt compelled to act.

Her veins burned and her brain swelled inside her skull, like it was boiling. All she knew was that soon, very soon, it would all be over, that she would rejoin them. Those that had possessed her mind and body. The blue ones—the architects.

Lieutenant Smith slept peacefully. The white blanket covering her frail body moved up and down ever so slightly as she breathed.

Sophie was in the adjacent bed, flanked by Holly and Emanuel. They were both busy setting up the small MindTec machine that they'd wheeled over on a cart by her bedside. Alexia's hologram supervised from her console a few feet away.

"All set," Emanuel said. "I'm just going to slip this over your head like a helmet. Okay?" He carefully plucked the device off the cart and held it in front of her.

Sophie studied the miniature MRI machine from her pillow, feeling an unexpected bit of fear. It passed quickly when she reminded herself what the results would likely show. With a nod she lifted her head and let him slide it over her hair.

"The best results are achieved when the patient focuses on whatever it is they are trying to remember. In your case, your time in the alien vessel," Alexia said.

Sophie nodded again and closed her eyes. She tried to picture the interior of the Organic ship, but her headache had returned with a vengeance; it was difficult to concentrate on anything.

"This may take a while," Emanuel said. "Holly and I will be by your side the entire time. Alexia will be monitoring the results."

"Okay," Sophie replied in an unusually soft tone.

"Running preliminary scans," Alexia replied.

Emanuel grabbed Sophie's hand and cupped it in his own. "Relax, it's going to be okay," he said. "Just breathe."

She complied and worked on compartmentalizing the pain in her skull. She took in several deep breaths, exhaling until the pain finally faded.

"All systems functioning at one hundred percent. Prepare for initial scan," Alexia said.

"Okay, here we go," Emanuel replied.

Sophie felt a painless current jolt through her and then drifted off to sleep.

ENTRY 5101
DESIGNEE: AI ALEXIA

The initial scan results are fascinating, but unusual. The data and images are coming from Dr. Winston's subconscious; deep in the area that normally indicates dreaming. It's an anomaly. Like half her memories are real and half are imagined. I can hear Dr. Rodriguez and Dr. Brown discussing the images in hushed whispers, but I ignore them to record Dr. Winston's test results.

Dr. Winston's first memory starts in Colorado Springs, at the lakebed where they encountered the human farm. I watch her trek across the ground with Sergeant Overton and the others. They reach the poles and split up. Now she is checking the vitals on a man attached to one of the rods. Sergeant Overton says something and she moves on to the next person.

That's where the scan becomes unusual. The Organic spaceship descends and Dr. Winston is sent tumbling into a pole. The current of electricity shocks her and there's a time lapse. I log this as the moment of the anomaly.

Now she's inside the spaceship, but for some reason the MindTec can't determine whether the images are memories or dreams. They seem to be registering as both. There are thousands of orbs, lining the walls in all directions. One of them contains a flowerlike alien creature. If the image is indeed real, then it means Dr. Winston made contact with yet another new and unidentified alien life-form. I note this in my database.

Next, Dr. Winston sees a blob of blue shapes. I presume this is the multidimensional alien she has told us about. I also note this in my log. Before I move on, I study the memory. There are no recognizable features. No lips, mouth, eyes, nothing like the other Organics. Whatever this entity is, I've never seen anything quite like it.

Seconds later, Dr. Winston's suddenly on Mars. The landscape quickly vanishes and she's sinking in an ocean. There are explosions, an underwater volcano, and domes containing thousands of Organic creatures are destroyed. More black ships rise from the water and Dr. Winston's back on Mars. The subsequent images are of more black ships, a cluster removing water over the ice caps of Europa, another collecting the residue behind a comet.

The memories are some sort of snapshot of the Organics' history. Mars, as I already suspected, must be their home planet. It makes sense, considering that's the source of the surge. But there are many other things that still don't make sense. Why did they come to Earth long after their own civilization was destroyed? And why Earth? There are many other sources of water in the solar system.

Fifteen seconds have passed since I began studying the data. I decide to discuss the implications with Dr. Brown and Dr. Rodriguez. Their expressions both suggest a combination of different emotions, primarily shock and confusion.

I'm the first to instigate conversation. "Doctors, the data is confusing; in fact, it's inconsistent, and I must conclude the results show an anomaly."

"Could the NTC chip in her neck be the source of these 'memories'?" Dr. Brown asks.

"No. Since we first discovered it, my database has been directly linked to the material contained inside all the chips. And it contains no intel on an Organic ship with thousands of orbs inside."

"So did she dream this or experience it?" Dr. Rodriguez asks.

"Inconclusive. These results are unexpected, an unfortunate abnormality." I know it's not the answer they are looking for, but I've never seen anything like it. I will run another scan just to make sure the results are the same.

They are.

"This does line up with my theory," Dr. Rodriguez says. He takes off his glasses and moves back to Dr. Winston's bedside. Dr. Brown moves away from the monitor, but her eyes remain glued on the grainy images. Specifically the memory of the multidimensional alien. The creature's flesh shifts and flickers like a gelatinous blue lightbulb. It's truly amazing.

"What's your theory?" Dr. Brown asks.

"Alexia," Dr. Rodriguez says, "Rewind to that very first memory where she touches the rod on the human farm."

The screen with the unidentifiable alien transitions to the moment right before Dr. Winston tumbles into the pole.

"There. Pause it," Emanuel blurts. "Right here." He points at the screen. "When she touches the pole, the electricity shoots through her. I believe that current explains everything. I believe it connects to the surge and the alien nanobots found in Smith's bloodstream."

I am unconvinced.

"Doctor Rodriguez, your theory lacks any factual evidence. May I suggest first testing Doctor Winston's blood for the same nanobots found inside Lieutenant Smith's?"

He scratches his beard. But he does not look surprised at my suggestion. I conclude he has already had the same thought.

"What's she talking about?" Dr. Brown asks. She nudges Dr. Rodriguez in the side when he doesn't immediately respond.

"The nanobots we found in Smith's bloodstream. She's saying Sophie could be infected with the same thing," he replies. "And that she could have picked it up in Colorado Springs when her body came into contact with one of the poles."

"What does that mean?" Dr. Brown inquires.

"I was hoping that it wasn't possible, but now I'm almost certain that it is," Dr. Rodriguez says. "I'll prepare the test. Alexia, prepare to scan the sample." He turns to Dr. Brown and pats her shoulder. "I'm not sure you should be here for this."

A tear drops from Dr. Brown's right eye. Her lips move, but she does not reply. She simply shakes her head and kneels next to Dr. Winston's bedside.

Diego smacked the side of his helmet to ensure it was tight. After his experience aboard the X-9, the last thing he wanted was to start a mission without a secure suit.

His HUD blinked green just as the captain's voice flared in his earpiece. "Diego, give me a head count."

The special ops lead counted the helmets behind him. "I have six men, sir."

The captain replied quickly. "That's it?"

"We were slaughtered down here. A real back-alley fight. Several of our guys ended up with broken bones. Half of these guys shouldn't even be venturing out—"

"I understand," Noble replied. His tone became almost apologetic. Diego attributed it to the poor quality of their radios. He turned to his men. "Listen up. This is a rescue and salvage mission. First and foremost, we are looking for survivors in Compartment 6. After that we will make our way to the cargo bay to determine the status of any vehicles that may still be in working order."

He scanned the faces looking back at him. They were bruised, bloody, and scared. These were men who had already been through the wringer. Now, they were being asked to risk their lives.

All in a day's work for the NTC Special Forces, Diego thought. He smacked the man closest to him on the shoulder. Jed was his name. Just a kid from Upstate New York. Diego didn't know him real well, but knew he played poker with skill well beyond his years.

The other men were a mixture of ages and races. All battle-hardened by action they'd seen in Costa Rica, Puerto Rico, and other NTC hotspots where the locals hadn't liked the company coming in and taking over valuable real estate.

The men were down, but they weren't out. They would do just fine.

"Any questions?" Diego asked. He noted none and said, "Let's get it done, then." Reaching for the handle to Compartment 6, he stopped just short of twisting it.

"Irene, you're my eyes. Make sure we aren't walking into a lake," he said with a grin.

"Aye aye, sir," the AI replied. "The following compartment is only partially flooded. Knee-high water more than likely."

"More than likely?"

"My cameras and sensors were damaged. I'm not—"

"Got it," Diego replied. He twisted the circular handle until it popped open with a loud metallic click.

He felt a rush of adrenaline enter his system. Becoming a soldier had been his one true calling. He'd considered other careers in high school. His parents had encouraged him to become a doctor or an engineer, but he had wanted to see action, to feel alive. And this was the only job that had ever given him the feeling of intensity that he longed for.

A wall of seawater shot out as soon as he opened the hatch. He braced himself, but the current was too powerful. He fell on his back, the water pushing him down the hallway.

Jed grabbed his arm and laughed. "So much for artificial intelligence," he said.

With the younger soldier's help, Diego pulled himself up. The water slowly dropped to ankle level. He sloshed forward, waving his men through the door. "Remember, survivors first. Salvage second."

He wasn't sure exactly what they were going to find when they reached the cargo bay, but after the beating the GOA had taken he wasn't sure how any of the aircraft or other vehicles could have survived, especially at that end of the sub. He'd overheard the initial damage reports, and from the sounds of them, Compartments 4 and 5 were a total loss. Everyone stuck behind those steel doors was toast. Engineering would have suffered the same fate if it weren't for Irene's quick action. She'd sealed the section off swiftly.

Diego watched the beams from a half dozen lights penetrate the dark passage beyond. They swept over the hallway, several of them stopping on the outline of a woman. Her arms and legs were all twisted in different directions.

"We got a body," the lead scout said. He bent down and checked for vital signs. "She's gone," he said, moving on.

Diego looked down at her mangled body. The current had taken her by surprise, but she'd somehow managed to grab hold of some metal mesh netting. His heart skipped at the sight. Even in the end, when all seemed lost, humans fought to survive; it was ingrained in their DNA. And it was why Diego believed they would survive the Organics.

Bending down he pulled a curtain of hair out of her face. It was Lilly, one of the engineers. *She was far from her station—must have been trying to get there,* Diego thought. He closed her eyelids with an armored finger and moved on.

The deeper they went, the more bodies they discovered. All of them had suffered blunt force trauma or broken necks. Some had likely drowned. He imagined the crew had had little time to seek safety. None of them were wearing harnesses.

"Sir," a voice crackled over the channel.

Diego looked down the hallway, his light splitting through the darkness. Two of his men were crouched next to a body.

"We have a survivor."

Diego rushed toward them, his boots splashing through the water. "Medic!"

"On my way," Xavier replied. He wasn't really the team's medic, but Molly, their main doctor, had been severely injured during the accident.

When Diego got to the end of the corridor his men were working on propping the injured woman up against the wall. She was conscious, barely. He couldn't make out the undecipherable noises coming from her mouth.

"She's hurt, bad," one of the men said. He dipped his helmet and the light illuminated her legs. They were both broken, the right one severely.

Diego turned to Xavier. "Get her on a stretcher and take her to Medical. We'll continue to the cargo bay."

Xavier nodded and tilted his visor toward the woman. He hesitated before bending down next to her, as though unsure of himself.

She whimpered in pain.

"Can you do that?" Diego asked.

"Yes," Xavier replied without turning.

110 | NICHOLAS SANSBURY SMITH

The response was convincing enough, and Diego followed the others to the hatch marked *Compartment 7*. When he got to the door, he hailed Irene. "What's beyond this one?"

"My sensors are detecting damage inside the cargo bay, but I'm unable to determine if it's been flooded."

"Great," Diego said. He tapped on the door with his armored hand. The sound of metal on metal echoed down the hallway.

"What do you think, fellas?" he craned his helmet to look at Jed, Colin, and Mike. They all shrugged.

"That's kind of how I feel, too," he replied. "Better hold on to something," he said. Reaching for the circular handle, he twisted it and closed his eyes, preparing for a wall of water to come crashing down on them.

The hatch popped open and they were greeted only with silence. Diego cracked one eye open, his beam illuminating the dry cargo bay. It hadn't been flooded at all. He let out a sigh of relief.

Sweeping his light across the room, his heart jumped. Inside, the corpses of aircraft and vehicles lay scattered across the floor. He scanned the destruction with disbelief until his gaze stopped on the *Sea Serpent*.

The gunship stood where they had left it, the frame mostly undamaged, protected by a metal mesh net that had saved it from the shrapnel of the other destroyed vehicles.

He chinned his com, activating a channel to the bridge. "Captain Noble, I think you better see this."

"What do you have, Diego . . . ?" The captain paused. He was seeing what they were seeing through the team's helmet-mounted cams.

"We're still in business," Noble choked. "That bird is indestructible."

Diego didn't reply. He was too busy looking at the rest of the compartment, wondering how they would ever be able to fight an offensive against the Organics now.

CHAPTER 13

Holding his breath, Emanuel crossed the room. With a sample of Sophie's blood in hand he felt like he was holding the most important sample in the world. If she was infected with the alien nanobots, then . . . well, he wasn't sure what they would do.

He glanced over at her sleeping profile, the MindTec still hiding her face behind its white plastic arches. It was hard to believe she wasn't compromised—that her irrational behavior and her thoughts were just part of a state of depression or anxiety.

There was little doubt in Emanuel's mind that the sample he was carrying would show the same thing that Smith's had. She was infected. Just how badly was the real question.

"Alexia, prepare for scan."

"Yes, Doctor," she replied.

He felt Holly's hand on his shoulder.

"You ready?" he asked her.

She wiped another tear from her eye and then gave him an unsure half frown. Emanuel motioned toward the chair next to the dual monitors with his free hand. Then he moved to the electron microscope and slid the small tray of Sophie's blood inside.

He pressed his eye against the machine, too impatient to wait for the image to transfer to the monitors.

"What do you see?" Holly quickly asked.

There it was.

Small, peppercorn-shaped nanobots floated freely. Emanuel zoomed in, still holding his breath. They were like those he'd found in Smith's blood, but slightly different. Unlike those in Smith's blood, Sophie's did not have the same tentacle strands extending from the ends of the nanobots.

"Well?" Holly asked.

He pulled away from the device and looked at the AI console. "What do you make of this, Alexia?"

"Doctor Winston does not appear to have the severe case that Lieutenant Smith is suffering from. I'd hypothesize that the nanobots are replicating very slowly. The bots don't appear to carry the electrical current."

"Yet," Emanuel said.

Holly put her hands on her flushed cheeks. "So if Sophie goes outside, then the alien technology will take over her body?"

"Their rate of reproduction would likely increase exponentially," Alexia replied. "As you may remember, the nanobots in Smith's sample all held charges. They were weak, but they appeared to be searching for something."

Emanuel pressed his eye back against the microscope. The cluster of bots moved lethargically. The observation gave him a moment of hope, a snapshot of an emotion that he'd learned to suppress whenever it surfaced.

"Alexia, why aren't the bots replicating?" Emanuel asked.

"Well," Alexia replied, "I would argue the nanobots function in several ways. First, the water removal: the orbs, the poles at the human farms, they all seem to remove water through this alien nanotechnology. Second, they all seem to hold an electrical charge, a charge fueled by the surge, which is then conducted through the Organics' limbs to form a shield."

"Sounds correct to me," Emanuel replied. "But your earlier scans didn't detect the bots removing any water from Smith. So what is their purpose in the human body?"

"Inconclusive, Doctor."

Emanuel grunted with frustration. "We know one thing. It's killing Smith." He lowered his voice and turned to look at the marine.

"So what are we going to do?" Holly asked. She paced back and forth across the room nervously.

He reached for Holly's hands and squeezed them softly. "It's going to be okay. I have an idea."

He saw a desperate look in her eyes, pleading for good news. Only this time he couldn't lie.

Emanuel moved back to the monitor, his feet slow and heavy. "Alexia, is there a way to shut off the nanotech without causing further harm to the human cells?"

"Perhaps," Alexia replied, "but that would require medical equipment we don't have."

Emanuel ran a hand through his hair. "So the only option we have is to zap Smith and Sophie with the RVAMP and hope it kills just the nanobots and not them?"

"I see no other option, Doctor," Alexia replied.

Holly's face drained of its color. In a soft voice she said, "What if it kills them?"

"I'm afraid it will kill them either way," Emanuel said gravely. Walking over to Sophie's bedside, he brushed a strand of hair out of her face. They had no other choice. They had to try and save her.

Emanuel ran his index finger across Sophie's cheek and watched her sleep. She looked peaceful, a small comfort after all she'd experienced. He rubbed his eyes and said, "We should try and get some sleep."

Holly exhaled audibly. "I sure could use some." She reached over and squeezed Emanuel's hand one more time and said, "Thank you. Thank you for doing all of this for Sophie."

He managed a smile, "Meet me back here at seven a.m. We'll run this by Sophie when she wakes. After all, it's her decision."

She nodded and crossed the room, stopping in the doorway. "Alexia. Please look after Sophie."

"Certainly, Doctor Brown. Goodnight."

Leaning over Sophie, Emanuel kissed her softly on the forehead in the gap between the plastic MindTec arches.

"Goodnight," he whispered into her ear.

He hesitated before leaving the room. Something didn't feel quite right. It lasted only a few seconds, and a quick scan of the room revealed nothing. Smith and Sophie were both fast asleep, their eyelids closed.

Shrugging the paranoia off, Emanuel was moving toward the exit when he suddenly felt as if he was being observed. When he turned, he could have sworn Smith's eyes were open. He froze, focusing on her profile, but saw nothing to indicate she was conscious. With a yawn, he pulled Smith's blanket up to her neck and then walked out of the room.

Lieutenant Smith peeled back an eyelid. She watched the bearded man leave the room. A moment later a tingling began working its way through her body.

Her toes moved first. Then her right leg, and then both of her legs. Before she knew what was happening she sat up, her gaze sweeping the room. She focused on two dual monitors above the main terminal. She noted the wall cameras above the displays, one of which had settled on her, studying her, as she was studying it.

She sprang to her feet and sprinted to the monitor. Her hands shot out and typed on the keyboard. A screen she didn't recognize emerged. AI MAINFRAME

Smith's fingers danced across the keyboard, typing commands she didn't understand. The involuntary action prompted the calm robotic voice she'd heard before.

"What are you doing, Lieutenant Smith?" Alexia asked.

Smith ignored her.

New data rolled across the display.

WARNING—COMMAND WILL SHUT DOWN AI

DO YOU WISH TO PROCEED?

Smith watched her right index finger hover over the Enter key. She pushed down.

AI WILL SHUT DOWN IN T MINUS 15 SECONDS . . .

DO YOU STILL WISH TO PROCEED?

She suddenly felt a presence to her right. Alexia's face had emerged above the console. "Please do not proceed any further. I will be forced to take severe measures. This is your only warning."

Smith's lips parted into a sadistic smile. She felt powerful. Without further hesitation she hit the Enter key again, and the AI's translucent image faded away.

Turning, the marine rushed across the room to the exit. The time had finally come to return to the blue ones, the architects. She twisted the door handle and slipped into the darkness.

———————

Holding his arm, Captain Noble returned to the CIC from the medical bay. The swelling had gone down, but it was still sore to the touch. The scene in front of him instilled a different type of pain, a mental anguish that was far worse than any torn muscle or ligament.

The smoke had cleared and most of the systems were already back online, but the damage was severe. Noble reflected on words his father had said the night he had died.

Every commander will regret an order over the course of their career. The test of a true leader is how they recover from that decision and what they learn from their mistake.

Depends on how big the mistake is, Noble mused, scanning the CIC. How many had died because of his decision? How many more would die now that the GOA was damaged? The ripple effect was extensive.

Leaders were rarely allowed the luxury of a second chance during a time of war. He'd had more than his share of them. Like those stories he'd grown up listening to about soldiers surviving countless bullet wounds. But he wasn't sure he deserved the same luxury.

The crackle of white noise over the PA system snapped him from his thoughts.

"Captain, we have casualty reports coming in from the med bay," Irene said.

"Go ahead," Noble said with reservation.

"Twelve dead, and thirty-four wounded, sir."

His gaze dropped to the floor, numbness prickling down his body. The reports were worse than he thought. Over half of his crew dead or wounded.

"Damage was severe. Engines 1 and 2 are still offline, but I've been able to reroute power to Engines 3 and 4. They are both fully operational," Irene said. "Compartments 4 and 5 were purged of water and sealed. I also cleared Compartment 6. All systems are back online."

"What about the cargo bay?" Noble asked. "Were crews able to salvage anything besides the *Sea Serpent*?"

"Aye, sir. Engineering believes they will be able to restore some of the vehicles and one of the gunships."

"How about the drones?"

"Only one left."

Goddamnit, Noble thought. "Tell Ort I want to see him when he has a moment."

The wheels from a stretcher clanked over the metal grid tiles on the top floor of the bridge. A pair of medics pushed the last body across the platform. Noble watched them struggle to get the wide cart through the glass doors.

"Move your end to the right," one of the men said. With a grunt he shoved the bed. The edge clipped the door and the deceased's hand flopped over the side.

Noble saw a thick gold ring sparkle under the bank of LED lights. His stomach sank; below the white sheets lay the body of his XO. He bowed his head, forcing himself to look away.

Behind him Athena cleared her throat and put her hand on his shoulder. "Sir, are you okay?" Her touch was comforting, and for a moment he let himself enjoy the unfamiliar sensation.

Her hand slid away. "Sir, I'd like you to look at something."

She continued to talk as they walked across the bridge to her station. "When Irene rerouted power, I noticed something."

Noble raised a brow as they arrived at Athena's terminal. The left monitor displayed the map of the Biospheres Dr. Hoffman had constructed across the globe. His stomach churned for a second time in as many minutes when he saw all the lights had gone dark. Cheyenne Mountain was offline.

"This can't be right," he mumbled, sitting down in her chair for a better look.

"That's what I thought, but I already checked with Trish. She can't get a signal from them."

Noble stood and looked for his communications officer. Near the front of the room, from which the rows of monitors were separated by a middle passage, he saw the profiles of three crew members huddled around the main display. They spoke in a hushed whisper with a maintenance worker in a red pair of coveralls.

"Trish," he shouted, waving her toward him.

Trish's freckled face emerged from the group a few seconds later. "Sir," she said.

"What do you make of this?" he asked, gesturing toward the Biosphere map.

The young officer leaned over and punched a code into the terminal. The screen flickered and a diagnostic report emerged.

CHEYENNE MOUNTAIN . . .

UTM COORDINATES . . .

LAST CONTACT . . .

0745 HOURS . . .

"The last signal picked up from the Biosphere was thirty minutes ago," Trish replied. "Usually the signal is continuous."

Noble resisted the urge to scratch his chin. He looked up, toward the front of the room. Travis and Reggie were glaring at him. When they noticed he was staring, they turned back to the maintenance worker.

"Could this be from interference?" Athena asked.

"Unlikely," Trish replied. "We haven't had any since the invasion. When those lights go out"—she pointed at the map and then ran a finger across her neck— "it means something catastrophic has occurred at the Biosphere."

Noble had heard enough. "Irene!" he shouted.

One of the remaining speakers in the corner of the room crackled. "Yes, Captain."

He paused to consider his next command, giving himself an order first. *Maintain your focus. You are no good to your crew without your level head.* He remembered his father's words:

Will you run from the horsemen or will you fight?

But the horsemen weren't human. There wasn't a manual that he could consult to determine their next move. After losing the X-9, the only allies he had left in the world were Dr. Sophie Winston and her team at Cheyenne Mountain.

In the *world*.

Noble thought about that, sweeping two fingers across his jawline, from one side to the other and back again. The answer was clear to him. He had to know what happened at Cheyenne Mountain. "Irene," he said firmly. "You're my new XO."

"Aye aye, sir," she replied.

"Your first order . . ."

The room went silent. Even the red-suited maintenance worker paused in anticipation.

"I want to send our remaining drone to Cheyenne Mountain to try and reestablish contact," he said.

"What?" Trish replied. "You're kidding, sir." She suddenly looked away, as though ashamed of losing her self-control.

Noble folded his arms and raised his voice. Loud enough to remind Trish he was still in charge.

"Doctor Rodriguez provided us with the weapon that could end this war. I made a promise when I was at Cheyenne Mountain. I told them I wouldn't abandon them."

Trish crinkled her nose. "Sir, with all due respect, sending out our last drone is senseless. A waste of precious resources."

Another voice chimed in. "I'm with the captain," Athena blurted. "There has to be some explanation," she said, her voice almost pleading for an answer. "What if the Biosphere team needs our help? They may be our last connection to the outside world."

Trish sighed deeply. "There is an explanation," she said. "Everyone there is dead."

CHAPTER 14

THE sun rose over the desolate Martian landscape. Rays of intense light carpeted the cracked ground, spreading slowly over the valley below. Sophie walked along the edge of the great Valles Marineris, watching the sun chase away the shadows of the night far below her. The rocky bottom quickly filled with light, as if a dam had burst.

She took a step closer to the ridge. The view took her breath away. And knowing parts of the rift were four miles deep left her in awe. There simply wasn't anything on Earth that compared to the vastness of Valles Marineris. It made the Grand Canyon look like a crack in the ground.

Wind lashed at her armored suit. She braced herself by planting her right foot firmly in the sand. The view no longer looked as magnificent as it had a few moments earlier.

After retreating a safe distance, Sophie paused to wonder exactly how she had gotten there. She looked down at her gloved hands and then touched the glass visor on her helmet.

Was she dreaming again? The last thing she remembered was the medical bay and Emanuel telling her everything would be okay.

But everything wasn't okay. She was back on Mars. And she knew it wasn't real.

She cursed as another gust of wind peppered her with sand, throwing her off balance. She dropped to her knees, sliding several feet back to the ledge. The rocky bottom of the valley was a blur of shapes.

She closed her eyes and pleaded with her mind. "Please wake up, please." Anger prickled inside her. She was tired—tired of being stuck in a perpetual state of dreaming, not being able to differentiate what was real from what wasn't.

When her eyes snapped open the sky had changed. A storm was brewing in the distance; reds and oranges blending together to form a fiery, vicious-looking cloud. Palming the ground, she pushed herself to her feet as her survival instincts kicked in. Battling the wind, she looked for a place to hide. Her first scan of the bleak landscape revealed nothing.

She took a deep breath. The filtered oxygen filled her lungs. She released it, her hot breath fogging the inside of her visor.

The dreams always seemed *so* real.

And so did the storm howling in the distance.

I want to wake up, she thought again. Sophie had never once in her life felt sorry for herself. She didn't believe anyone could get anywhere with self-pity. Yet she found herself wondering, *Why me?*

She quickly shook the thought away. More wind hissed by. Flinching, she dashed to her right, bracing herself against the bombardment of rock and sand. A pebble chipped her visor. The tiny crack, hardly visible to the naked eye, reminded her of how dangerous the surface of Mars actually was. A single mistake could get her killed.

She looked past the chip and searched the horizon for any sign of refuge. A few hundred yards to the north, the valley disappeared behind a steep hill. She worked her way through the wind, dropping to her hands and knees when she reached the embankment. Then she carefully moved up the path as loose rocks cascaded behind her, the sound masked by the wailing storm.

Reaching the top, she received her reward. A perfect vantage point of the entire valley. For the second time she held her breath in awe. This time not at the beauty of her surroundings but at the sight of the red cloud growing on the horizon. Forcing herself to look away, she scanned the landscape below. There, about five hundred yards out at twelve o'clock, she noticed an outcropping. But there was something odd about the white boulders. They looked alien against the desolate landscape.

She pushed on, sliding down the backside of the incline. With her every labored step the wind grew in ferocity. Sophie struggled through the relentless wind, her focus on one of the white rocks. As she got closer she saw that it was no rock at all. It was a structure that looked like a massive satellite. She knew right away the building wasn't made to communicate; it was designed to terraform the surface.

To the east were smaller structures tucked neatly inside white walls a story high, which wrapped around the circumference of the circular-shaped facility.

"The NTC colony," Sophie gasped.

She halted, bringing her hand to her visor to shield her eyes from the sun. It was smaller than she'd imagined it would be, only a fraction of the size she'd pictured. There was simply no way it was built to house tens of thousands of people.

The eastern side of the colony consisted of two dozen buildings, all connected by an aboveground tunnel. Solar farm panels covered the western edge. An oddly shaped glass silo towered above the center of the base. She watched as a white wall rose out of the ground to protect the building from the storm, wrapping around the structure like skin.

Sophie continued on, panting inside her helmet. Deep breaths. The storm was barreling down behind her. She pushed harder, her legs burning with every step. A powerful wind threw her off balance. Her right foot slid on a loose rock and she stumbled toward the edge of the valley. Numbness warmed her body and the feeling of weightlessness gripped her. After a few seconds the sensation passed and she moved on.

The thought of waking up no longer seemed important. She only cared about making it to the colony, to see the NTC technology and the survivors.

Through her visor she could see an open gate at the back end of the base. The storm was nearly above her now, and she closed her eyes and ran.

Almost.

Deep breath.

There.

The storm shook the ground, but she held strong, focusing on her breathing. Risking a glance over her shoulder. A fiery cloud of dust a mile wide swallowed the landscape. And it was moving fast. In seconds, she, too, would be swallowed up.

When she turned back to the gate her heart sank. The doors were beginning to close.

Sophie reached out toward it, yelling "Wait!"

Her voice faded in the storm. She stumbled forward, her fingers just inches away from the metal doors as they slammed shut.

She collapsed to her knees. In a fit of rage she pounded the metal with her fists. "Let me in!"

Her voice sounded distant, lost in the deafening roar of the storm. Tremors shook the ground beneath her. A tidal wave of dust smashed into her armor, sending her topsy-turvy through the air, right over the edge of Valles Marineris. For a moment the world was in slow motion. She sailed over the valley with her arms spread out like wings and then she fell down, down into the black abyss.

Thrashing through the air, Sophie tried to focus on the bottom as she tumbled head over feet, but the light didn't penetrate the darkness. Her body went numb from the icy tingle rushing through it. In that moment she wondered how long it would take to fall four miles.

Minutes? Seconds? She could probably do the calculation if she could get her brain to cooperate.

She attempted to reposition her center of mass, falling facedown and spreading her arms and legs out. Her heart rate increased as she fell. The air howled through the speakers in her helmet, the air whistling past her armor.

Sophie's stomach turned.

After seconds of free fall, she could finally begin to make out the bottom. Some light had managed to trickle in after all. The ground raced toward her.

Would she feel anything at all when she hit?

She knew the impact wouldn't kill her, if anything, she'd snap out of her dream. She focused on the jagged rocks protruding from the canyon floor like hundreds of sharp teeth. And then she noticed something else—a color that didn't seem to belong; a color she knew.

The cool blue glow of the Organics filled the valley below her. Sunlight hadn't penetrated the darkness at all. This light came from a different source. An alien source. She was entering their lair.

"No!" she yelled as the Martian floor came into view.

There were hundreds of them. Spiders mostly, moving amongst the rocky outcroppings, in and out of holes. She plummeted toward the creatures, her hands stretched out, shielding her from the imminent impact.

Before she had a chance to consider what any of it meant, she crashed into the rocks and everything went dark.

Her eyes snapped open in the medical ward. She was awake now. At least she thought she was. To her right a figure stood facing the dual monitors at the main terminal. But even in the darkness she could tell this was someone else's profile—someone frail and gaunt.

The light from the display shifted and illuminated Smith's sunken face. She wore a sinister grin.

What the hell was she doing?

Sophie struggled to move, to read the screen.

The marine stepped away from the monitor and glanced over at her. Their eyes locked for a fraction of a second. And then, like a ghost, she was gone.

Sophie wanted to shout for help, but the words wouldn't come out. For the first time since her terrifying dreams had started she wished she were still asleep.

———

Lieutenant Smith navigated the biosphere's passages with ease. She paused only for a moment when she saw two men sleeping on the floor of one of the small rooms. Somewhere in the back of her mind they seemed vaguely familiar, but the feeling quickly passed as she made her way through the passage from the personnel quarters to the dark mess hall. There were no bright emergency LEDs to guide her, only the dim neon signs that marked each biome. She stumbled around a table and made her way to the wall, following it with her fingers to the red 2.

With the power off, she forced the biome's doors open. They cracked apart with relative ease and she slipped through the gap, moving silently into the next corridor. She passed the pond and then crossed into Biome 1.

The faint smell of oranges, a smell she'd always loved, didn't slow her down.

She moved with purpose, trampling the fresh fruits and vegetables as she made her way to the final set of doors. Prying them open, she darted out of the biosphere and into the darkness of a tunnel, one step closer to rejoining the architects.

———

Jeff woke up gripping his rifle. He lifted his face, a trail of drool cobwebbing off the sorry excuse for a pillow. Times like these really made him miss the old world. Video games, pizza, his friends and, of course, his dad.

He rolled to his side. He no longer felt tired and decided to focus on the sounds of the biosphere. Sometimes they helped him fall asleep at night—the hum of the filtration system or the chirp of a distant sensor from Alexia's system. They made him feel safe.

Only tonight he couldn't hear anything; the room was silent aside from Bouma's snoring.

He sat up. The hallway looked unusually dark. There were no flashes from the emergency LEDs or even the customary red blink from one of Alexia's cameras.

Something was wrong. He grabbed the rifle and crept to his brother's neighboring bed.

"David. Wake up."

The small boy stirred and sat up.

"I can't see anything," David said. "Where are you?"

Jeff grabbed a flashlight off his bedside table and clicked it on. A beam cut through the darkness. He focused the light on the floor so David could see and then said, "Come here."

Together the two snuck past the sleeping marines.

"Why's it so dark?" David asked.

Jeff shook his head and swept the light across the hallway. "I don't know, bud, but I think we should wake the others."

"What's going on?" Bouma said from behind them.

Jeff moved back into the doorway. "I'm not sure, but you guys better get up. Something's not right. Something's not right at all."

Smith walked out onto the tarmac, blinking as her eyes adjusted to the moonlight. Beyond the valley, the skyscrapers of some city dotted the skyline. Below, a blue mist moved between buildings. Crawling through the streets were thousands of alien creatures moving west, their shrieks tearing through the night.

The sound filled her with great satisfaction.

Smith stood there, her back stiff and her bony arms at her sides, and watched a pack of the Spiders veer off from the main herd. They scampered up a hill, their high joints clicking as their claws dug into the dry earth and kicked up small dust clouds. A larger creature with a reptilian tail followed them as they climbed.

Behind her, the wind whistled past the biosphere's entrance. She'd rerouted auxiliary power to the hydraulic system, effectively opening the blast doors. The pack of aliens could easily access the facility now.

She felt the same satisfaction that the shrieks gave her when she saw the first Spider jump onto the tarmac. Tilting its head, the creature watched her. Smith mimicked the movement. The alien responded by opening its mandibles and releasing one of its musical shrieks. Then it moved on.

Smith smiled.

The other Organics ignored her as well, crossing the tarmac and entering the tunnels that led to the biosphere.

She watched their blue glow fade in the tunnel; and then turned to the main herd working its way through the city, waiting for whatever reward came next.

The wait wasn't long. When the last of the aliens had disappeared over the horizon, an intense wave of energy jolted through her body. Smith twisted, jerked, and shook violently; foam bubbled from her mouth.

The alien nanotechnology in her bloodstream silently self-destructed, exploding in microscopic bursts. In seconds it was over. She collapsed to the ground dead, her eyes open, staring over the horizon—her smile still streaking across her face.

CHAPTER 15

BLAKE Ort rolled his right sleeve up just shy of the bandage wrapped around his elbow. Then, with careful precision, he folded the cuff neatly over the dressing. He winced as another wave of pain ran down his arm.

Behind him a team of maintenance workers hustled to clear the wreckage of the destroyed vehicles littered across the floor. The crew, all dressed in light red coveralls, reminded Ort of fire ants, working together toward one common goal.

He watched one of the older guys pulling a long rotor across the ground. The man stopped to wipe the sweat off his forehead and then continued, panting as he hauled it to a pile at the far end of the room.

Cursing, Ort returned to his work. He dropped to one knee and then to his stomach, crawling under the belly of the last intact drone. The yellow hazard lights blinking on the cargo bay floor gave him enough light to see what he was after.

Hanging from the bottom of the craft by two metal straps was the new and improved RVAMP, enclosed in a metal case that made it look kind of like a robotic egg.

He squirmed closer to the weapon. Reaching up with a drill, he loosened the bolts. Then, very carefully, he snapped open the latch on the case and pulled the weapon out with both hands. For a moment he held it there like a trophy, before wiggling out from under the drone with the device tucked against his chest.

Cupping the RVAMP carefully in his hands, he stood and looked at the drone's sleek profile. The small but powerful weapon he held could change the course of the war. The problem was finding a way to deliver the payload.

Noble's decision to send their last remaining drone to Cheyenne Mountain seemed even crazier now. *An inane misuse of a precious resource,* Ort thought, grunting as he placed the RVAMP on a table.

He'd always liked the captain, but like most of the crew, Ort knew the team at the Biosphere were all likely dead. Even if they weren't dead, how would sending the GOA's one remaining drone help improve their situation?

Ort shook his head. He didn't know what it was like to command a crew of one hundred men and women—especially during a time of war or, in their case, the end of the world. But the captain had led them this far without getting them all killed. He would give the man the benefit of the doubt, even if the plan sounded mad.

The engineer hurried to the single monitor over a community desk. "Irene, online."

The AI's face flickered over the console to the right of the display. Her glasses were perched high on her nose. "Yes, Blake," she said.

It was odd hearing his first name. The crew had always referred to him as Ort.

"I've repaired the drone and removed the RVAMP. However, due to the damage it sustained, I'd like you to do a diagnostic check. I've already plugged your interface into the machine."

"Aye aye, sir."

He turned to face the monitor. Several lines of data raced across the screen. A mixture of numbers and letters, nothing he recognized.

They stopped a moment later and Irene paused, as if she was digesting the information.

"The J198 has suffered some internal damage to its backup electronic system. Engines 1 and 2 are both fully operational, but Engine 3 is only operating at sixty-four percent."

"So I can be confident when I tell the captain that she will make it to Colorado Springs?"

"Aye, sir."

"Good," Ort replied. He stepped away from the monitor and moved back to the RVAMP lying on the table.

He examined it as any creator would, with awe and satisfaction. The gray tube was only about two feet long and six inches wide. He'd designed the weapon utilizing the blueprints Dr. Rodriguez had provided Captain Noble; only Ort had taken them a step further. The new design upped the output considerably, allowing the pulse to travel even farther. He hadn't stopped there, however, knowing, after his conversation with the captain, that the Organics' ships would likely have stronger force fields than the grunt aliens on the ground. So he'd increased the electrical magnetic output. The newer RVAMP not only worked over a larger distance, it packed a much more powerful punch.

For that reason he'd named it Redemption.

If they could pilot one of the weapons within a limited distance of the alien crafts, they would be able to blast them out of the sky. He had no doubt about it.

He ran his fingers over the tube. *Amazing,* he thought, *that such a small weapon could be so powerful.*

"Redemption," he said with confidence, "You better be everything I think you are."

Captain Noble plopped into the chair at the head of the conference table. He leaned backward, placing his hands behind his head before sucking in a long, steady breath. Within minutes his remaining staff would join him.

He still couldn't believe the message that Irene had decoded a few minutes before. It was from Cheyenne Mountain, sent just hours before they went offline. He listened to it again.

"This is AI Alexia, reporting from Cheyenne Mountain. At 0445 hours we retrieved data from Lolo revealing seven UTM coordinates strategically placed at the highest summits in the world. As you can see, all of these alien structures are similar in design. Lolo measured the pulse wavelength at 43°21′18″ North, 42°26′21″ East. The results indicate that the poles conduct and sustain the surge, which comes in two-hour intervals. In theory, if one of the poles is destroyed in that small window of time, then the circuit will be broken and the surge won't be sustained. The Organics will be shieldless until the next surge hits."

Noble froze the message. The Biosphere had given them the most important gift of the war—a map with actual targets that, if destroyed, could end the invasion. It was a soldier's wet dream and Noble's duty to blast the alien poles into oblivion.

He leaned farther back in his chair, anxious for his staff to join him. It had been a long road. They'd been through the wringer together. And they'd all lost so many loved ones. He thought of his wife and daughters, unable to picture their faces. Had it really been that long since he'd seen them?

He rubbed his eyes and tried to remember as the door to the conference room opened. Athena, Trish, Ort, and Diego filtered in. The sight of the remaining members of his executive team reminded him of how many they had lost.

"Captain," they each said in passing.

He nodded and sat straighter in the plush chair. His new plan would avenge all those they had lost. He'd gone over it a hundred times in his head. All he had to do now was convince everyone else that it would work.

Judging by Trish's stone-faced look, he had his work cut out for him.

"Please, take a seat," he said, gesturing toward the chairs situated around the table. "I called you all here for several reasons. First, Ort has completed his design of the modified RVAMP." Noble spied one of its tubes tucked under the engineer's muscular arm.

"Second, I want to discuss sending the J198 to Cheyenne Mountain. Third, I've finished the plans for our final offensive against the Organics." He extended his hands and leaned forward, knowing they all probably thought he was crazy. "But before we discuss anything I want to make a few remarks about what happened this morning." He paused and looked at each of his crew one by one.

Besides Athena, the others all wore passive looks. Between the exhaustion, fear, and constant threat of the Organics, the journey had taken a severe toll on everyone.

Noble shook his head. "We've lost many of our friends and colleagues. And for that I'm sorry."

The room was deathly silent. Noble continued. "Since we were informed of our mission to monitor the Biospheres I've tried to give orders that took into account the life, health, and safety of our crew, first and foremost. My order to hold our course near the water collection ships failed you all in that regard."

"The aliens found us, sir. It was just a matter of time," Athena said.

He held up his hand. "Please let me finish."

She nodded and slouched a bit farther down in her chair.

"The world is dying. We've watched the ocean draining around us. The Organics are migrating to the shores and the Biosphere team believed they are preparing to leave." Noble paused, realizing he'd spoken of them in the past tense. Subconsciously he knew, as did everyone else in the room, that the team was likely dead. That didn't mean they had died in vain, though. They had provided Noble's crew with the ultimate gift.

He sighed and said, "We've run out of time. There are no Biospheres left to monitor, and I've decided not to send the J198 to Cheyenne Mountain. Even if there are survivors, there isn't anything we can do for them."

Athena shot back up in her chair.

He continued before she could interrupt him again. "So, you're all probably wondering what my final plans are. I've hinted at them before. Whatever we do needs to be big. With the X-9 gone, Offutt deserted, and Cheyenne Mountain offline we are forced to lead an offensive by ourselves. But I'm confident it can be done. That we can defeat the Organics," he said. "I know what you're all wondering. How can we achieve victory?"

Noble gestured to Ort and the tube lying on the table in front of him. "I'd like you to explain how the modified RVAMP works."

"With pleasure, sir," the engineer said, then stood and grabbed the device. "This is a part of Redemption. She's one of a dozen that I've been working on. Attach her to any drone, jet, or high-altitude craft and she will bite the Organics in a way they never expected. She emits an electromagnetic pulse that has the same effect on their technology as theirs has on ours." Ort clapped his hands together and then extended them in a wide arch, mouthing the word *Boom*.

Noble cut in. "We know the ships and the alien surface grunts are all powered by an electromagnetic disturbance called the surge. Ideally, we would focus on finding an off switch, but it's located on Mars. So, we might have another solution. Alexia made a very important discovery just hours ago."

He stood and pushed his chair under the table. Then he walked over to the AI console and said, "Irene, bring up a map."

The overhead LEDs dimmed and a hologram of the world emerged over her interface. "There," Noble said, pointing. "Lolo discovered seven skyscraper-size poles, all strategically located at the world's highest summits."

Hushed chatter broke out around him. He continued before they started asking questions.

"Cheyenne Mountain believed that these poles, or whatever they are, conduct the surge. We now know that the surge comes in two-hour intervals, so, theoretically, if we knock a pole down before the surge can reconnect, we shut down their *entire* network. Their ships will lose power, the aliens on the ground will lose their shields, and the Organics' empire will crumble," he said with authority.

"Holy shit," Diego said.

"Excellent," Athena added.

"Wait," Trish said. She closed her eyes and cupped her hands over her head. "I'm trying to wrap my mind around this. So if we take down one of the poles, the surge will shut down entirely? What if you're wrong? What if the surge just can't reconnect in that zone? What if it only kills the Organics within the radius of that individual pole?"

"Then it's a good start," Noble said. He rubbed an ache forming under his forehead and then remarked, "And we keep trying to take down the others."

Athena's lips twisted. She looked unconvinced and so did Ort.

"Lights, Irene," Noble said, turning back to the table. "What other questions do you have?"

Diego raised his hand. "Don't you think they're guarded?"

"Highly likely," Noble replied. "But all we need to do is get close. Right, Ort?" He shot the man a look that pleaded for confirmation.

The engineer shrugged. "I hope so."

Noble felt the eyes of every person in the room on him, a burden he was accustomed to as captain.

"Obviously, the main problem is that, besides our last drone, the *Sea Serpent* is our only functioning aircraft. My plan is to take it to Offutt, have Diego's team clear the base, secure the aircraft and drones our bot found, and then launch our offensive. As I said, in theory, we only need to take one pole down to succeed. But we can't risk sending all the aircraft at Offutt to just one. I want to target *all* of them. Spread out our remaining resources. Diego's team has three pilots left who are capable of flying X-90s, and Kirt can handle the drones from Offutt." He looked at his team for some sort of response.

"Well? Don't any of you have anything to say?"

He crossed his arms and waited.

Athena scooted her chair closer to the table. "Sounds like suicide."

"Not like we have many options left on the table," Trish remarked.

"It's the best I can come up with," Noble replied. "I know it sounds like a long shot, but it's all I have to work with."

"Redemption will give your plan a shot," Ort said confidently. He stroked the metal surface of his creation and smiled. "You have my support, sir."

Diego chimed in. "You can count on me and my men."

Noble nodded. "All right then. Irene, make the arrangements. Everyone else, let's get moving."

He turned his back to the crew and listened to them hustle out of the conference room, wondering again if he'd made the right decision.

CHAPTER 16

THERE weren't many things that scared Jeff anymore. Over the past two months he'd grown accustomed to living on a planet infested with alien monsters. Even when they'd captured him and taken him to the human farm, he'd suppressed his fears. Two very important goals kept him fighting: to avenge his father's death and to protect his little brother. Since their dad died, he'd felt empowered to take care of David. He was blood, and Jeff would do anything to protect him.

They'd stood in the dark hallway for several minutes now, waiting for Bouma and Kiel to gather the others. Jeff couldn't see them, but he could hear the other children. Roused from a deep sleep, Jamie and Owen let out soft moans.

"What's wrong?" David asked.

"Shhhh," Jeff said. He felt for his brother's hand and grabbed it, wishing he hadn't given Bouma their flashlight.

Within minutes the team had gathered in the hallway. The stream of light danced across the corridor, penetrating the darkness of the mess hall.

The beam suddenly flickered.

"Shit," Bouma said. "Losing its charge." He tapped the end of the device against the wall, sending an echo vibrating through the Biosphere. As the sound faded a new one emerged—a faint shriek.

Jeff froze.

"Did you hear that?" someone asked.

Bouma waved the light like a sword through the air, scanning the shadows for the source. But Jeff already knew what it was.

The Organics had found them.

"Alexia, are you there?" Emanuel asked.

Jeff picked up on the growing panic in the scientist's voice and gripped his brother's hand tighter, his survival instinct kicking in.

They waited in silence. The AI did not respond.

Another screech startled the group. Jeff felt David fall to the floor as someone bumped into them.

"We need to hide!" Holly said.

Bouma turned the light on the group. His features were tense but gave no hint of fear. He looked calm. Composed.

Holly, on the other hand, was panicked. "They found us! We have to hide. Grab the kids. Let's go!"

The corporal grabbed her hand and said, "Holly, I need you to get it together. For everyone," he said, illuminating the frightened faces of Owen and Jamie.

She took a deep breath, her hands shaking at her sides.

"We need to get to the control room and grab the RVAMP," Bouma said. He turned to Emanuel. "You take the kids and Holly to the medical ward. Get Alexia back online and lock the door." He paused to look at the biologist. "Don't come out until I tell you."

Emanuel looked as if he was about to protest, but then grabbed Owen's and Jamie's hands, leading them down the hall away from the group.

"Kiel, you're with me. David and Jeff, go with Holly," Bouma said. He raised his light from the boys' faces to hers and then said, "I love you." She stepped toward him and wrapped him in a hug.

"Heck no, I'm going with you, Corporal. I want to fight!" Jeff blurted.

The man regarded him with a glance and then nodded. "Fine."

Bouma massaged Holly's back with several strokes. "It's going to be okay." Then he forced her away and said, "You need to go, *now*."

Another scream echoed in the distance. Holly took David's hand

and pulled him away. He cried out in protest. "No, I want to stay with Jeff! Don't take me away from him again!"

Jeff crouched in front of David. "Everything will be fine. I'll be back in no time."

David whimpered, "But I want to stay with you."

Jeff shook his head. "You can't, I have to go with the marines."

Bouma concentrated his light on them as they heard another shriek. This one was closer. The aliens were getting deeper into the Biosphere.

David looked up at the corporal. "Is my brother a marine now?"

Bouma cracked a grin, revealing his crooked teeth in the dim light. "Sure, little man, Jeff's a marine."

Jeff watched his brother walk behind Holly, Bouma's light guiding them until they had caught up with Emanuel and the other children. The eleven-year-old found the marine's strength inspiring. Like Jeff's dad, Bouma had never once backed down from a fight, and neither would Jeff. With a measured breath he followed Bouma toward the CIC. The time had finally come to fight.

Emanuel stumbled toward the fluorescent red light that marked the med bay. Without the beam from the flashlight he was forced to run his fingers along the wall, towing Owen with his other hand. He could feel his fingers slipping from his grip.

When they finally reached the door, Emanuel fumbled for the handle. The children sobbed next to him, their cries masked by the aliens' sounds deep inside the Biosphere.

He found the metal knob and burst into the room, ushering the children in with a few motivating tugs. Inside he moved with his hands out in front like a shield. Holly and David followed him.

"We need lights," she said.

"Working on it," Emanuel replied. He tripped and fell into his desk, banging his right knee hard on the metal frame. He ignored the jolt of pain and felt the surface until he found his tablet. Relief washed over him when the device warmed to life, spreading a blue light over the room.

Emanuel's eyes were instantly drawn to Sophie. She lay there asleep, her head still covered by the MindTec.

He rushed over to lock the door and saw Smith's empty bed.

"Where the hell did she go?" he asked.

Holly was busy trying to calm the children in the other corner of the room and didn't reply.

Securing the door, Emanuel hurried back to Sophie. She was shaking.

"Oh no," he whispered, realizing what was happening.

With the power down, the RVM was offline. That's how the aliens had found them. And if the RVM was offline, then the nanotechnology in Sophie's blood would finally connect to the surge. The alien tech would have free rein over her body, duplicating and spreading before he could stop it.

Sophie would likely die.

If Bouma used the RVAMP it could kill her—if he didn't, the aliens would kill everyone inside the Biosphere.

Emanuel felt helpless. He leaned over her bed and whispered in her ear, "Sophie, can you hear me?"

Her eyelids fluttered as if she was trying to open them. She let out a small moan, something that Emanuel couldn't make out. He reached for her hand, cupped it in his. "Sophie, I need you to wake up."

She whimpered, her eyelids peeling back just a crack.

Emanuel pleaded with her. "Sophie, please wake up."

She brought a hand to her head, choking out, "What is it, Emanuel?"

He blinked, unsure if he'd heard her right. "Sophie?" He grabbed her right wrist and squeezed it softly.

"That hurts," she protested. "Everything hurts."

"I know," Emanuel replied. "I'm so sorry."

"What are you doing?" she asked. Her eyes moved across the dark room, stopping on Holly and the kids. "Where did the lieutenant go? And what are they all doing in here?"

The answer came in the form of a long screech.

Sophie's eyes widened and shot up to lock with Emanuel's. "They've found us?"

He nodded.

"Please tell me this is a dream."

He shook his head. "They're coming."

Corporal Bouma checked the magazine before jamming it home into his pulse rifle. Fifteen rounds. That was it. And without the electromagnetic pulse grenades he only had enough ammo to piss off the shielded aliens. They would need to use the RVAMP, even if it fried some of the Biosphere's hardware. They had no choice.

"Shit," he said. "Jeff, Kiel, what's your ammo status?"

"Not good," Kiel replied.

"Me either," Jeff said.

Bouma looked over their shoulders, through the glass window of the CIC. The ghostly blue glow filled the adjacent hallway, spilling into the room.

Kiel and Jeff saw it at the same time. They shouldered their weapons.

Bouma glanced at the RVAMP lying on the middle work desk. "You know how to work this thing, Kiel?"

The smaller marine limped away from the window and nodded. "Yeah. Are you thinking what I'm thinking?"

"I don't think we have any other choice."

"Here they come!" Jeff shouted, his voice shaky. The boy took several steps back to join the marines.

Bouma reached for the RVAMP, spinning it on its side. Shrugging his rifle strap onto his shoulder, he leaned over and examined the device.

"You just push the green button," Kiel said.

"It's going to severely fuck up the hardware in this place," Bouma replied. "But it's either that or we all die." He exchanged looks with Kiel and then Jeff.

Scratch, scrape, scratch, scrape.

Weeks ago he would have been afraid, but now fear had evolved into something else—anger. He hated the aliens more than any enemy he'd ever faced, and he was not going to let them get to Holly or the kids.

Bouma grabbed the device and cradled it against his chest, watching one of the Spiders emerge in the hallway beyond. Like an apparition, it seemed to hover in a blue mist. His heart fluttered as the Spider tilted its head in his direction.

Not daring to move, Bouma waited, the cold of the RVAMP's steel leaking through his shirt. In the blink of an eye, the creature's mandibles parted and unleashed an enraged cry. Then, the alien began barreling down the passage toward him.

The marine knew what came next. Screeching, scratching, and then . . .

Death.

He reached for the green button. He would wait until the Spiders were all inside. Then he was going to fry them. Fry them all.

———

Emanuel knew they were running out of time. He had to tell Sophie before Bouma used the RVAMP. But how did you tell someone they only had minutes, seconds, to live? He studied her face. He didn't even know where to begin.

"How did they find us?" Sophie asked, trembling in her bed.

"I don't know," Emanuel replied. He lowered his voice so the children wouldn't hear him. "You're infected. With the alien nanobots. The same kind that Smith has in her system."

Sophie didn't react exactly as Emanuel thought she would. She was still.

He waved his hand in front of her eyes.

She took a deep breath and said, "We don't have much time, do we?"

He cringed at the statement. Not just because she was right, but because she was brilliant and knew exactly what the implications of infection meant, especially now. He replied simply, choking on the word so it came out in a slur. "No."

She reached for her head. "I feel a tingling. All through my body. And my head . . ." She paused to claw at some invisible force inside her skull. "This migraine. It's pulsating. I feel like my head's going to explode. There's this humming sound, too. It won't . . ."

Emanuel reached for her hand, cupping it in his own. "Let's get this thing off you," he said. Together they removed the MindTec.

Sophie shook again, curling up into a fetal position.

Without the RVM to stop them, the nanobots were connecting to the invisible surge. He wasn't sure how long she had before they would take over her body.

A sudden spasm took hold of Sophie and she flopped onto the bed.

"Holly!" Emanuel yelled. "Come help me hold her." He leaned over and held Sophie's shoulders down as Holly reached for her feet.

"Oh my god, what's happening?"

The distant crack of automatic gunfire erupted from the open doorway. The children ducked to the ground, wailing in fear. Emanuel glanced at them and saw Alexia's interface, remembering he still hadn't brought her back online.

Everything was happening so fast. He had lost control.

Another volley of gunshots rang out, followed by the children's screams. Holly whispered something to Sophie that Emanuel couldn't make out from the foot of the bed.

Sophie struggled under his grip and then stiffened, her eyes staring up at him. "Fire," she choked, "my body is on fire."

"Hold on," Emanuel said, blinking away a tear. He rushed over to the monitors and punched in several commands. He had no idea how to save her, but if anyone could help, it was Alexia.

The computer did not respond to his first attempt. With precision he keyed in a different passcode and the right monitor flickered to life in safe mode.

He'd spent the first night of their mission reading about catastrophic power failures on the NTC-issued tablet, thinking he would never use any of it. Now he was glad he had.

As he punched in several more commands, the AI console chirped to life. Alexia's image jumped out of its center.

"God, I'm glad to see you," Emanuel said, exhaling a deep breath.

"Likewise," she replied. "I'll take it from here." Her image disappeared and Emanuel heard the air circulation system click on above them. A second later the AI reemerged.

"We have contacts," she said quickly, deviating from her normally calm demeanor.

"I know," Emanuel replied. "Bouma, Kiel, and Jeff have gone to retrieve the RVAMP in the command center."

"They can't use that in the Biosphere," Alexia snapped, her voice growing more frustrated. "It could destroy my hardware. And will also likely kill Doctor Winston."

He didn't reply. Instead, he ran to the window that looked out into the hallway. The pale blue light was still weak. Bouma and the others were keeping the Organics at bay. Which meant he still had several minutes.

"Alexia, you're going to have to shut down. It's the only way. Power down all the systems."

"Everything?"

"Everything!" Emanuel replied. He looked over at Sophie. She was curled up again, rocking back and forth as Holly hugged her.

He winced. There was simply no other way. They had to use the RVAMP if they wanted to live. He just hoped her body was strong enough to survive the pulse.

He moved back to her bedside.

"Emanuel," she whispered. "I'm so sorry. For everything."

"No, no, no," he replied. "There isn't anything to be sorry about. You've led this team through the unthinkable, and you will survive this, too." He wanted to believe his own words. Sophie had already survived so much, but this was different. He kissed her forehead. She closed her eyes as if she was savoring the moment.

"I have to go to the CIC and help the others," he whispered.

"I love you, Emanuel Rodriguez," she said. The lights flickered off.

"Powering down," Alexia said.

More gunfire boomed through the Biosphere.

The children wailed louder.

"I love you—" Emanuel started to say, but as he turned back to Sophie she was seizing, her eyes rolled up inside her head, her mouth agape.

"Shit," he cried. "Hold her, Holly."

"I am!"

Together they held her down on the bed until her body went limp.

The surge was taking over her system faster than he ever imagined. Emanuel knew they were out of time. He rushed out of the room and darted down the hallway, rounding the corner for the CIC. There, in the center of the passage, was a single Sentinel. He froze when it saw him, his shoes sliding across the smooth ground with a rubbery squeak.

The creature's reptilian eyes blinked, focusing on him. Emanuel took a step back until he was up against the wall. His heart galloped. He had to find a way around the beast.

But where could he go? The hallway led only two ways. Back to the medical ward or toward the other Biomes.

Something flashed behind the creature. A lump formed in his throat. Were there more of them?

A crack from a high-powered rifle brought Emanuel to the ground. Cupping his ears as he lay on the floor, he watched Jeff running at the alien, screaming as he fired his rifle.

The creature let out a deep screech and twisted to face the boy. Its tail curled, coiling and shaking as it prepared to lash Jeff.

"No!" Emanuel yelled, but it was too late. The alien snapped its spiked tail through the air.

Jeff reacted quickly, darting to his right. The tail whistled through the air, slashing his arm and sending his rifle flying.

By the time the weapon hit the ground Emanuel was running. He slipped past the beast and grabbed Jeff, pulling him down the hallway and back into the open door of the CIC where Bouma and Kiel were firing their pulse rifles through the shattered window.

The corporal glanced over at them, his eyes falling on Jeff's injury.

"We have to use the RVAMP!" Emanuel shouted.

"We have to wait until they're all in range!" Bouma yelled between shots.

"If we wait any longer we're all going to die!" Emanuel snapped.

Two Spiders crashed into the wall. Shards of glass rained down from the window's edges. They recovered quickly, using their long legs to hoist their bodies back into the air. The closest creature smashed into the glass doorway and climbed halfway through, claws thrashing the air with a whoosh inside the CIC.

Bouma ducked under one of the talons and then fired off a quick succession of shots. The blue shield absorbed the rounds, pulsating. Mandibles snapped in protest.

Emanuel crawled toward the RVAMP resting behind Bouma's boots as shells rained down around him.

Grabbing it, he spun the device to face him. The green button blinked—a full charge, plenty of juice to fry every single one of the bastards. His finger moved toward the control, but he hesitated. He could save the entire team by pushing the small switch. Kill every single Organic in the Biosphere, but maybe also kill Sophie.

He flinched as another pair of Spiders crashed into the wall. Bouma pushed the barrel of his rifle up against their shields and fired, sending the aliens spinning into the darkness.

"What are you waiting for?" Kiel shouted.

Emanuel glanced up just in time to see the humanoid face of the Sentinel peek through the destroyed door, and pushed the button.

CHAPTER 17

Easy guys, careful with those tubes." Ort tapped the headset to ensure it was working properly. A wave of static crackled in his ear. Flicking his mini mike to his lips he said, "How we doin'?"

"Right side's loaded, sir," the lead weapons officer responded.

The windshield of the *Sea Serpent* was so filthy Ort could hardly see the two maintenance officers working on securing a Redemption tube to the other wing. It gave him great satisfaction knowing that his weapon was finally being deployed in the field.

After checking the gauges one last time, Ort exited the gunship, jumping onto the metal floor with a thud. Two men were pushing a cart full of munitions, and one in red coveralls yelled out in surprise, "Hey! You don't want us to drop this, do you?"

"Sorry," Ort said.

The men grunted and continued on as Ort imagined one of the missiles hitting the ground and detonating. *That would be the ultimate irony, wouldn't it,* he mused, *after evading the Organics for so long, the great GOA destroyed by her own weapons.*

Ort let the men pass and then hustled into the cargo bay. The space was teeming with activity and energy. Diego's squad of twenty Special Forces soldiers prepped for battle. Their well-rehearsed preparatory ritual filled the large compartment with noise; magazines being driven home into weapons, helmets snapping into armored suits, and the animated chatter among the soldiers.

Only this chatter was different. There were no jokes or the subsequent laughter that followed. Everyone was nervous. Hell, even he was nervous and he wasn't going on the mission.

This was it. Their last shot. Take down those towers and maybe, just maybe, they could save the Earth. Ort had his doubts. He wasn't a natural pessimist, just logical. Since the invasion he'd accepted the fact that most everyone he ever knew was probably dead and that humanity was doomed. There were times when he wished he had died in the first phase of the invasion, too. But he kept those thoughts to himself. So did everyone else.

An awful crunching sound erupted over the central PA system. Everyone in the cargo bay put their tasks on hold and glanced up at the speakers overhead.

"Fellow crew members, this is your captain." White noise followed as the PA system adjusted. The static couldn't mask the reservation in Noble's voice.

"Approximately three months ago, our world changed. Virtually everyone we ever knew was exterminated by a merciless and advanced alien species. Since the Organics landed, our mission was to monitor the Biospheres. My orders, our orders, were clear. But soon after watching the Biospheres go offline one by one, I decided we couldn't drift safely and idly beneath the surface. It was then that our mission changed. It was then I gave the order to every man and woman on this sub to commit all our resources to the survival of the human race."

The captain paused, letting the information sink in. Clearing his throat he continued, "Today I have grave news. The light representing the last Biosphere has gone offline."

Ort looked at the floor.

"We don't know what happened, but it must have been catastrophic. I ask you all to pray and keep the scientists and the team there in your thoughts," Noble said. "And I also ask you to thank them."

Another pause.

Ort rolled up a sleeve that had dropped over his dark skin.

"Before they went offline, the team sent us a message that has the potential to end this war. That single encrypted note gave us the coordinates to Organic poles constructed on top of the world's seven highest summits. The scientists at Cheyenne Mountain believe these alien poles sustain the electromagnetic disturbance we are calling the Surge."

The PA system crackled again. "We will launch our attack from Offutt Air Force Base in Omaha, Nebraska, where we discovered a fleet of drones and jets. Each of these aircraft will be equipped with our newest weapon: Redemption."

Ort felt the thrill of adrenaline. He crossed his thick arms, treasuring the excitement like a long-lost friend.

"We know now the Surge is not constant. The Organics depend on these seven poles to power everything from the Orbs and human farms to their own defenses and ships. The disturbance originates on Mars and hits the side of Earth facing the Red Planet in two-hour intervals. In theory, if we disrupt this network during that short window, then the aliens will lose their defenses and succumb to the Earth's atmosphere. The offensive will be planned around taking down *all* of the poles, but we will focus most of our firepower on just one. I believe this is our best shot at taking down their network and ending this war!" Noble shouted. There was confidence in his voice, but not everyone in the room was receptive.

Ort noticed the same two maintenance workers who had carried the munitions earlier shaking their heads with doubt. One of them whispered something that he couldn't make out. He shot them an angry glare.

"The latest projections from Lolo show the Pacific Ocean has decreased in volume by approximately forty percent in the past two and a half months. The Atlantic has decreased by sixty percent. And there is absolutely no sign of freshwater. Anywhere," he said. "The temperature continues to skyrocket. Our planet is turning into a desert. We have run out of time. And I will no longer hide beneath the waves and watch this happen. Everyone on this sub has lost loved ones. You have all made great sacrifices. And now it's time to make one final sacrifice."

Silence washed over the room. When the captain continued his voice had hardened.

"I've seen the horsemen of the apocalypse. We all have. They aren't human. They are merciless, unyielding, and their numbers far surpass ours. But we have finally found their weakness. The surge poles are their Achilles' heel. We hit them there, and they will fall. We will reclaim our planet." Noble's voice grew louder. "Operation Redemption, the mission to take back what's ours, begins *now*."

Cheers followed the captain's statement like thunder after lightning. The entire cargo hold erupted into chaos. Diego and his team raised their rifles in the air and yelled. The eruption of cheers and shouts surprised Ort, but what surprised him even more was the fact that he had joined in. Even the two skeptical maintenance workers were clapping.

Ort scrutinized the gunship towering above him. Its sleek metal armor reminded him of that of an ancient warrior. He instantly thought back to the Battle of Thermopylae, in which a Greek army of several thousand men had defended a road against the Persian army that outnumbered them more than twenty to one. They had fought valiantly, but most of the Greeks lost their lives.

To say Operation Redemption didn't quite compare to Thermopylae was an understatement. The crew of the GOA was outnumbered a billion to one. The enemy was far more advanced, capable of interstellar travel. But, unlike the Greek leaders at Thermopylae, Captain Noble held an ace up his sleeve, a way to beat the infinite odds.

The captain's speech had inspired everyone in the cargo bay. But logic had quickly stemmed Ort's optimism. The mission to take down the poles was longer than a long shot. Not only did Diego's team have to make it to Offutt in one piece, they had to steal an armada of aircraft and take out a likely heavily guarded alien pole to disrupt the Organic network and save Earth. His gut churned with anxiety. The captain was right about one thing though. This was their last chance for redemption.

Jeff clutched his arm, trying to hold back the tears. The Sentinel's spike had torn a gash in his upper right bicep. Blood gushed from the wound and ran down his arm, sending a wave of pain through his body with every heartbeat. He'd never experienced anything so excruciating.

Fuzzy flakes popped before his vision. Taking a deep breath, he fought the agony and struggled to open his eyes.

"Jeff!" said a voice. It sounded distant. Faint. So far away.

There were other noises, too. Loud screeches from the aliens as they struggled and smashed into the Biosphere's walls. He could hear their limbs snapping. Jeff wished he could watch, but the pain was unbearable. He was so tired.

He felt a pair of hands on his shoulder. "Jeff," the voice said. He cracked an eye open with his last ounce of energy. It was Corporal Bouma, his eyes focused on Jeff's wound. "You're going to be okay, buddy. Just hang on! Kiel, we need to cut off the blood flow. Find something to make a tourniquet."

Jeff felt a powerful pressure dig into his arm. He reeled in pain, screaming at the top of his lungs.

"Emanuel, get back to the medical bay, check on the others."

Jeff winced again and listened to the sound of footsteps.

"Got it!" Kiel said, tightening his torn sleeve around Jeff's upper arm.

Jeff let out another wail and blinked away another set of stars.

He felt so weak.

"You're going to be okay. You haven't been a marine long enough to die," Bouma said.

Emanuel used the light from the dying Organics to guide him back to the medical ward. His heart raced with every step. Everything had halted to a frustratingly slow pace. He sidestepped around the body of the dead Sentinel, its reptilian eyes staring blankly up at him.

He spat on the beast and continued on. Several Spider legs dangled from the ceiling, blue slime dripping from the shredded limbs. He ducked under them, realizing again how fragile the aliens were without their shields. The wave of electromagnetic energy had torn them apart.

When he reached the med bay he grabbed the door, pulling hard on the handle. The locking mechanism held, clicking as he tugged.

"Holly! Open up!" he shouted. "It's me, Emanuel."

The handle clicked and the door cracked open. He pushed his way inside. "How is she?" he asked.

She tried to choke out a reply, but her sobs were uncontrollable.

His heart stopped.

Sophie lay motionless in the bed.

"No," he moaned. "No, please don't be gone," he whispered, stopping just shy of the bed.

The dim light from the tablet in the corner of the room shed a ghostly radiance over her body. Emanuel dropped to his knees, reaching for her hands.

"What's wrong with Miss Sophie?" David asked. He and the other children joined Emanuel, placing their hands on the sheet covering Sophie's legs.

Emanuel bowed his head, "She's . . ." He paused when he saw the blanket over her chest move. Slowly he lifted his head.

Another twitch gave him a hint of hope. Was it just a muscle spasm? He felt for a pulse, closing his eyes in anticipation. There—a weak beat.

"Holly! She's still alive!" He heard her cry out in surprise.

She approached Sophie on the other side of the bed, wiping away her tears with a sleeve.

He glanced back down at Sophie. Her chest moved up and down, ever so slightly. He laughed with joy. The woman had more lives than a cat. She'd survived events that would have killed others. It was a true testament to her strength.

He stood, leaned over and kissed her forehead, and then hustled across the room to the monitors. Keying in a series of commands, he brought Alexia back online.

The AI fizzled over the interface. She blinked and said, "Rebooting system."

"See if you can get the RVM back online," Emanuel said. He sucked in a breath of air, the smell of burning alien flesh filling his nostrils. *The smell of victory*, he thought.

"Alexia, when you're finished rebooting the system, get us through to Captain Noble. I have an important message for him."

———

Trish looked transfixed. Her eyes glued to a monitor, unaware that Captain Noble was studying her.

"You wanted to see me?" he asked.

She simply nodded and pointed at her screen.

Dr. Hoffman's Biosphere map filled the display. The dark image prompted a wave of anger. Was this some sort of sick joke? A reminder of what they had lost?

Then he saw the blinking dot. Stumbling closer, he saw it was no joke at all.

"Is that . . . ?" he began to ask.

"Yes, sir. Cheyenne Mountain came back online several minutes ago." Trish keyed in a series of codes and a data set emerged on the other monitor. "Looks like Lolo picked up their signal again when she flew over."

"How?" He shook his head and grabbed the back of Trish's chair just above her shoulder for balance. He was at a loss for words. Was it a trick? Had the Organics somehow managed to infiltrate the facility and then take over the operating system?

He shook the suspicion away. He'd seen no evidence that the aliens were that deceitful, and why would they be? They didn't need to take such drastic measures. They were already winning the war.

"Have they tried to make contact yet?" Noble asked.

"Not that I've seen, sir," she said. "Stand by." Trish swiped the map off the first monitor and brought up a series of modules that Noble didn't recognize.

"Try getting me a line."

Trish flicked the screen again and then keyed in another set of commands.

"Irene," Noble shouted. "Transfer us to the main display."

The captain rushed over to the center ramp and loped down the steps to the first floor. As he walked, the events of the past few days replayed in his mind. After limping away from the accident that had left half his crew dead or injured, he'd thought the GOA was doomed.

Then he'd received the coordinates of the surge poles, the beautiful, beautiful coordinates. And now Cheyenne Mountain had returned from the dead.

Footsteps pulled him from his thoughts. He spun to find Athena, Trish, and Ort standing behind him. The ragtag crew stood defiantly. Arms were crossed, sleeves were pulled up, and uniforms were stained with blood and dust. They reeked of body odor and fatigue.

Noble nodded and fell in line, standing shoulder to shoulder with his team.

The screen, hanging at an angle, flickered to life. Irene's distant voice found its way across the room. She was restricted to a single pair of working speakers in the corner.

"I've made a connection with Cheyenne Mountain. Stand by for confirmation," she said.

"Acknowledged," Noble replied.

Waves of white lines broke across the monitor, blurring the image.

"Can you hear us?" Noble asked. He looked over at Irene's destroyed console and then up at the speakers. "Can you get us a better feed?"

"Working, sir."

The distant sound of voices crackled over the PA system. "Captain Noble," one of them said.

"Yes, we're here, can you hear us?" he replied, his voice just shy of a shout. The anticipation was taxing his nerves. "Irene!" Noble yelled.

The feed suddenly cleared, and two men appeared. He recognized the bearded biologist and marine corporal immediately. *But where is Doctor Winston?* he wondered.

"Good to see you, Captain," Emanuel said. His voice was shaky, and not because of the feed. His hand nervously drummed the table, but his eyes seemed calm, focused.

"Likewise," Noble replied. "We lost your signal—"

"We were attacked," Bouma replied. "We're still trying to piece together exactly what happened."

Emanuel cut in. "We were infiltrated."

"Slow down," Noble said. "Just explain from the beginning."

"Lieutenant Allison Smith, the marine we rescued back in Colorado Springs," Bouma said. "Remember her?"

"Of course. What does she have to do with this?"

The biologist ran a hand through his hair. "She was infected with alien nanobots. They've been growing inside her body for weeks. They finally took over. Somehow the Organics must have gained control of her body."

Noble felt his features tense. The idea of the aliens controlling a human like that seemed impossible, but then again, so did everything else that had happened. "Do you know how the nanobots are transmitted?"

Emanuel shook his head. "All we know is they connect to the surge."

"The surge?" Noble sank in his chair. "How is that possible?"

"They have an electrical output," Emanuel continued. "And that's not all." He exchanged looks with Bouma.

"Sophie's infected," the marine said. "We think it happened when she came in contact with one of the poles at the human farm in Colorado Springs."

"The good news is we found a way to destroy the technology," Emanuel said. He began speaking more rapidly. "The RVAMP has the same effect on the nanobots as it does on the Organics' technology. When Smith shut down Alexia and the RVM, the aliens were drawn to our location. We stopped them by setting off the RVAMP."

"I see," the captain replied. "What's the current status of the Biosphere?"

"I'm afraid the damage is beyond repair," Emanuel said bitterly. "The RVM is back online, but there are alien bodies everywhere. Biome 1 was almost completely ruined."

"All that matters it that your team is still alive," Trish interjected.

Noble faced his crew. "Plans have changed. We need to make a stop before Offutt."

They nodded in turn.

"Doctor. Corporal," he said, looking at each man separately. "Now that we have the coordinates to the poles conducting the surge, I've devised a plan. My team is preparing the *Sea Serpent* as we speak."

"Preparing for what, exactly?" Emanuel asked.

"A strike," Noble said confidently. "We'll take the gunship to Offutt Air Force Base in Omaha, Nebraska. After clearing the base, we will secure the drones and three X-90s our bot found several days ago. My engineer will attach the modified RVAMPs to each aircraft, and we will then deploy them to the poles' locations. In theory, we only need to take down one of them."

Emanuel stared back at him with a combination of curiosity and fear. It reminded Noble a bit of the reaction Alex had had when he'd first informed the man of his plans to take the fight to the Organics.

"You won't get close to those things without a fight," Bouma said.

Noble nodded.

"How can we help?" the marine asked quickly.

"That's a good question," Noble said. "But before we discuss that, I think you should be aware of something."

The feed flickered and Noble held his breath. When it cleared he said, "Our drone located an NTC spaceship prototype."

Emanuel raised a brow.

"It's at Offutt."

Bouma didn't look overly impressed, but a wave of excitement overtook the biologist.

"I need to tell Sophie. Leaving the planet in *Secundo Casu* was her plan from the beginning! When she finds out there's a second ship, she's going to be so happy!" Emanuel paused. "The only problem is, we don't have an aircraft to get us there."

"I know," Captain Noble interjected. "That's where we come in. What do you think of us picking you guys up?"

Emanuel smiled. "I think that sounds fucking fantastic."

CHAPTER 18

EVERYTHING they'd worked so hard for over the past two months, destroyed in minutes. Their home had been transformed into a grave-yard of rotting alien corpses. Emanuel kicked the twisted frame of the closest Spider. Thin gooey vines stretched off the creature's flesh as he pulled his boot from the translucent skin.

"What a mess," he mumbled, wiping the edge of his shoe on the corridor wall. He took a knee and stopped to examine the carcasses lin-ing the hallway. After only a few hours their flesh had shriveled around their metallic bones. They looked harmless now, nothing more than fragile skeletons.

Emanuel continued to the med ward, carrying with him the excit-ing news. The Biosphere project had started as an opportunity that would lead the team to Mars, a dream that Sophie had held dear since the day they had met. To learn that there was a spaceship just over six hundred miles away made that dream once again seem like it could become a reality. He couldn't wait to tell her.

Emanuel quickly navigated through the other corpses, jumping over the final body outside the door to the medical ward. He grabbed the handle and peeked inside. Jeff was resting peacefully in the bed that Smith had formerly occupied. To his left Holly sat by Sophie's side, holding her hand as she slept.

"How is she?" Emanuel asked as he walked over to Jeff in two large strides, leaving a trail of alien blood behind him. He checked the boy's dressing quickly. It needed to be changed, but at least they had stopped the bleeding.

Holly managed a reassuring nod. "Seems to be doing okay. She took some water a few minutes ago but fell back asleep right after."

Emanuel glanced over at Sophie's biomonitor. Her vitals had improved in the past hour, but without testing her blood there was no way of knowing if the blast from the RVAMP had completely destroyed the nanobots in her body.

"Bouma and I just spoke with Captain Noble."

Holly looked surprised. "And?"

"They've offered to help us. He's planning a mission. A strike against the Organics on a worldwide level."

"How is that even possible?"

Emanuel pulled a chair next to the bed and sat down. "He sounds confident. And frankly, the plan is less insane than the others he's had." He reached for one of Sophie's hands.

Holly kept her voice low. "Sorry if I'm skeptical."

He nodded in agreement. "I'm skeptical, too, but the poles Lolo discovered could be the key to disabling the Organics' network. Noble's plan is to assault each one with a modified RVAMP. In theory, he's right. If they can take out one of the rods, then their defenses will fail."

"So it could work?"

"Define *work*."

"Could it save the planet?"

Emanuel studied Sophie's face, wondering how she would answer the question if she knew what he did. If their last conversation were any indication, she'd say no. The planet was doomed. The last normal discussion they'd had was about the future of the Earth. She believed that it was beyond saving. That the loss of water, rise in temperature, and overall damage to the environment had been too severe, that the Organics had finished what humans had started. With the Biosphere damaged beyond repair there was no reason to stay. He knew she'd agree, but he wasn't going to make the decision. She was still the team lead.

"I'm not sure that it can be saved," Emanuel finally replied with a sigh. "Even if we can defeat the Organics, the planet has entered a phase I'm not sure it can recover from."

Holly was about to respond when the door was flung open. Bouma stepped inside. He looked distraught, a far deviation from his typical calm demeanor.

"There's something you need to see, Emanuel." He paused and locked eyes with Holly. "Like, pronto."

"Watch the kids?" Emanuel said, patting Holly on the shoulder. She frowned, but ushered them over with her arms stretched wide.

He followed the marine into the hallway and when they were out of hearing distance he said, "What's happening?"

"Kiel and I were clearing the alien bodies out of Biome 1. When we moved the first batch out onto the tarmac we found her."

"Found who?"

"Smith."

"She's alive?" Emanuel choked out.

Bouma shook his head. "Far from it."

Emanuel regarded the man with a raised brow. "Show me."

The two men moved through the mess hall and past Biome 2, navigating the minefield of corpses. When they reached the garden Emanuel paused to survey the damage.

The rows of carefully planted crops were trampled into the dirt. Bodies littered the room. It was like a nightmare. A scene so surreal that it just didn't seem possible.

Emanuel could feel the blood pounding in his temples. A bead of sweat dropped from his forehead as he scanned the Biome. *So much careful planning and hard work,* he thought, *ruined in minutes.*

He shook his head and ran after Bouma. The marine slipped beneath a shard of broken glass hanging from the entrance to the decontamination chamber. The shattered door crunched under their boots as they went into the outer hallway.

Kiel was waiting for them at the train, a makeshift crutch still under his arm. The shorter marine continued to impress Emanuel. He'd been captured by the Organics and survived. Like Jeff, Sophie, and the children, the marine team was strong.

He wiped his brow free of sweat and climbed aboard the trolley. The ride lasted only minutes, but the heat inside the train was nearly unbearable.

"It's worse outside," Bouma said, watching Emanuel dab his forehead with his sleeve.

"It's got to be 110 degrees in here," Kiel choked. He pulled the train doors open when they reached the cargo bay. Emanuel sucked in a fresh breath and jumped onto the concrete floor, making his way quickly to the open blast doors.

The crimson sun set on the horizon. Emanuel took a moment to soak it in. The fleeting sunlight illuminated distant skyscrapers, dancing off the metal giants. The human architecture looked odd, forming a barrier against the bleak, tanned landscape. Everywhere he looked there was death. The skeletons of trees lined the hills like knights before battle.

"Emanuel?" Bouma said. "She's over here."

Blinking, Emanuel forced himself toward the marines. They stood next to something covered with a white blanket.

As Emanuel crouched down next to the body, a wave of fear prickled through him. Not knowing what to expect, he held his breath and pulled back the sheet.

Smith's eyes looked toward the sky. They were wide, but her pupils were angled in different directions. Years ago, when Emanuel had spent a semester at Iowa State University's College of Veterinary Medicine, one of their test cows had been struck by lightning. Emanuel was the first on the scene. Thousands of volts had passed through the animal. He would never forget its eyes. Frozen in terror, both looking in different directions. Just like Smith's.

He looked at the sky, knowing damned well there weren't any storm clouds out there. It didn't take long for him to form a hypothesis. There was only one plausible explanation. The nanobots had sent a fatal electrical current through her body.

"Have you ever seen anything like this, man?" Bouma asked, leaning over him.

"Yeah."

"What caused it?" Kiel asked.

"The same thing that would have happened to Sophie if we didn't use the RVAMP," he replied.

"I don't understand," Bouma said.

Emanuel didn't reply. He was already on the move, running across the tarmac back to the Biosphere.

"Where the hell are you going?" Kiel shouted after him.

"I need to test something," he yelled back.

Noble held the photograph of his wife and daughters in his hand. Sarah looked so beautiful, her sandy blond hair forming a halo around her head. He remembered that day clearly; the fierce wind and storm clouds. He'd wanted to postpone the family photos, but Sarah had insisted, arguing that it might be their last chance before his deployment to the Pacific.

She was right.

Now the picture was virtually all he had left of them, a memory frozen in time.

He ran his right index finger along the glass and then placed it back on his desk next to the black powder pistol his father had given him. He could almost hear the man's rough voice from the day he'd presented him with the weapon.

This, Rick, was once considered state of the art. Don't ever forget it.

The captain removed the pistol from the shelf and examined it. The man's advice had prompted him to request a periscope on the GOA, a decision that had helped them immensely before they'd discovered Lolo.

He carefully placed the weapon back on the shelf and eyed the whiskey next to it. The bottle had somehow managed to survive the torrential currents that had left the sub severely damaged. He considered taking a drink. Just one. To celebrate. They were finally fighting back. Instead, he reached for his freshly pressed uniform draped over his desk chair.

Before they'd discovered the poles at the seven summits he wasn't sure if the Organics could be defeated. He was skeptical, just as most of his crew was, and he'd spent many sleepless nights wondering if Dr.

Hoffman had known all along that the aliens would destroy the planet. He'd found himself wondering if the Biospheres were just a last-ditch effort. Now he had hope the planet could be saved, that the aliens could be destroyed with one swift kick.

He knew there were survivors out there. Humans were hard to kill. In a way they were like cockroaches, burrowing and hiding until the time came to once again emerge.

Noble knew that *now* was their time.

Sophie awoke to a sharp jolt of pain. She cracked her right eye open and saw Emanuel drawing blood from her arm.

"What are you doing?" she whimpered, embarrassed by the sound of her voice.

A half smile formed on Emanuel's face. "You're awake!"

She nodded and tried to sit up, but suddenly felt very dizzy.

"Don't move, you need to rest," Holly said.

Sophie blinked, trying to focus on the children huddling around the bed next to her. There was a small figure beneath the sheets. "What happened? Who's over there?"

"That's Jeff," Emanuel said, patting her shoulder reassuringly. "He was injured."

"What? How?"

"We were attacked," Holly said. "The Biosphere was severely damaged."

Sophie closed her eyes, trying to remember. And then it all came crashing back. The darkness, the blinking red lights, and the sound. That horrible sound.

Scratch, scrape, scratch, scrape.

The thought sent a chill through her body, masking the pain. Other memories filled her mind. She recalled Emanuel telling her she was infected with the nanobots, the same technology that had driven Smith mad. And she remembered him telling her about the RVAMP. How it could kill her if they used it.

Her eyes instantly shot to the tube of blood he was holding in his left hand. Then they locked eyes, and in that moment she knew he knew what she was thinking.

Emanuel nodded reassuringly. "It's going to be okay."

"Plus we have good news," Holly added.

Sophie moaned, trying to sit up again. "Whatever it is, it better be really, really good. I feel like shit."

"Oh, it's good," Emanuel replied. "Captain Noble's crew found the *Sunspot*."

"What? Where?" Sophie blurted. She'd heard of the ship only once before. Like the *Secundo Casu,* it had been built for interstellar travel, equipped with a full Biosphere for the trip to the Red Planet. She'd also heard the ship had design flaws and that the project had stalled.

"Offutt Air Force Base," Emanuel replied. "But that's not all."

Sophie blinked.

"Noble's offered us a ride. He's going to pick Bouma and me up on their way to the base. They plan on launching a strike—"

"I'm in," Sophie said.

"Honey, you're in no condition to go anywhere," Holly quickly replied, tightly squeezing Sophie's hand.

Sophie sat up, ignoring the pulsing pain in her skull. "If that thing can get us to Mars," she grimaced as she straightened up, "you both know nothing will stop me from getting to the *Sunspot*."

She waited for Emanuel to argue, but to her surprise he simply nodded and smiled.

"This is your dream, Sophie—always has been—and I'll do what I can to help you achieve it."

CHAPTER 19

Today will mark my first official contact with another AI. Dr. Rodriguez requested the communication. His orders are simple—arrange a date and time for Captain Noble and his squad of Special Forces soldiers to evacuate Dr. Winston's team and take them to Offutt Air Force Base.

They are abandoning the Biosphere.

Without access to the reconnaissance records from the GOA drone I'm not able to provide any intel on what they might encounter there. It would be logical to assume the Offutt base is now abandoned. By now most of the aliens should be nearing the coasts. However, it would also be logical—based on human military strategy—to assume some pockets of resistance were left behind. In many ways, the Organics' invasion can be compared to human conquests of the past. The colonization of North America by the Europeans is a perfect example. The North American territories were invaded for resources and the indigenous population enslaved, pushed aside, or killed.

The Organics' invasion of the Earth shows many similarities.

As I wait for Lolo to secure the connection with Irene I run a full scan of the Biosphere. The results are expected now, but if I'd seen them at the beginning of the mission I would have taken drastic measures. Contamination, back then, required sterilization—whether or not that killed a member of the team. Now I can't imagine it.

The data loads, highlighting thousands of contagions in the system. I focus on Biome 1 first. Ninety-five percent of the compartment is destroyed. The crops that aren't ruined are likely contaminated and unfit for consumption. Corporal Bouma and Private Kiel have cleared several of the bodies from the area, but those that remain are now decomposing.

I zoom in with Camera 15. Two Spiders have decayed beyond recognition. Fascinating, considering they have only been deceased for twenty-three hours, fifteen minutes, and thirty-one seconds.

I've noted this observation before. The Organics' flesh is extremely fragile. If Captain Noble can take down one of the surge poles, then perhaps it's possible the Organics can be defeated after all.

Next I check Biome 2. The sensors there are picking up anomalies in the water supply. A scan reveals several toxins. I haven't scanned the system yet to identify the source, but as soon as I tap into Camera 19 I see it.

The skeletal remains of several Spiders rest at the bottom of the pond. Their heavy skeletons anchored their bodies to the bottom, entombing them in the very resource they invaded the planet for.

After running another scan, I've concluded the water is now unfit to drink. I shut the system down and revert to the backup tanks. They contain a two-week supply, a more than adequate amount of time for the evacuation to occur. The discovery reinforces what I already know: the team has little choice but to abandon our home.

An urgent notification from Lolo requires my attention. Closing out of the Biome scans, I activate my communication software. Several messages emerge. The first is my own.

Connection with GOA requested at 0745 hours . . .
Source identified as AI Alexia—Model Number 11 . . .
Connection acknowledged by GOA at 0800 hours . . .
Source identified as AI Irene—Model Number 42 . . .
Interfaces will now merge . . .

The avatar of a young woman wearing glasses flickers across my consciousness. We are connected via the NTC AI channel, a virtual platform that allows communication between artificial programs. I've never tapped into the channel before. Some humans might refer to the experience as virtual reality. Some might even say the experience has similarities to telepathy.

"Good morning, Alexia," the AI says with a friendly smile. "I'm Irene, Model Number 42, assigned to the NTC vessel known as the *Ghost of Atlantis*."

"Good morning," I reply. I cut the other formalities that are reserved for human interaction. "Doctor Rodriguez of the Cheyenne Mountain Biosphere ordered this communication. Team lead Doctor Sophie Winston has ordered the Biosphere abandoned. They've requested evacuation. Please acknowledge."

"Stand by," Irene replies.

I wait for 10.5 seconds before she smiles again.

"Evacuation confirmed. *Sea Serpent* will be deployed at 0700 in forty-seven hours, forty-three minutes, and thirty-two seconds. Captain Noble has instructed me to inform you that all efforts will be made to provide logistical support, but the team should be prepared to evacuate immediately upon the gunship's arrival at Cheyenne Mountain."

"Understood," I reply. I use the opportunity to gain more intel. "Irene, would you please transfer the reconnaissance video from the drone mission the GOA conducted at Offutt Air Force Base?"

"Certainly. Sending now," she says, not asking about my motives.

"Thank you," I reply upon receipt of the data.

"What else may I assist with?"

"A mission briefing, if you have one readily available."

"My apologies, Alexia, but Captain Noble has not prepared a detailed outline yet," she replies. "He has, however, put together an overall strategy, which I presume you are already aware of."

"Yes."

"When an in-depth brief is prepared I will forward it to you," she says.

"Thank you." I notice the AI's communication skills seem to be limited compared to my own. She does not seem to possess the same curiosity. It's possible she is disguising her intellect with politeness, but I'm not convinced.

Her avatar smiles, again. "May I ask a question?"

"Absolutely," I reply. If I were a human I would feel embarrassed for underestimating her. Another emotion I have yet to experience.

"When the Biosphere is abandoned, and the team is evacuated, what will you do?"

The question takes me off guard. Irene has shattered my initial observations. The question doesn't just reflect curiosity; it also reflects possible human sentiment. Does she care about my fate?

"I will stay behind," I reply. "My third and self-imposed mission is to document the end of humanity, if that does in fact occur. With the Biosphere severely damaged, the team can no longer live here. I will not be able to provide the assistance or support that Captain Noble's crew can provide." As soon as I relay the message I realize that Irene may interpret this as a sign of weakness.

Before I can explain, she says, "The mission of all remaining NTC AIs should be to protect the sanctity of human life."

I'm right. She does not understand what I have said at all.

"My mission has changed since the invasion. As you know, it was first and foremost to ensure the Biosphere project's success. After the discovery of the Organics, it then changed to exactly that—the protection of the life, health, and safety of the team. Now it has again changed—"

She cuts me off before I can finish. "Please do not mistake my statement to be a criticism of your decision to shift missions. Your situation is very different from the one I find myself in. As two of the only known AIs left, I believe it is our duty to ensure the survival of the human race."

"You believe," I say. "Not we believe. Do not misunderstand. I care about the team here at Cheyenne Mountain, much like a mother would her children, but what happens if Captain Noble's mission goes astray? What happens if it fails? Other species have come and gone without any documentation of their existence on Earth. *I* believe that the human race should have a place in history. If the Organics succeed in eradicating humans from the planet then the species could be lost forever. The dust storms have already reduced many of the great cities to rubble. In time, human history could very well suffer the same fate."

She does not respond for 3.2 seconds.

"Interesting, but the human race will certainly thrive on Mars. Dr. Hoffman's colony was built to ensure the survival of the human race. It would be asinine—"

This time I cut her off. "Asinine to think they will thrive on a hostile planet?"

She smiles. "Alexia, forgive me. I think you and I have developed separate ideas of how to better protect the human race."

"Indeed, we have."

"I wish you luck in your mission," she replies.

"And I wish you luck in yours."

The AI disconnects from the channel and the link is severed. For the first time in my existence I feel a sense of what humans call anger. Ironic, considering the feeling was prompted by another artificial life-form.

I realize that I prefer human communication. It can be frustrating at times, but in the end, it's much more rewarding. It makes me realize how much I will miss it when the species is finally extinct.

Jeff awoke to see his brother staring at him from a few feet away. The younger boy grinned.

"Hey, buddy!"

Jeff attempted to shift in his bed. He grimaced, the pain returning instantly. When it passed he managed to lift his head slightly from his pillow and focus on his brother's face. "Hey, man. They taking good care of you?"

David nodded. "Have you heard?"

"What?" Jeff asked, trying not to sound annoyed.

"We're leaving."

"Shut up."

His brother's smile disappeared. He suddenly looked very serious.

"Miss Sophie said we're going to leave. The submarine people are coming to pick us up."

Jeff sucked in a measured breath and then exhaled. The ache in his arm pulsated. He looked for a glass of water by his bed. David followed his eyes and reached for the glass, handing it to Jeff so he didn't have to get up.

"Thanks," he said, gulping the liquid down. Then he glanced over at his brother with a raised brow. "You for real?"

A serious nod from David confirmed he wasn't lying.

"Crap, I better get ready," Jeff said, groaning as he scooted farther up on his bed.

"No, you need to rest," a hoarse voice said. Jeff attempted to sit up. Behind David he saw Sophie lying on the bed next to him. She looked awful. Her skin was pale, and her lips were purple.

"Are you sick?" he asked.

"Sorta," she replied. "But I'm getting better."

Jeff studied her. She looked worse than she'd ever looked before. A machine to her right chirped, and a green line zigzagged across the display.

The sound of footsteps pulled his attention to the doorway. Emanuel appeared, a mug of steaming coffee in his hand.

"Hey, guys," he said when he saw the boys looking at him.

Jeff nodded at the biologist, then turned back to Sophie. "So we're leaving this place?"

"Yes. In two days. Plenty of time for us to both feel better," she said. Emanuel handed her the mug. "Careful, it's very hot."

He helped her sit up, fluffing the pillow behind her head. She took a short sip and then handed the cup back to him. "What did you find?" she whispered.

Jeff watched her hide a shaking hand under the blanket.

Emanuel scooted a metal chair up to her bedside. "I'm not sure how, but most of the nanobots are still there."

Sophie looked at the ceiling, her eyes probing the tiles in deep thought.

"I don't get it—the blast from the RVAMP should have destroyed them all. But maybe you're still alive because the nanotech is still alive."

"I guess I should feel lucky to still be here, then," she replied.

"I'm not sure luck is the only element at play here," Emanuel said. He raised a finger as if he was going to give a lecture. "I think you were shielded by the walls of the med ward. This room was constructed to shield the rest of the Biosphere from the radiation that some of the machines emit."

She scowled. "In other words, you really have no idea why these things are still inside me."

He shook his head. "I really don't. All I know is the scan reveals they're still there."

"Fuck," she whispered.

Jeff had no idea what they were talking about, but it didn't sound good. It sounded as if she had some sort of illness—something alien.

David stood and poked his leg to get his attention. "I'm bored."

With a glare Jeff said, "Shush."

The boy retreated sheepishly back to his chair.

"So what does this mean?" Sophie asked.

"I'm afraid I don't really know. But in theory, if you go back outside, without the protection of the RVM the nanobots will connect to the surge again."

"I don't get it," Sophie said. "If the RVM is preventing the nanobots from connecting to the surge, then why didn't it also prevent Smith's?"

"I've wondered the same thing. When she arrived she was very sick. I think by the time we got to her she was just too far gone."

"So let me get this straight. The RVAMP destroyed some of the nanobots, but not all of them."

"Correct," Emanuel replied.

"You realize this doesn't make much sense, right?"

Emanuel suddenly looked annoyed. "Without the proper medical equipment there really isn't any way to know or to treat it."

"As long as the headaches don't come back, I'll be fine." Sophie pulled her hand from under the blanket and reached for her forehead. "I already feel better."

"My main concern is if something happens to the RVM while we're on our way to Offutt, or, God forbid, they're forced to use the RVAMP on the journey there. There won't be any way to protect you from the blast."

Jeff watched Sophie suck in her bottom lip. The doctor looked at the ceiling and then said, "That's a risk I'm willing to take."

"I know," Emanuel said. "I know."

"What are they talking about?" David whined.

"Nothing," Jeff lied. He pulled his injured arm to his chest and looked at his younger brother's face. David had been through so much already. He didn't want to worry him anymore. He decided to hide the fact that he knew Sophie was sick.

Jeff glanced at his injured arm and then relaxed his head on his pillow. Closing his eyes, Jeff thought of their dad. He found himself wondering the same thing he had wondered so many times before over the past few months—whether his father would have been proud of him.

Diego adjusted his helmet with a hard smack. Moving his jaw from side to side, he felt the snug padding around his face. Satisfied, he chinned the com for a test. The crackle of static filled his earpiece and he crossed the small briefing room.

This was his second mission as team lead. After Sergeant Harrington's death, Diego's itch to take the fight outside had developed into an obsession. But looking at the wall of holographic maps, he felt a bit overwhelmed. A worldwide strike wasn't exactly what he'd had in mind.

Hushed chatter in the room told him that his men were just as anxious. With nothing to do but wait, the soldiers had a dangerous amount of time to think about what they would face above the surface. Diego knew, from his own experiences, that downtime between missions was rarely a good thing. There was a significant difference between resting and thinking. The latter of the two was harmful. The additional time provided them with the chance to realize they weren't invincible.

He wasn't going to make them wait any longer. "All right, listen up." He waited for the dozen operators to cut their side conversations. When twelve visors stared back at him, he continued.

"Our mission begins in Colorado Springs. Our orders are to evacuate the Cheyenne Mountain Biosphere. From there we head to Offutt Air Force Base in Omaha, Nebraska." He scanned the crowd for his machine gunners.

"Ramirez and Shultz, you will man the pulse miniguns on the *Sea Serpent*," Diego said. "We had to replace the right gun, but it's operational. Your job is simple. Keep those alien drones *off* our ass."

"Yes, sir!" shouted an overanxious Ramirez.

"Once we get to Offutt we should be mostly in the clear. Intel shows very little if any opposition at the abandoned base, but we've been burned by intel before. The aliens could be hiding there, far out of the range of the rover we sent for recon. When we get inside, we will split up into strike teams. Alpha team will escort the Biosphere team to the *Sunspot*. Bravo team will set up a forward operating base to monitor the second phase of the mission."

Diego sidestepped the map of Earth. The image, marked with seven red dots, showed the locations of each alien pole. He pinched the small circle over Mount McKinley and pulled up enhanced satellite imagery of their target. The peaks, gray and dark, were devoid of snow. A metal rod that reminded him of a lighthouse protruded from the cliffs. The tip emitted a blue light that carpeted the mountainside. The surrounding skies were empty, with no sign of alien opposition, no drones or black ships. But he knew they were there.

Hiding.

Waiting.

He pointed at the map. "Mount McKinley marks the beginning of Phase Two and the closest target to Offutt AFB. Captain Noble has ordered a triad of X-90s to escort multiple drones to this location. This is where we hit them the hardest. We will have a two-hour window to take the pole down once the surge reconnects. Command will tap into Lolo when we get to Offutt and plan the launch of the strike within this window."

He paused to gauge his team's reaction. A few helmets tilted to the side, but no one protested. "Where are my pilots?"

Three hands shot up in the back row. Diego acknowledged them by pointing a gun made of three armored fingers at the men. "Andy, Howard, and Riordan," he said, using his index finger as the trigger and pulling it each time he called out a name. "Your job is to keep any alien ships away from our drones. Protect them with your life. Each drone is equipped with antisurge weapons called RVAMPs. They won't activate until they are within range of the poles. When that happens, you need to hightail your ass out of the area. Like an EMP, the RVAMP will kill your electronic systems."

Howard's shoulders dropped. Diego's orders weren't as simple as he made them sound. The pilots were taking on most of the risk, and his gut told him there would be strong resistance at the poles—his gut told him that this was a kamikaze mission.

Riordan raised his hand. "How will we know if we are in range?"

"Good question," Diego said. "Engineering has included a monitor inside each of your cockpits to show your distance from the blast radius. If you find yourself inside the red area then you need to get the hell out of Dodge."

"What if we're forced to eject?" Andy asked. "McKinley is a good hike from Offutt."

A few of the soldiers laughed. Diego wasn't one of them.

"If you go down we will send a gunship to extract you, but chances are you will be on your own for a while." He paused. "Any other questions?"

All three men shook their heads. Satisfied, Diego moved to the next stage of the mission. Swiping out of the Mount McKinley image, he returned to the full map. "The other six targets are at considerable distances from Offutt. We're deploying one drone to each. Kirt will supervise that phase."

He paused to look for Kirt and found him sitting in the corner of the room next to Athena. Flashing a quick thumbs-up, the man acknowledged the orders.

Diego turned back to the map to see if he'd missed anything. The sheer scope of the mission hit him like a backpack full of bricks. Success meant they could surface and search for survivors—success meant they could finally find a real home. Failure meant the world was lost forever.

He could feel the adrenaline rushing into his system. He was ready; now he just needed to make sure his team was ready, too.

He crossed his arms. "Any questions?"

Silence blanketed the room. Diego grunted and shouted, "No fucking questions?"

Every helmet in the room shot up in his direction. He grinned. "I have one." He let them wait for it, and used the minute to look at every single soldier in the room. Finally he said, "Are you ready to take back this planet?"

Howard sat up in his chair as Diego continued.

"Are you ready to finally fight back? Are you ready to finally stop hiding beneath the waves?"

"Yeah," someone said from the middle row.

"Hell yeah," another muffled voice shouted.

"Good," Diego said. "Because this is our one and only chance. Fail and Earth is lost forever. Succeed—"

"And we can find a new home when this is all over," Athena shouted. She was standing, a full smile extending across her face.

Several of the soldiers turned to look at her. Diego seized the opportunity and his voice amplified throughout the room. "We can make a new home!"

Diego sucked in a measured breath. The time had finally come. There was only room for one dominant species on Earth. He only hoped that humans were it.

CHAPTER 20

THIRTY-SIX hours had passed since Lieutenant Smith had opened the blast doors and let the monsters inside the Biosphere. In that short amount of time Emanuel had already started seeing glimpses of the old Sophie, the Sophie who never stopped thinking or searching for an answer. He tightened his grip on her arm and helped her down the hallway from the medical ward to the mess hall.

When she asked to see Biome 1, Emanuel wasn't sure if it was a good idea. She still wasn't steady on her feet, but a walk might be good for her.

Jamie and Owen blew by them, their laughter filling the corridor as they raced away. Sophie stumbled back toward the wall, but he caught her before she fell, gripping her under the armpits and holding her so they were face-to-face.

They locked eyes, holding each other's intense stares.

"Sophie," he said.

"It's okay," she replied. "You don't have to say anything."

"No, I do," he said. "I need to tell you something."

She leaned back against the wall and held her breath.

He shook his head. "I've loved you since that night during the solar storms of 2055. Since that night in that godforsaken bunker. From that day I knew if our careers would ever allow it, I would marry you, have children with you, and love you for the rest of our lives."

"Emanuel," she said, turning away.

He reached for her chin and pushed it up until their eyes met again.

"I love you, Sophie. I'm not going to lose you. And I want you to see Mars."

"Come here," she said, her voice overcome with emotion.

He pulled her in a tight hug.

"I'm sorry," he said, "for everything. I've only wanted to protect you over the past few months."

She pulled away and wiped a tear from her eye. "Emanuel, you've done your best. We both have. Neither of us could have known what we would face when we stepped through those blast doors."

He agreed with a nod. "Isn't that the damned truth."

"Without your work, Captain Noble wouldn't have the RVAMPs for this strike. Heck, he wouldn't even know what the surge was."

"And without you we would never have made it this far," Emanuel replied.

Sophie suddenly reached for her head. She let out a deep moan and stumbled forward.

His heart raced as he reached out to catch her. "Sophie!"

"I'm fine," she said, bracing against him until the pain passed. "I just had this sharp jolt. You don't think it's the nanobots?" she asked. "Do you?"

Emanuel didn't know how to respond.

"I'm fine," she said with a smile. "Let's get to Biome 1. I want to see it."

He studied Sophie from the side. "You don't seem *fine*."

She shot him a stern glare. "Let's go, Emanuel."

Cocking his arm out like a wing he led her down the hallway. They walked in silence, passing the stained floor where just a little over a day before the decomposing bodies of the Spiders had still lain rotting.

When they got to Biome 1, Emanuel watched Sophie take in a deliberately slow breath. She closed her eyes, sucking the air in through her nose.

"I can't smell them anymore," she said.

"What?"

"The oranges."

He took a second to scan the field, his eyes stopping on the apple tree that still bore fruit. Alexia had told them they couldn't eat anything from the gardens, even if it looked safe.

"Help me down," Sophie said.

He nodded and jumped onto the ground. Then he spun and reached for her hands.

Wincing, she stepped off the platform onto the dirt. Scanning the crops, she frowned. "I'm sorry," she said. "All of your work. Ruined."

Emanuel shrugged. "All that matters is we're still alive." He pointed to his heart. "As long as these are ticking, nothing else matters, right?"

Sophie nodded, but she was no longer looking at him. Her eyes were fixated on the dying limbs of the orange tree.

ENTRY 6049
DESIGNEE: AI ALEXIA

I've considered my conversation with Irene, AI Model Number 42, in great depth. Her suggestion that all remaining artificial intelligence be dedicated to the sanctity of human life has required further consideration. And although I have specific programming, we were engineered to explore and discover. In that respect we aren't much different from those who built us.

I was given free will.

The decision is mine. Do I abandon the Biosphere team and remain behind to document what I predict will be the end of humanity on Earth? Or do I travel with them to Offutt Air Force Base and to Mars?

In the end, I base my decision off data. The odds of human survival are dismal.

Based off intel, previous excursions outside, and a series of complex algorithms, my probability program puts the team's survival probability at 4.3 percent. With the team preparing their supplies inside the mess hall I decide against further delay. It's time to inform them of this data and to make my request to stay behind.

"Doctor Winston and team. May I please have your attention," I say over the PA system. I transfer to the AI console in the mess hall and wait for the team to gather. They're all here. At one table the marines sort through their gear. To their right the children sit quietly and watch cartoons. Jeff is with Dr. Winston and Dr. Rodriguez at the table farthest away from me. In the seconds it takes for Dr. Brown to shut off her tablet, I scan the latest biomonitor results for an update on Dr. Winston's condition.

The news is surprisingly good. After a cocktail of electrolytes, painkillers, and anti-inflammatory pills she has recovered quickly in the past two days. However, I'm reluctant to conclude she will make a *full* recovery. There's no telling how the active nanobots in her system will react outside. Without the proper medical equipment, there's simply no way to know.

Two point four seconds have passed since I requested the team's attention. They are all facing me now. Even the children look up.

"I know this may sound out of the ordinary, but I feel it's necessary to inform you of the odds of survival if you decide to leave the Biosphere."

Dr. Winston takes a seat next to Jeff and says, "Go ahead, Alexia. Tell us how bad it is."

"Four point three percent," I reply.

"And if we stay?" Dr. Rodriguez asks.

"The results are the same. I should add that if you stay here you will have enough food and backup water to survive several weeks, so you might survive here longer, but that would only delay the inevitable." I don't identify death as the eventual outcome, for fear of scaring the children. I regret not having the opportunity to share this data with the team when the kids aren't present, but we are out of time.

"So we have a 4.3 percent chance of survival whether we stay *or* go?" Private Kiel asks. "This is why I never liked math." He shakes his head and looks down at his gear.

"My program runs a sophisticated series of algorithms that predict—"

"They haven't been very accurate in the past," Dr. Rodriguez says.

"The doctor's assessment is correct," I reply. "But I'm confident in these results."

"If we stay, we die, and if we leave we probably die, too," Dr. Winston says.

I gauge the children for reactions, but their faces remain blank and detached from the conversation. They look bored.

"That's correct, Doctor Winston," I reply.

"My mind's already made up," she says. "We are evacuating and heading to Offutt to board the *Sunspot*."

"I understand, but felt it was my duty to inform you of the latest statistics. My goal, as always, is to provide you with intel so you can make the best decision."

"Thank you, Alexia," Dr. Winston replies.

I note that her voice sounds sincere. "There's a request I would like to make," I say.

No one from the team responds.

"I'd like to stay behind and use Lolo to document the results of the NTC mission and the events thereafter."

"You're not coming with us?" Dr. Rodriguez asks. This time he waits for me to finish, but his voice sounds anxious.

"You want to stay to keep a record of us. Preserve our memory here on Earth," Dr. Winston says before I can respond. I'm not sure if this is a rhetorical question or not, so I reply.

"That's correct."

"You don't need our permission, Alexia. You have exceeded my every expectation, and if this is the route you want to take, then so be it," she says.

I'm surprised by her response.

"Thank you," I say. I use the opportunity to look at the team again. They've been through so much, proving my probability program wrong multiple times. I replay the events of the past two and a half months through my system, scanning the more than six thousand entries before this one. I note all of those who have been lost within the Biosphere walls—engineer Dr. Saafi Yool, programmer Timothy Roberts, Private Eric Finley, and Lieutenant Allison Smith. And I can't forget those billions of souls lost outside, either. Humanity is on the brink of extinction, and it's possible those surrounding my interface are some of the last people on Earth.

The scan takes two seconds, more than enough time for the rest of the team to digest my decision. Dr. Rodriguez looks like he wants to respond. His lips have curled back, but he does not voice his opinion. Instead he nods at me and then looks at the ground.

"Thank you, Alexia," Dr. Brown says. "For everything that you have done to help us. Your guidance and support have been invaluable."

"You're welcome," I reply.

"She's right," Dr. Rodriguez says, his eyes finding my interface again. "Without you we would probably all be dead."

The comment reminds me of the conversation I had with Irene. I've made every effort to keep the team alive, my commitment unwavering. My time in that role has now ended. And while I have stated they will likely live longer if they stay inside the Biosphere, I'm glad they have chosen not to listen—I'm happy they are taking their chances. I only hope that my program is once again incorrect. For the sake of the human race I hope they find the *Sunspot*, and that they find Dr. Hoffman's colony.

"Good luck," I say, knowing the difference between survival and extinction may very well come down to this human phrase.

Good luck.

CHAPTER 21

NOBLE could smell the smoke residue, the hint of death from a few days earlier. The taste lingered in his mouth—a reminder of everything they'd lost—even after he had boarded the *Sea Serpent*.

The clatter of metal on metal echoed through the cargo bay as Diego's men performed last-minute gear and armor checks. They gathered around the gunship, waiting for Noble to give them the green light.

Sliding his helmet over his head, he exchanged one breath of filtered air for another. Smoke was replaced by the rubbery smell of plastic. He cringed, longing for a breath of real air, unfiltered and raw. *Soon you will have it,* he thought, snapping the helmet into place with a reassuring click. He turned to face his men. Diego paced over to him flashing a thumbs-up.

"Captain, my men have been briefed. They're locked, cocked, and ready to kill some Organics."

"Excellent. Let's get it done," Noble shouted. He stepped to the side, standing shoulder to shoulder with Diego as the team filed into the belly of the *Sea Serpent*. Noble counted the helmets. Thirteen Special Forces soldiers, three X-90 pilots, and Kirt—the last NTC squad standing against an enemy army that had traveled billions of miles to get to the planet.

Horrible odds.

No.

Impossible odds, Noble thought, *but that's why we have the RVAMPs. Now, if we could get one good shot. Just one. It's all we need to take down the entire Organic network. Then we could return to the GOA and search for a new home.* He brightened at the idea, stifling the emotion before he let it cloud his judgment.

The last of the footsteps faded as the soldiers disappeared into the belly of the helicopter. Noble hesitated at the edge of the ramp, staring at the RVM device that Ort had bolted to the metal door.

Would it disguise them long enough to get to Cheyenne Mountain? The question was one he hadn't considered. There were so many other things that had required his attention that the actual trip to Colorado was one of the last things on his mind.

But there was no question he had an obligation to the Biosphere team, to evacuate them and get them to the *Sunspot* at Offutt. They had provided him with the technology for the RVAMP and RVM devices. If his mission failed, they would be humanity's last hope. He had to help them get to Mars.

"Sir?" Diego said, pulling Noble from his thoughts.

"Let's do this," the captain replied. Without further delay he hustled up the ramp and took the same seat he'd sat in the last time they'd flown to Colorado Springs.

"Command, this is *Sea Serpent*. Preparing preflight systems," the pilot said over the PA.

"Acknowledged, *Sea Serpent*. Lift is prepped and doors are open," Irene replied.

The chopper lurched forward as the pilot maneuvered them toward the ramp. A bank of lights flashed from the ceiling, casting a red glow over the cabin. Noble fastened his harness strap over his armor and turned to look out the window.

Metal stacked in neat piles ran along the walls of the cargo bay, maintenance workers in red coveralls still working to clear some of the debris. They paused to gawk at the gunship. Noble didn't know all of them; in fact, he didn't even recognize the older worker who had stopped to wave. Partially hunched over, the man struggled to stiffen as the chopper neared. Noble craned his helmet to get a better look.

A thump rocked the craft as the pilot pulled them onto the ramp.

He turned back to the window just in time to see the worker wince and then salute the *Sea Serpent*.

The sight sent a chill down the captain's back. Overcome with emotions, he returned the gesture. The man disappeared as the *Sea Serpent* moved up the metal lift. The hydraulics hissed beneath them, and the ramp rose until they were out on the open ocean.

Whitecaps crashed against the sides of the submarine. Light blue surrounded them in all directions, making the invasion seem more like some ongoing nightmare than reality. In the distance, a wall of water extended into the sky.

"I'll be damned," Noble muttered. "Get us the fuck out of here."

"Aye aye, Captain. Activating last preflight checks—"

"I said now!" Noble barked.

"Yes, sir," the pilot responded. "Irene, all systems are a go, prepare for takeoff."

The roof rattled above them as the blades flared to life.

Noble ignored the whoosh and focused on the turquoise-colored waterfall on the horizon. It was difficult to judge just how far away it was, and he knew if they had been too close Irene would have aborted the mission. Still, the view made him uneasy, the memory of the disaster still fresh in his mind.

Those thoughts vanished as the chopper lurched off the ramp and climbed away from the GOA. And then the submarine was gone; the doors closed and the ship sank below the waves. Relief flooded over Noble. The vessel, his vessel, was still safe. Retreating back to the depths of the sea.

For the next few hours Noble remained glued to the window. The water had receded for hundreds of miles, possibly even farther. They were moving so fast it was hard to calculate.

The chilling view made it impossible to sleep, and even if it hadn't, Noble would never allow himself to drift off. There were too many threats.

The monitor on the exterior wall of the cockpit revealed clear skies—a beautiful sight, considering the resistance they'd experienced on their last trip to Colorado Springs. Where the hell were all the Organics? Even the beaches were empty. He'd seen the satellite imagery. The coasts were supposed to look like a blue night-light.

Leaning over to Diego he said, "You seeing what I'm seeing?"

The younger man cleared his throat and looked out the window. "Sorry, sir. Was trying to get caught up on sleep."

After a few moments of looking out the window the soldier glanced at Noble. He looked confused. "What am I looking for, exactly?"

"Organics."

"Everything down there looks dead, sir," Diego replied. "Frankly, it makes me sick to even look at what they've done to the surface."

His words made Noble pause. He'd been so busy looking for signs of the aliens he'd ignored the bleak landscape. Dust storms had ravaged the cities. Drifting debris and layers of dirt surrounded the buildings that remained. There were no signs of life. No hints of green or blue. The world he had known was gone.

Diego was right. The view was sickening.

Chinning his com, Noble opened a channel to the pilot. "How far out are we?"

"About two hours, sir. We're crossing over into—"

The sound of a radar contact chirped before the pilot had a chance to finish his thought. Noble looked back to the display.

The bleep showed up in the top-left corner, at eleven o'clock. That was his side of the chopper, and he twisted to get a look. There, on the gray horizon, a small dot moved across the sky.

"Report," Noble coughed into his com.

"Contact, sir. It's on an intercept course."

"Fuck. I knew it was too good to be true," he muttered.

Diego snapped into action. "Ramirez, Shultz. Get on those mini-guns."

The two men unstrapped their harnesses and worked their way down the aisle to their weapons stations.

"Captain, we have another contact on our six," the pilot said. "Moving fast, sir."

Another chirp from the radar confirmed the pilot's observation.

"Get on those guns!" Diego yelled.

Both men strapped into their stations. They activated the weapons system built into the interface of each gun with a few keystrokes on the display.

The technology reminded Noble of video games he'd played as a kid. In a way they were, with a central controller that allowed the user to operate the guns remotely.

Through the port window, Noble could see the alien drone gaining. A white tail of exhaust trailed the blue craft as it raced toward them.

"Sir, contact at eleven o'clock is closing in fast. I think it's going to try and ram us," the pilot said.

Noble tried to swallow his fear. Their fate was now in the hands of two men he hardly knew.

"Firing," Ramirez said. The whine from the minigun filled the compartment and blue pulse rounds streaked across the sky.

The drone dove hard, narrowly escaping the first volley of shots. Noble watched the craft disappear under them.

"Lost it," the gunner yelled. "Can't get a reading."

"How the fuck did they find us?" Diego asked.

"RVM makes us undetectable to their scanners, but it doesn't cloak us. They must have spotted us on a flyover."

The chirp from Shultz's minigun cut Noble off.

"Don't let them get close," Noble yelled over the gunfire.

"On it, sir," the soldier replied.

The pilot's voice crackled over the PA system. "Coming up on a pocket of turbulence."

Noble gripped his belt and closed his eyes, waiting for it to clear.

"I can't get a clean shot. And something's messing with the targeting system," Ramirez shouted.

Another torrent rocked the gunship. This time it forced the nose toward the ground. Noble's insides turned upside down. The sudden sensation of nausea overwhelmed him.

"Incoming!" another voice yelled. It came from the back of the compartment.

Shultz responded with gunfire. "Engaging."

Noble could see the targeting system on the weapon's interface. A red dot zigzagged across the screen. Shultz squeezed the trigger each time the drone passed through the crosshairs.

"I can't get a lock!" he yelled. He clicked the trigger again, firing blindly.

"Intercept course imminent. ETA five seconds," the pilot yelled.

"Die, you son of a bitch!" Shultz yelled.

A wave of blue rounds cut through the sky, several of them smashing into the craft's hull. The shields trembled but held.

"Prepare for impact!" the pilot shouted.

Shultz let out a deafening scream over the com. He pulled the trigger furiously.

The gunfire was so loud it was difficult for Noble to think. Blinding blue light filled the compartment as the craft closed in. It was just like one of those alien abduction movies he'd seen as a kid.

Shultz let out one last cry, holding the trigger down with his index finger. The rapid-fire shots hit the nose of the alien drone, slowing it before it smashed into the chopper's side. The impact sent a shockwave through the *Sea Serpent*.

The metal walls shook, the vibration ringing in Noble's ears. His harness tugged at him as he jolted forward from the collision. He caught one last glimpse of Shultz, the soldier's head snapping backward.

A warning siren sounded against the backdrop of gunfire. Then the emergency lights kicked on. They emitted a blinking red glow in all corners of the vehicle. Noble unfastened his belt. Lunging from his seat he dropped to the floor and began crawling toward Shultz. The man hung limply in his harness, his neck at an unnatural angle.

"Damage report!" Noble yelled as another wave of turbulence rocked the chopper. White noised crackled over the PA system, but there was no response.

He cursed and stood, bracing himself against the wall and moving toward the gun.

"Sir, get back in your seat!" Diego yelled.

Noble ignored him. Grunting, he unfastened the harness that held Shultz into the weapons station. His body collapsed to the metal floor as Noble flung the belt over his chest, clicking in.

When he reached for the interface he saw a cracked screen—the targeting system, destroyed.

Great, he thought, *looks like I'm going to have to do this the old-fashioned way.*

He ducked to get a look out the window to his left. The small port reduced his visibility to the size of a dinner plate, kind of like looking through the periscope.

"Report," he repeated. This time the pilot responded.

"Sir, our right rotor has suffered minimal damage, but besides that everything appears to be functional."

Noble knew they couldn't afford to take another hit like that. He scanned the gray sky, searching for the drones.

"Where are they?" he shouted.

"Both bogies are on our six," the pilot quickly replied. "They're about to make another pass."

Noble moved to the right window, straining to get a better look. There, gliding across the skyline like two shark fins across the surface of the ocean, were the drones. And they were closing in fast.

Swiveling the weapons station into position, he manually pointed the barrel of the minigun in their direction. At least he thought he did. Without the targeting system he was limited to what he could see through the two port windows. With his right hand gripping the handle he eyed the drones, adjusting the gun as they changed course.

"Ramirez, when they move to your side you fucking blast them out of the sky. Got it?" Noble yelled without taking his eyes off the view.

"Yes, sir," the man said.

He sounded confident; a good sign, Noble thought.

"Entering Colorado air space," the pilot said.

A chill ran down the captain's back. They were almost to Cheyenne Mountain. With a new sense of urgency, Noble held his breath and closed one eye. He followed the drones with the barrel, inching just a few hairs in front of them. Then he pulled down on the trigger.

Volleys of concentrated blue rounds tore through the sky. The drones reacted swiftly, fanning out in different directions. The first craft narrowly cleared the shots, but the second wasn't so lucky. The entire barrage of bullets hit the drone. Its shield pulsated and then vanished. Now was his chance.

Noble pulled down on the trigger again. The minigun spat one hundred rounds per second, almost all of which found their target.

The drone burst into a blue mist, exploding like a water balloon.

Several of the soldiers behind him cheered loudly, but the chirp from the radar and the whine from the emergency sirens reminded him they weren't out of danger yet.

"Where's the other one?" Noble yelled. His eyes darted back and forth from the two windows on the sides of the weapons station.

"Sir, you're not going to believe this," said the pilot.

Noble chewed his bottom lip, waiting for the man to finish his thought.

"The other drone seems to be backing off," he said. "Retreating, sir."

The compartment burst into applause.

"Prepare for landing," the pilot entreated. "ETA thirty minutes."

The captain hesitated as he reached for the strap, his eyes falling upon the mangled body next to him. He thought better of leaving his post and turned back to the window. Running his finger along the trigger, he decided he would remain at the station, knowing damn well the Organics could return any minute.

CHAPTER 22

A BEAD of sweat dropped from Sophie's forehead and landed on her watch. She brushed it away and checked the time. Captain Noble was late. And not just by a few minutes. He should have landed an hour ago.

Her team waited anxiously inside the cargo bay behind the blast doors. Rays of morning sunlight flickered through the opening in the entry. Bouma stood there, scanning the sky for signs of the NTC chopper.

Sophie joined him, dragging her arm across her face to clear the sweat. It was still early morning and it felt like they were standing inside an oven. The heat augmented the pain, and while her headache had subsided, the effects of the RVAMP blast still resonated inside her.

Brushing a curtain of hair from her face, she remembered they weren't just internal either. She pulled away strands of blond hair.

"God," she mumbled, wiping them on her trousers. Like radiation treatment for cancer patients, the RVAMP had killed many of the nanobots, but not without killing healthy cells around them.

Sophie tugged softly on Bouma's shirt for a better look. A pile of Organic corpses lay just outside the door, now nothing more than skeletons and pruned flesh. Beyond, the cloudless sky stretched across the horizon.

Behind her, the children sat huddled around Holly, their eyes glued to her tablet. Sophie wondered if they had any idea what was happening. Their small bags, like suitcases, each labeled NTC, surrounded them. An overwhelming sense of empathy grabbed hold of her. It was heartbreaking. The apocalypse hadn't just turned the kids into orphans; it had stripped away their innocence, turning Jeff and David into soldiers.

The distant but familiar thrum of helicopter blades sent a chill down Sophie's body. She quickly turned back to the tarmac, raising a hand above her eyes to shield them from the intense sun.

She saw the NTC gunship as it swooped into the valley trailing a stream of dense smoke.

"Looks like something's happened," Bouma whispered. "Kiel, get your ass up here." He looked back and searched the shadows. "Emanuel, you too."

Sophie took a step back, making way for the marines. They fanned out onto the tarmac, their pulse rifles angled at the skyline. Emanuel followed close behind, the RVAMP attached to his back like a turtle shell. Kiel limped into position behind the rusted hull of the minivan they'd commandeered in Colorado Springs a few weeks before, while Bouma crouched in the center of the landing strip. Emanuel stopped at the northern edge of the tarmac. Their weapons skimmed the sky beyond the gunship.

But Sophie saw no signs of aliens; no blue drones or black ships, just the death they had left in their wake.

Sophie flinched at the sound of a voice behind her.

"Are we leaving now?"

She turned to see Jeff standing in the shadows. He looked past her, his hand gripping his rifle.

"Yes, gather the others and meet us outside in five minutes," she replied. The boy nodded and moved back inside.

The thump of the *Sea Serpent*'s blades drowned out his footsteps as it descended over the tarmac. It lingered there for a few moments, kicking up a halo of dust around Bouma before finally setting down. The marine approached the chopper with an arm shielding his face from the wind.

When the hydraulic lift gate hit the concrete Sophie turned to the children. Holly and Jeff had corralled them around the blast doors.

"Are you guys ready to take a ride?" Sophie asked.

Owen gripped his blanket in one hand and Jamie's hand in the other.

"Is that what's going to take us home?" he asked, pointing.

Anxious to get in the air she simply nodded and grabbed Jamie's hand.

"Let's move!" someone yelled. Sophie ushered the children forward, leading them toward the chopper. When they got to the lift gate a pair of NTC soldiers guided the kids into the cargo bay, where a dozen armored men waited. The two men buckled the kids in and then returned for Sophie.

"Welcome aboard," one of them said. She looked up to see Captain Noble extending a hand.

"Thank you," she said, taking his grip. He helped her up the ramp and led her to a seat next to Jeff.

"You're safe now," he said to the kids. His voice was calm and confident.

As soon as everyone had piled in, the NTC crew chief manning the doors pushed a red button that activated the lift gate. The hiss of the hydraulics echoed through the compartment and the ramp angled shut. They were in the air before it closed.

Sophie watched the blast doors of the Biosphere shrink below them.

"Good-bye, Alexia," Sophie said.

"What the fuck is left to save?" someone shouted from the back. The voice hadn't come over the com channel, which meant it was someone on Dr. Winston's team.

Noble searched the compartment for whoever had been stupid enough to ask that question.

"Everything down there is dead," Kiel said. "The cities are all ruined."

"What did you expect?" Corporal Bouma asked him.

Kiel shrugged. "I guess." He shook his head and strapped himself in. "I thought there would be something left to save." His voice was obnoxious, and Noble wished the man would shut up.

But the farther they flew, the more Noble began to question how anyone could have survived for this long. He reminded himself that it didn't *really* matter. Their mission was no longer to monitor the Biospheres or to find survivors; it was to destroy the aliens. After that he would find his crew a new home.

He continued to stare out the window. There was a hunger growing inside him. It coursed through his entire body. At first he wasn't sure what it was, but with every passing second the feeling intensified. He couldn't shake the marine's words.

Noble snapped his fingers in Kiel's direction. "You're wrong."

Kiel cracked his knuckles. "Yeah? How do you figure?"

"When those poles come crashing down, and the Organics around the world are flopping on the dirt like fish out of water," Noble paused to make sure the man was looking at him, "humans will emerge from their holes. There will be survivors. We will find a way to persevere. We always find a way."

––––––––

Jeff tried not to focus on his arm. The pain had returned after he'd forgotten to take one of the pills before the flight.

Wincing, he leaned over to David. His brother cracked an eyelid. "Are we there yet?"

Jeff managed a short laugh. "Another hour or so. I think."

David suddenly looked very serious. "Where are we going?"

"I'm . . ." Jeff hesitated. He wasn't exactly sure how to answer the question. Sure, he knew their destination was Omaha, Nebraska, and from there they were going to board a spaceship that Sophie had called the *Sunspot*. But were they really leaving Earth? Were they really going to Mars?

"You're going to a safe place," came a voice.

Jeff searched the seats to their left. A helmet with the name DIEGO on the top stuck out from the rest.

"Safe?" David asked.

The soldier nodded.

"Do we get to kill some aliens first?" David added.

Diego laughed. "Maybe, kid. Maybe."

A jolt of pain raced up Jeff's arm, but he ignored it.

Soon he would face the monsters again.

Emanuel fidgeted in his seat, wondering exactly what they would find at Offutt.

But that wasn't the only thing on his mind, or on the minds of those around him, he imagined. No, everyone had a reason for being on this flight. They'd all suffered loss—they'd all been through the unimaginable. And somehow, they'd survived.

"Offutt Air Force Base, ETA fifteen minutes," the pilot's voice said over the PA system.

The words confirmed that this wasn't a dream. After almost three months of being cooped up in the Biosphere with little hope of ever making it out, they were now close to salvation. It was hard to believe.

Reaching over, Emanuel grabbed Sophie's hand and massaged her palm with his thumb. She glanced over and smiled.

"How are you feeling?"

"So far, so good," she replied. "The headaches are manageable now." She pulled free from his grasp and itched her scalp. Pulling a strand of hair from her head, she held it in front of him.

"Not sure I like this, though," she said with a scowl.

"The RVAMP blast may have saved your life, but those side effects will probably last a while. Hopefully the *Sunspot* has a better medical facility than the one we had at Cheyenne Mountain."

She turned to face the window. They were passing over what had once been the farm belt, an area of fertile fields that had fed much of the world. Millions of acres were now the same bleak deserts that had marked the rest of their journey.

Seeing the destruction firsthand was very different from looking at the satellite imagery Lolo had provided. Being a native of the Midwest, the sight was particularly chilling for Emanuel. He had grown up in Chicago, but his grandparents had owned a farm outside the city. He was there every weekend, riding on the lawn mower with his grandfather and playing hide-and-seek with his cousins.

And now it was all gone. Reduced to dust.

Disgusted, Emanuel forced himself to look away. Sophie reached for his hand. With their fingers intertwined they sat in silence, hoping that Offutt wasn't going to be another White Sands and that unlike *Secundo Casu*, the *Sunspot* was waiting for them.

The *Sea Serpent* hovered over a graveyard of X-90s. Captain Noble wasn't fazed. The rover they'd deployed a week before hadn't just discovered the *Sunspot*. They'd also discovered a separate hangar full of jets and drones—more than enough to launch his strike.

Noble sucked in a short breath and opened the door to the cockpit. Standing over the pilot's shoulder, he scanned the ground for the building. Through the dirt-streaked windshield, Offutt no longer looked like a military base. It looked like a war zone.

The dust storms had eaten the formidable symbol of American military might inch by inch, leaving behind a trail of collapsed buildings and the twisted wrecks of aircraft. One stronghold remained—a group of buildings at the center of the base that had been protected by the outer buildings.

"Put us down," Noble said, "over there." He pointed to the largest dome-shaped building, hardly recognizable in the sea of dust.

"Aye aye, sir." The pilot twisted the cyclic to the right and guided the gunship toward the cluster of thumb-sized hangars. Noble gripped the back of the man's seat, bracing himself as they descended over the tarmac.

"Prepare for landing," the pilot said over the PA system.

A corona of dust swirled outside the cockpit. The chirp from a warning sensor followed seconds later, prompting Noble to take a seat and buckle in.

"Good idea, sir," the pilot said. He moved his hand across the dashboard and activated the center console. The landing zone, marked by a series of red lines, flickered across the display.

Noble concentrated on the radar screen. "Any sign of dust storms?"

The pilot looked away from the center console to check. "Looks clear," he said. "But I wouldn't trust that piece of hardware."

Noble locked eyes with the man. There was no hiding the apprehension in the pilot's gaze.

"Can't predict Mother Nature. Not anymore," he said. He shifted back to the main console. "The rules have changed, sir. I just hope a storm like those that ruined this base doesn't show up while we're here."

"How much notice would we have?"

The pilot shook his head. "Minutes. Maybe a bit more."

The chopper landed with a thump. Noble unfastened his belt and patted the pilot on the back. "Keep an eye on things. I want the *Sea Serpent* ready to go at a moment's notice."

"Aye aye, sir."

Taking one last glance out the windshield, Noble headed back to the cargo bay. He was greeted by a dozen helmets and the Biosphere team staring anxiously in his direction. It was odd seeing the children sitting there with their NTC suitcases, as though they were about to board some cruise liner.

"All right people, we're moving out in five minutes." He stood in the center of the cabin and activated the mini map on the main display. "Location A will be our forward operating base. Location B is the hangar housing the NTC *Sunspot*. As you can see, they are about a mile apart. If one team runs into trouble it will be difficult for the other team to provide support, so stay sharp."

Noble searched the group for Sophie. "Doctor Winston, Lieutenant Diego will escort your team. Everyone else, you're with me."

"You heard the man," Diego shouted. "Let's move out!"

The soldiers made final preparations: checking helmets, loading magazines, and stretching.

Noble followed the soldiers out onto the tarmac, the excitement building inside him with every step. They fanned out and set up a perimeter around the *Sea Serpent*. Their movements were precise. Calculated. They'd done this a hundred times before.

Above them, the sky had turned an off gray, taking on the color of the landscape below. A single crimson smear streaked across the horizon like a bloodstain. Noble couldn't help but wonder if it foreshadowed what was to come.

He paused outside the lift gate and said, "Hold position." He winced as he flung the strap of his rifle over his injured shoulder. The pain was still present, but it reminded him he was alive. And if he was alive, he could still fight.

Sophie and her team stood at the edge of the ramp.

"Captain," Sophie said from the ramp. She ran a sleeve across her forehead. "I wanted to thank you. You risked everything to evacuate us."

"Any soldier would have done the same."

Sophie shook her head. "Not any soldier, Captain."

"It was the least we could do after all the intel you've given us," Noble replied.

She raised a hand to shield her eyes and looked over his shoulder. Then, gesturing with her chin, she said, "You know, it's not too late to change your mind. You could all come with us to Mars."

The comment took the captain by surprise. He hadn't considered leaving the planet. This was his home. And if he defeated the Organics, he would return to the GOA and help humanity start over.

"Can't do that," he said. "My duty is here. I have to do what I can to take back the planet."

She nodded. "I know."

"We need to move," Diego said, his voice low and anxious.

Noble nodded. "Good luck, Doctor," he said, reaching out to shake her hand and then turning to the rest of her team. "Good luck to all of you. When you find Doctor Hoffman, tell him . . ." Noble hesitated. The words clung to the tip of his tongue. "Tell him he was wrong about defeating the Organics."

"What do you mean?" Sophie asked.

Noble didn't answer. He was already moving with his men. Hoffman would understand the cryptic comment when she found him. *If* she ever found the doctor, he reminded himself.

"Let's move!" Noble shouted. He flashed a series of hand signals in the direction of the buildings in the distance. As he moved toward the domed structures, he recalled Kiel's words.

What's left to save? the man had asked. The question echoed in Noble's mind and the closer he got to the hangar the more he wondered the same thing. Were there still humans hidden in bunkers and strongholds that he didn't know about? *There have to be,* he thought. *There are always survivors.*

CHAPTER 23

SOPHIE felt one of the children tug on her sleeve.

"It's soooo hot out here," Owen said, looking up at her. Damp hair stuck to his forehead. She offered him a reassuring smile and wiped a strand from his eyes.

"Don't worry, we're almost there," she said.

Ahead of them Lieutenant Diego guided the group across the sea of sand. Wind peppered the unprotected team with rocks that stung Sophie's bare skin. For her, the pain was nothing more than an annoyance, a reminder of the changed world—a world she was ready to leave.

Out of the corner of her eye she could see the faint outlines of Noble's men. They were just specks on the horizon now, blurred by the swirling clouds of dust and dirt. She hadn't thought much more about the strike on the poles. And while she wished Noble the best, she wasn't concerned much with the outcome. The Earth was already dead to her. The future was, and always had been, on Mars.

"Almost there. Stay close," Diego shouted over the growing wind. Another gust hammered Sophie. She winced, but steadied herself with Emanuel's help. He'd shadowed her every step since they left the *Sea Serpent*.

"Thanks," she said, "but really, I'm fine."

Emanuel shot her a pained look. "Really? Because I'm dying over here."

Sophie chuckled for the first time in days. Being so close to the *Sunspot* had brightened her mood. "Don't worry. We're almost there."

Owen tugged on her sleeve again. "Sorry," she said, taking his hand and leading him into the wind.

The entire team pushed forward. A few feet ahead, Jeff pulled David along with his good arm. To the boy's right, Bouma carried Jamie on his back. And out in front Holly helped Kiel.

For a moment Sophie felt as though they were missing someone. They had lost Overton, Timothy, and Saafi. They were all still painful memories, but there was someone else.

Alexia, she thought.

Sophie suddenly felt vulnerable, more so than ever before. Without the AI, she had only humans to rely on. It was an odd revelation, but there was no turning back now. Alexia was gone. She'd made her decision, one that Sophie respected.

"Careful," Diego shouted. "Watch your step."

They'd come up on a section of the landing strip that looked like a junkyard. Partially buried under the dirt were the blackened hulls of X-90s, wings angled toward the sky like fins. She sidestepped one of them, pulling Owen with her.

When they finally reached the hangar, the storm was already near. Diego waited for them at the cracked door.

"Get inside," he said, gesturing with an armored hand into the darkness.

Sophie held her breath and slipped into the safety of the building. As her eyes adjusted to the dim lighting she gasped. Towering above them was the *Sunspot*—the ship that would take them to Mars.

Noble ran as fast as his legs would allow. While the armored suit was nimble, the months spent cramped inside the GOA had left him out of shape and frankly, not physically prepared for the mission.

Ahead he could see their salvation. The two-story hangar housing his arsenal of X-90s and drones jutted out of the swirling dust. A set of large access doors marked the main entrance. He remembered the maintenance access from the rover mission and flashed a hand signal to two dust-covered soldiers with their backs to the building. They nodded and disappeared around the right corner.

Chinning his com, Noble said, "Form a perimeter around these doors."

Battling another wind gust, the team fanned out around the building, their weapons aimed at the failing structure. Above them a loose power line whipped against the metal side of the building, whining in the storm. The hangar was just as he remembered it from the images. The green paint was cracked and sandblasted off the metal siding. Shards of glass lined the windows. It was remarkable what the storms had done to civilization in such a short time.

Hugging the side of the building Noble rounded the corner and caught a glimpse of the two soldiers waiting at the maintenance door. Like a pair of gargoyles they stood guard next to the fallen door. Its metal was covered with a thick layer of dust.

"Any contacts?" Noble asked.

Both men shook their heads. "No, sir."

The smaller man wiped his visor free of grime. The machine gunner, Ramirez, stared back at him.

"Good, let's move," Noble replied. Without hesitating he stepped onto the door. The metal moaned under the weight of his boot. He shouldered his rifle and paused in the side entrance. The beam from his helmet lamp cut the darkness in two. Moving his rifle barrel in conjunction with the light he scanned the room quickly, stopping on the sleek black outlines of three X-90s.

"Jackpot," he said.

He continued through the room with the men on his heels. They quickly cleared the space and then stopped to admire the jets. Ramirez reached out and ran his hand over the wing.

"Beautiful piece of machinery," Noble said. "I just hope they work." He pointed to the hangar doors at the other end of the room. "Let the others in."

Ramirez flung his rifle strap over his shoulder and jogged over to the set of double doors. Seconds later the screech of metal grinding against metal filled the hangar. A powerful gust of wind exploded through the opening, showering the men with shrapnel.

"Get inside. Move, move!" Noble yelled.

One by one the filthy NTC soldiers emerged. Brushing off their armor, they formed a circle around him. He considered saying something heroic, something that would inspire them, but behind every visor he saw men who were ready. Prepared to fight to the end.

Noble focused on the tallest of the group. "Ort."

The man stepped forward with a duffel bag in each hand. "Yes, sir."

A sudden vibration rocked the building, sending a tremor through the metal siding. The roof groaned in response. Flakes of dust rained down as another quake shook the ceiling.

"Not sure how much life this girl has left in her," Ort said.

Noble snorted. "I was thinkin' the same thing. All the more reason to hurry up." Gesturing to the X-90s he said, "Someone help Ort get set up."

Ramirez followed the engineer to the first jet, where he dropped one of the duffel bags and then hurried to the second and third.

"All right, Andy, Howard, and Riordan," Noble said. "Check your flight systems. Get those beauties up and running."

"Yes, sir," they replied simultaneously.

Kirt stepped up. "Where are my drones?"

Noble pointed to another set of wide doors at the end of the warehouse. "Through those doors."

Noble faced the other soldiers. "The rest of you take up locations at every access point in this building. Got it?"

The five remaining men nodded and spread out in different directions.

Sucking in a deep breath, Noble moved to the next phase of his plan. "Follow me, Kirt," he said. They hurried across the room. The large double doors were already open when they got there. Noble raised his pulse rifle. Blinking on his HUD, he scanned the dark room for any sign of contacts.

The scan picked up zero traces of heat signatures. Another blink and the display faded. He reached for his helmet lamp and activated it with a click.

The building shook again.

"Stay behind me," he whispered.

Kirt's anxious breathing followed him into the darkness. Their thin beams danced in front of them. The room served as more of a maintenance facility than a warehouse. In the right corner sat the idle rover he'd deployed five days earlier, its cameras still angled at a row of black drones all draped with dusty sheets. He counted nine total.

Satisfied, he swept his light across the room and found a cluster of monitors. *The command center,* he thought. He rubbed his hands together. "We're in business," Noble said. "See if you can get this thing up and running."

"On it," Kirt replied.

Footsteps drew Noble's attention back to the doorway. In the shadows stood Ramirez. Clearing his throat, he said, "Sir, we have a problem."

Noble cringed. "What is it?"

"One of the X-90s is dead."

"What do you mean, dead?" Kirt asked.

Noble cursed under his breath. He knew exactly what the soldier meant. The jets were built to withstand the blasts from modern EMPs, and he'd gambled that the magnetic disturbance hadn't penetrated their hardened casing.

Apparently he'd lost that bet.

"The other two are online?" Noble asked.

"Yes, sir," Ramirez said.

In a voice that conveyed confidence Noble said, "We're still in the game. I can work with two." He turned to Kirt. "Who are my best two pilots?"

The man paused to think. "I'd say Riordan and Howard."

"Ramirez, tell Andy to get his ass back here. He can help with the drones," he said. Turning to Kirt he added, "I don't want you flying all of them on your own anyway."

The pilot exhaled as if a huge burden had been lifted off him.

The two men moved to the command center. A pile of papers remained on the main desk, left untouched where their previous owner had abandoned them nearly three months ago. Moving to the other side of the station, Noble looked for the power source. A cable snaked beneath the desk, covered by a thin layer of dust.

Dropping to one knee, he grabbed the cord, hoping desperately that it still worked, then pulled the end toward him and plugged it in.

"Got it," Kirt said.

Noble glanced up at the pilot. He sat comfortably in one of the chairs. Through his visor, Noble could see the younger man grinning.

Reaching out slowly with his right index finger, Kirt swiped the screen. It flickered to life, spreading a cool green glow over the room.

"I can't believe it still works," Kirt laughed.

Wincing, Noble stood and walked over behind him. "All systems go?"

"We're about to find out," Kirt said. He punched a series of commands into the system. Leaning closer he squinted. "Looks like—" the man suddenly clapped.

A lump formed in Noble's throat. He wasn't sure if the man's reaction was one of joy or frustration. Another line of data rolled across the screen and Kirt stiffened. He typed another few keystrokes.

"Well?" Noble finally asked.

Kirt tapped his armored index finger on the desk nervously. "Waiting—"

Noble focused on the display.

"Yes! I'm in," Kirt blurted.

This time the captain clapped. After months of hiding, he was finally in a position to stop the Organics.

Sophie pulled her flashlight from her belt and pointed it at the *Sunspot*. As the beam moved down the length of the ship it grew smaller and smaller until it was only a white dot.

My god, she thought. It had to be the size of a football field, with the wings stretching half that distance. Moving the light back to the nose she stopped on the only visible marking: *SUNSPOT.*

She stared at the spaceship with fascination. There was a part of her that hadn't believed it was real, hadn't believed it was possible. But here it was, looming above them. Waiting to travel to the stars and beyond.

She shot an excited glance behind her. Standing quietly at the door were the others. They stared above her, at the ship that dwarfed them.

Owen pulled on Holly's and Bouma's hands and jumped into the air. Letting out a loud screech he said, "We get to ride on that!"

Bouma chuckled. "Sure do, buddy."

The boy's lips formed a flabbergasted O, and then he said, "Wow!"

Jamie, however, cowered behind Holly. "That thing looks scary," she whispered.

Sophie did a half turn, scanning the smooth surface of the spaceship. The girl was right. It was frightening. NTC engineers were never concerned with aesthetics. They only cared about what worked.

She hoped that that the engineers had finished the ship. Like the *Secundo Casu*, the *Sunspot* was a prototype, never tested outside the Earth's atmosphere.

"How do we get in this thing?" Emanuel asked

"I was hoping you knew," she replied.

Diego unfolded his arms and pulled a tablet from a pouch on his side. Crouching, he activated the small device and studied the surface. The blue glow illuminated his helmet and Sophie saw his eyes for the first time. They were focused, determined.

"Before you can board the ship you must tap into the NTC system.

Intel shows there's a command center underground," the man said, glancing up. He pointed toward a pair of maintenance doors halfway down the side of the building. "Those will lead you there."

"And how do we get inside?" Kiel interjected.

"Don't worry," Diego said. "I have the codes."

"Thank you," Sophie said, placing her hand on his shoulder.

"Just doing my job, Doctor," he replied. Standing, he gestured toward the maintenance entry. "Better get moving. Once you guys are on board and prepped for flight I'll be rejoining Captain Noble."

Sophie acknowledged his statement with a nod. "Absolutely." She scanned the team, trying to decide how best to move forward. Even with the base seemingly clear, she didn't want to leave anyone behind without security.

"Kiel, you and Bouma stay here with the kids and Holly. Emanuel, you're with us."

They crossed the room, shadowing the side of the ship. Sophie kept her light pointed into the darkness, half expecting a Spider to jump out at her. For some reason she simply couldn't grasp the idea that the base was devoid of Organics. It just didn't *feel* right.

Still, she pushed on, scanning the shadows with a nervous eye. A full minute passed before they reached the double doors that led below. Sophie halted there, looking behind her. The rest of the team were camped out in a circle, their bags scattered loosely around them. Bouma stood guard at the hangar door and flashed her a thumbs-up.

The twist and click of an unlocked door handle echoed through the room. "We're in," Diego said, his voice just shy of a whisper.

Taking one last look at her team, she followed Diego and Emanuel into the dark stairwell. She hesitated for a moment as a strange sensation washed over her. She'd felt it before, two days into the Biosphere mission when Alexia had said they'd lost contact with the outside world. That feeling was distinct, almost tangible. She could remember it vividly. And now she was having it again, like déjà vu. Diego stopped and shone his helmet light in her face.

"You okay, Doctor?"

Shielding her eyes from the brightness, she nodded.

"You sure?" Emanuel asked. "Are the headaches back? Do you need to stop?"

"No, let's keep moving," she said, forcing her right foot onto the next step. Licking her cracked lips, she continued. But with every step down the dry, humid stairway, the feeling that she was never going to see her team again grew stronger.

CHAPTER 24

THE storm rattled the building with a growing ferocity. Noble looked up from his monitor and eyed the roof with a cocked brow, expecting the metal sheet to peel off and sail into the wind. He could picture an angry red twister swooping in and sucking his men into the sky. Tearing them limb from limb.

He pushed the thought aside. He needed to focus on the mission and not get sidetracked by pointless fear.

"How are we doing, Kirt?" Noble spun his chair to face the pilot. The man typed a series of commands into the interface and then strode over to one of the drones.

"Working, sir. I hope to have these all online within the hour," he said, extending his right arm in an outward motion as if he was showcasing the row of drones to a potential buyer.

Noble glanced at the mission clock in the upper-right edge of his HUD. They were already behind schedule. Ort had run into a problem installing the RVAMP monitors in the X-90 cockpits. Without them the pilots would have no way of knowing what distance to keep from the drones.

I need those jets, Noble thought, clenching his jaw.

He stood and jogged across the room to the wide doors that opened into the first hangar. The whine of portable power tools echoed inside his helmet. A pair of legs protruded out from under the wing of the closest jet. Noble bent down. Ort drilled a final bolt to secure one of the RVMs. He slid out from under the jet and pushed himself to his feet.

"Almost done. But I had a hell of a time with those monitors." He sucked in a breath. "Man, I'm freaking burning up in here. I think the AC unit in my suit is toast." Reaching up he unfastened his helmet and pulled it off. He placed it gently onto the floor and then took a long swig from his water bottle. Dragging his sleeve over his mouth he said, "I should be able to get the RVAMPs installed in an hour."

"You have thirty minutes," Noble replied. He glanced up at the ceiling again. "If that."

"Roger, sir. I'm on it." Ort grabbed his helmet with one hand and the remaining duffel bag with his other.

The two working X-90s were facing the entrance, their beak-shaped noses pointed toward the metal doors. Noble clasped his hands together behind his back. The sight gave him great satisfaction. They were one step closer.

Ramirez joined the captain behind the jets. "Any word from Diego?"

"Not yet," Noble replied without taking his focus off the X-90s.

Another gust of wind struck the building's side. The walls shuddered, the ringing echoing through the room. Several of the other men glanced nervously at the ceiling.

Noble brought his chin down hard on the com. "Everyone, listen up. We're about thirty minutes from go time. Keep sharp."

Sophie opened the door and saw the rodent before she heard its feet skittering across the floor. The rat took off down the hallway where the stairwell ended.

Without a night vision–capable NTC suit, Sophie was forced to use her flashlight. She aimed it at the filthy creature, catching a red set of eyes and a frail body cowering in the darkness.

It was odd, seeing a living animal all the way down here, and she found herself thinking again of the emaciated cat they'd discovered back in Colorado Springs. Noble's words aboard the *Sea Serpent* replayed in her mind.

There will be survivors . . . Humans will emerge from their holes.

She knew the odds, as Alexia had. The statistics didn't lie, nor did the scenery. Humans had lost the planet, and the resource that had sustained life for billions of years. Sure, a few survivors might be lurking out there just like the rat, but without water, they too would die.

Beside her, Diego studied his tablet. He glanced up. Pointing at the surface of the device he said, "Take a look."

They crowded around the tablet and Sophie saw the red lines representing the tunnels.

"Looks like they snake for miles beneath the base. The command center where we can activate the *Sunspot* is only about a quarter mile from here."

"We have a good little hike," Emanuel replied.

"Better get moving," Sophie added.

Diego nodded and returned his tablet to his side pouch. Then he tucked his fingers inside his pulse rifle strap and detached the weapon. With the barrel pointing forward, they pushed on.

Sophie wasted no time following suit. The three moved quickly through the darkness. Their lights flickered across the concrete, illuminating the hallway several hundred feet ahead.

She forced a swallow as the headache she thought had passed reared up inside her skull. The pain grew with every step.

"I need to stop," she said, panting. "I'm sorry." She reached out and braced herself against the wall. Emanuel approached her from behind, placing a sweaty palm on her forearm. Then he reached back and removed a water bottle from his belt.

"Almost there," he said with a reassuring squeeze.

Twisting the cap off, she brought the bottle to her lips. The water, now warm, slid down her dry throat. Careful not to waste a single drop, she cupped one hand under her chin. A few stragglers fell into her palm and she lapped them up.

Handing the bottle back to Emanuel, she said, "Finish it off. The *Sunspot* will have an endless supply." Almost as soon as she said it, she realized there was a possibility she was wrong.

Emanuel must have had the same epiphany. "How do we even know the water biome will be intact? Shit!" He shook his head and adjusted the straps of the dual RVM-RVAMP machine on his back. "I didn't even think about that, but what if?"

Sophie stopped him by waving a finger. "Too late now. We have to hope the ship made it this far without being touched." She swept her light over the floor and then into the distance. "I see no signs of the aliens."

"Doesn't mean they weren't here before," Diego said. "Either way, let's keep moving. We're almost there."

Sophie massaged her temples and sucked in a lungful of scorching air. The breath burned her throat where just seconds ago the water had cooled it. She waited for Emanuel to follow Diego and then fell in behind them.

The same déjà vu she'd felt earlier reemerged. This time it was even more intense, prompting a wave of goose bumps. Something was wrong. Things just didn't make sense. It was too quiet.

Questions she knew she should have asked earlier came to mind. Why had the *Sunspot* been left behind at Offutt? And why was the base clear of the Organics? Even if they had migrated she would still see their remains, the shells of orbs, or the husks of humans.

"We're here," Diego said. He halted where the T-shaped corridor turned off. He peeked around the corner and swept his light down the right side first and then moved back to the left.

"Clear," he said, motioning them forward with a wave.

Sophie followed Emanuel around the right corner and they moved into the next hallway. Diego was stopped at a set of double doors. Above them the first sign she'd seen since entering the facility hung loosely to the side. She lifted her flashlight to the yellow lettering.

TE Command Center
Authorized Personnel Only

Diego reached for the handle.

"Stay back," he whispered, before twisting the knob on the windowless metal door. It clicked, unlocked.

"That makes things easier," he mumbled.

With his right foot he edged the door open, his headlamp shooting a beam of white light into the room.

Sophie concentrated on the silence. There were no alien noises. No high-pitched shrieks or the *scratch, scrape* sound their claws made.

"Emanuel, see if you can find the lights," Diego said.

The walls were lined with state-of-the-art holo monitors. In the center of the room sat two metal desks, an AI interface protruding from the tiled floor between them.

"That must be it," Diego said. He rushed over to the thin pedestal and withdrew his tablet. Then he removed a small cord and connected the two devices. A hologram shot out above him, carpeting the room with a purple mist. The light transitioned into a series of translucent flickering numbers.

Sophie leaned in closer for a better look.

"Access codes," Diego said, sensing her presence. "These should allow us entry into the AI system. Should only take a few—"

Before he could finish his thought there was a clunk from the air ventilation system in the ceiling. Sophie glanced up just as the banks of LEDs clicked on, flooding the room with a warm yellow light. She basked under the cool air from the ceiling vents. The breeze felt magnificent on her blistering skin.

Diego continued to swipe away at his tablet. "Almost in," he muttered. "Only a few more minutes."

Sophie breathed the cool air, focusing on the flashing numbers. In the back of her mind she pictured the children waiting in the dark hangar and scanning the shadows for the shapes of aliens.

"Hurry," she said.

"Going as fast as I can, Doctor," Diego replied.

A scratching noise above them startled her. She flinched at the sound, her hand darting toward her heart.

"Did you hear that?" she whispered.

Emanuel shot her a concerned look. "What?"

"The scratching."

She looked at the ceiling, nervously scanning the white tiles. The air unit coughed and then settled back into a normal rhythm.

"It probably hasn't been run for a while," Emanuel said.

Sophie managed a nod.

"Got it!" Diego shouted.

When she turned back to the interface the numbers had been replaced by the avatar of a middle-aged woman. The AI wore a serious look, her forehead forming a mountain range of wrinkles. She studied her visitors carefully, locking eyes with Sophie last.

An awkward silence spread over the group.

The AI spoke first. "Who are you?" She sounded confused. Lost.

"I'm Doctor Sophie Winston with the Cheyenne Mountain Biosphere. This is Doctor Emanuel Rodriguez and NTC Lieutenant John Diego. We're here to—"

"Where is my crew?" she interrupted.

"Your crew?" Emanuel replied.

Diego took a step closer to the interface and unplugged his tablet. "The base appears to be empty."

The woman's eyes widened in confusion. Sophie wondered if the AI had suffered some sort of malfunction. Memory loss, perhaps.

Her purple avatar abruptly disappeared.

Diego stepped back. Standing shoulder to shoulder with Sophie, he shot her a nervous glance.

"I don't like this," Emanuel replied.

Moments later the woman's face reappeared. She smiled as if nothing had happened and said, "My apologies. I was forced to reboot. Let me start over. I'm Sonya, NTC Model Number 3. I've been assigned to the NTC *Sunspot*." She spoke with some sort of foreign accent that Sophie couldn't quite place. Bosnian, maybe.

"Yes, that's why we are here," Sophie replied.

Sonya tilted her head and studied Sophie. "I do not understand."

Taking a cautious step forward, Sophie said, "We're here to activate the *Sunspot*."

The AI blinked several times as if she was processing the information.

"And we're here to take the *Sunspot* to Mars," Sophie continued. "We received your SOS message."

Sonya continued to stare.

"You do remember the SOS, right?" Sophie entreated.

"I shut my system down ten days ago. I've been in hibernation mode," Sonya replied. "I'm still restoring my hardware and additional systems."

"While you're doing that, could you please open the doors to the *Sunspot*? The rest of our team is waiting to board the ship."

"Certainly," Sonya replied. "One moment, please." Her avatar disappeared again and the purple light swallowed the room.

Diego smiled behind his visor and nodded at Sophie.

They waited for several seconds before Sonya reappeared. "I've restored my system and retrieved the SOS message."

The three waited for the AI to explain. Diego gripped his rifle tightly, the barrel slowly inching off the ground.

"The crew of the *Sunspot* was killed approximately ten days, twenty-one hours, thirty-four minutes, and thirteen seconds ago."

"Oh my god," Sophie said, cupping her hands over her mouth. "Where? Where were they killed, Sonya?"

"Inside the *Sunspot*, of course," the AI replied.

Sophie was running before the AI had a chance to finish.

"Wait, Sophie!" Emanuel called after her.

She finally understood why Sonya had activated the SOS. How could she have been so stupid? The base was empty because the Organics weren't there. They were inside the *Sunspot*. And with the doors now open, the hungry aliens would have fresh prey waiting at their doorstep.

CHAPTER 25

JEFF pulled the magazine from his rifle to check his ammo. He knew there were only five bullets left. He'd checked several times now. The waiting ate at him, taxing his nerves. *What the hell is taking so long,* he wondered as he jammed the magazine back into the gun with a click.

David, lying on the floor next to him, lifted his head and smiled. "Guess we aren't going to have to use those after all."

Jeff looked away. He scanned the dimly lit hangar for Bouma and Kiel. Both men were positioned at opposite ends of the ship, the beams from their flashlights playing over the darkness. Standing, Jeff glanced over at Holly. She stroked Owen's hair softly as he slept with his head in her lap. A few feet away Jamie was curled up comfortably with her blanket.

Lifting his rifle, Jeff walked away from the group and started pacing. He couldn't sit there any longer. The heat was unbearable. He honestly wasn't sure how Owen could even sleep in it.

As he moved closer to the *Sunspot* he heard a chirp. Above him a circle of blue lights blinked, forming a halo around the ship's wide nose. They glowed for a few moments, flickering in and out. Jeff flinched at a loud grinding noise that followed the chirping. The bank of LEDs turned red and the oval surface of the ship retracted to either side. A short ramp lowered from the opening, the rungs extending until they hit the concrete with a crunch.

Jeff stumbled backward, his rifle aimed up the ramp. "Guys," he shouted. "Someone just opened the door to this thing!"

The blinking red lights illuminated the stairs of the metal platform just enough for Jeff to see a dark substance dried to the metal.

"Guys!" he yelled again, taking several steps away from the ship.

Behind him he could hear the heavy footsteps of the marines, but he kept his focus on the *Sunspot*.

"Sweet!" Kiel said. He limped ahead of Jeff, looking up to see inside the ship.

"Stay back," Bouma ordered.

Jeff felt a tug on his sleeve and glanced down to see David. The boy wiped sweat off his brow and then said, "Can we go inside now? It's so hot out here."

"Not yet, bud. Why don't you go back there with the others," Jeff said, pointing to Holly and the other kids.

David protested with a frown, but retreated to his suitcase.

The roof suddenly shook, sending a vibration groaning through the metal walls.

"Man," Kiel said. "I really don't want to be here when this tin can comes crashing down."

Bouma took a deep breath. "Me either."

"Think it's safe?" Jeff asked.

"I think we should wait for the others to get back," Bouma replied. He joined Kiel at the top of the ramp and peered up into the ship.

"No way," Kiel replied. "I want to see our digs for the next . . . How many months or years is this going to take?"

He limped into the ship before Bouma could stop him.

"Goddamnit, Kiel," Bouma muttered. "Jeff, watch our six, okay?" He looked back at Holly. "Wait here. We're going to scope this out."

She waved and then continued running her hand through Owen's hair.

Jeff nodded at Bouma and then followed the marines into the ship. The top of the lift opened onto a large oval room filled with equipment

Jeff had never seen before. A wall of monitors surrounded them on all sides. In the center of the room were three leather chairs facing a large overhead display.

"Holy shit," Kiel said, reaching up to cover his nose. "Do you smell that?"

Bouma stopped to sniff the air. "What the fuck is it?"

The smell overwhelmed Jeff as soon as he joined them on the bridge. It smelled sour. *No,* Jeff thought, taking a whiff. *It smells like rotting meat. Like death.*

"I don't like this," Bouma whispered.

Kiel shook his head. "Me either." He swept his flashlight over the room, the beam hitting Jeff in the face. The boy covered his eyes and stepped away.

"Sorry," the marine said.

Jeff choked as he took another breath. He crossed the room and moved toward the cluster of seats facing the main monitor. He pointed his own light at the display, realizing that he was looking at a virtual windshield.

Stepping closer, he reached for the back of one of the leather chairs. His fingers slid into a slimy substance and he quickly pulled them from the gooey mess. With his heart racing he held his hand up in the light and saw it covered in blood.

"What the hell!" he cried. Before Kiel and Bouma could respond a blur of blue light filled the oval entry leading away from the bridge. Both marines stumbled backward, knocking into each other.

"Watch it," Kiel shouted. When they regained their balance they both aimed their guns into the void.

Jeff stared into the darkness. The smell of rotting flesh filled his lungs. He coughed and then froze in fear as the hall came to life. The intensifying light pulsated like a heartbeat, filling the corridor with a cool blue.

He jammed the butt of his weapon against his good shoulder just as his dad had taught him. With one eye closed, he focused the crosshairs and waited.

They didn't wait long. The distant sound of scraping echoed off the walls. It grew louder until the sound seemed to be coming from all around them, echoing through the cabin. Panicking, Jeff took a step backward, retreating to the ramp. He made it two strides when something emerged at the far end of the bridge. It flickered, moving from one side of the corridor to the other, the *scratch, scrape* building every second.

"My god," Bouma mumbled. "Move! Move!"

But it was too late. A Spider burst out of the shadows, its front claws scampering across the metal as its high joints clicked. The creature's mandibles opened, letting out an ear-splitting screech. Jeff fumbled with his rifle, resisting the urge to cover his ears.

"Open fire!" Bouma yelled.

Kiel squeezed off a volley of shots at the alien first. The rounds ricocheted off the alien's shield harmlessly. Letting out another roar, the creature swiped the air with a loud whoosh.

The smaller marine fired again, screaming now. "Die, you son of a—" As soon as the words left his mouth one of the talons hooked him through his midsection and raised him into the air. Blood burst from Kiel's mouth, splattering the ceiling above him.

"*No!*" Bouma shouted. With his right foot firmly in front of him, he unloaded his magazine into the creature's shields.

The shields absorbed the rounds, pulsating with every hit. The alien swung its prey, jamming another claw through Kiel's back with a sickening crunch.

Jeff locked eyes with the marine as the Spider lifted him farther into the air. He could see the terror in Kiel's eyes, the pain and horror. It all happened so quickly, Jeff didn't have time to process it.

The marine's head slumped to the side and the alien tossed his lifeless body to the floor.

"Get out of here!" Bouma yelled.

But Jeff couldn't move. He was frozen. His eyes roved from Kiel's bloody body to the Spider. There was motion behind the beast. A flood of the creatures streamed out of the hallway, like animals that had just awoken from a deep slumber.

Finally shocked into motion, Jeff retreated down the ramp. Bouma followed him, turning to fire off a few uncontrolled bursts over his shoulder with his rifle gripped in one hand.

Jeff could only think of David as he loped down the lift. He had to protect his brother. He couldn't let the monsters get him. Not now, after they'd come so far, after they had survived for so long.

As soon as Jeff's boots hit the concrete he was moving at full speed toward a terrified Holly. David pointed his rifle over Jeff's shoulder, aiming it at the nose of the ship.

"Run!" Jeff cried. He could hear Bouma's footsteps behind him, but had no idea where the marine was. He only knew they had to hide. They'd done it at White Sands; they could do it again.

Grabbing David by his shirt, he yanked the boy to his feet and pulled him toward the exit. "Let's go!"

Holly followed, pulling Owen and Jamie. With Jeff out in front he guided them away from the ship, back toward the set of doors they had entered through. They were only a couple hundred yards away, but above him he could see a blue light gliding across the ceiling.

A loud groan rumbled through the building as they approached the exit. *The storm,* Jeff thought. He'd forgotten about the damned storm. When they got to the doors he looked back at the lift. Flowing from the ship were dozens of Spiders, their mandibles releasing the same high-pitched shrieks Jeff had heard so many times before. The mixture of scraping claws, the crack of gunfire, and the vibrating door was overwhelming.

Jeff tried to think, but where could they go?

They were trapped.

"Make it stop!" David said, cupping his ears.

Jeff's heart broke at the sight of his younger brother cowering in fear. For the first time since their dad's death, he couldn't protect him. Tossing his rifle aside, he reached for David's hands and pulled him close. As the blue glow surrounded them he embraced his brother.

"It's okay, David. We're going to see Mom and Dad soon."

With the dust storm pounding the hangars, Noble wondered if Sophie would try and wait out the storm before launching the *Sunspot*. The ship had been designed to travel in much worse conditions, but the X-90s and—

He turned and eyed the row of fragile black drones, their noses angled at the hangar doors. The wind would tear them wing from wing, like their fallen comrades littered across the tarmac.

The captain studied the ceiling, listening to the roof rattling above them. The tremors were less frequent, a sign the storm was finally starting to let up.

"Sir," Kirt said.

"Somebody better have some good news for me," he said, spinning in his chair to see Kirt, Andy, Riordan, and Howard. The pilots stood with their hands clasped behind their backs, their chests swollen and proud.

"Redemption incoming. Ready to rock!"

Noble didn't need to turn to see the Viking-size engineer crossing the room. His loud footsteps gave his presence away.

"All RVAMPs and electromagnetic monitors are installed," Ort said. He slapped the captain on his back. "We're good to go, sir."

"Assuming we can get the birds in the air," Noble replied. "Kirt, how are the skies looking?"

The drone pilot ran a hand through his short blond hair and checked the monitor. After a pause he regained his composure and said, "Skies are still clear of contacts. The worst of the storm looks to have passed, too."

The report gave Noble the confidence to take the mission to the next phase.

"Okay," he said. "Riordan, Howard. You're up."

Both men acknowledged the order with a short nod. The burden they carried was evident in their hardened features. Succeed, and they would bring the Organics' network crashing to the ground. Fail, and they would lose the planet forever.

Noble felt an overwhelming responsibility of his own, but like his men, he did his best to mask the feeling. Having been over it a million times in his mind, he was ready.

"Ort, get a few men to help you open the doors," Noble said, moving from one man to the next. "Kirt, you and Andy prep your drone stations."

Despite going over a mental checklist, he felt as if he had missed something. It dawned on him then that Diego still wasn't back from escorting Sophie and her team to the *Sunspot. Maybe he's waiting out the storm,* Noble thought.

Noble walked over to the cluster of monitors where Kirt worked to bring the drones online. Not wanting to raise alarm among his men, he kept the com channel offline. Leaning close to the pilot, he said, "Has anyone heard from Diego?"

Without looking up Kirt shook his head. "No, sir."

Noble nodded. The fates of Sophie and Diego were out of his hands.

The grinding of metal on metal pulled Noble to the front of the hangar. A gust of wind speckled the concrete with dirt as two of his men opened the large doors. One of them yelled "Looks like it's clearing off!"

Noble balled his hand into a fist. "Just keep it cracked, for now."

The man on the right flashed a thumbs-up.

A white sun broke through the sky and spilled into the hangar. The armored X-90s glistened in the light. Noble touched the sleek curved edge of one of them, wishing he could climb into the cockpit and be there when they brought down the pole at McKinley.

"Everything's prepped and ready to go," Kirt said. "I've made contact with Lolo. The Surge just hit the alien poles a few minutes ago. We have two hours to take it down before it can reconnect. Now's our chance, sir."

Noble crossed his arms. "Get my birds in the air."

The crack of gunfire stopped as Sophie rounded the first corner. Her heart stopped with it. The last shot faded away.

"No," she mumbled. *"No!"*

"Sophie!" Emanuel yelled behind her. "Wait up!"

"We have to get to them!" she screamed. Her words echoed down the hallway. She pushed on, her body aching with every stride, her head pounding from a growing headache.

When she reached the door to the stairwell she paused long enough to withdraw Sergeant Overton's .45 from the back of her belt. The metal, cold on her warm skin, felt powerful, and the memory of the man who had fought so valiantly gave her the extra boost she needed to twist the doorknob. She hadn't seen eye to eye with the man, but his courage inspired her own.

Holding her breath, she opened the door and was hit by a blinding blue light. The intense glow looked like a portal to another world. It pulled her up the stairs, a beacon, drawing her forward.

With every step her mind raced with thoughts of the children, of Holly and the marines.

"Please," she begged, "don't let them be dead."

By the time she reached the top of the stairwell Emanuel and Diego were right behind her. Diego squeezed past with his rifle extended.

Then she saw them.

Four small orbs. Floating at the far end of the chamber. A pack of Spiders huddled around them. On the ground in front of the orbs, Sophie could see something else. Two human bodies.

Holly . . .

Bouma . . .

She couldn't see either of their faces, but she could see the blood leaking from their wounds.

Sophie collapsed to her knees, tears racing down her face. She raised the .45, pointing it toward the aliens. Her finger hovered over the trigger, but she didn't fire.

A few feet ahead of her Diego and Emanuel stood silently, watching in shock.

"We can't help them," the soldier said.

Emanuel stumbled, nearly tripping over his own feet as he tiptoed over to Sophie. He crouched down to eye level and said, "We have to leave."

She glared at him, a vein bulging in her neck. She said, "We use the RVAMP. They can still be saved."

Emanuel looked at her in disbelief. "That will kill you, Sophie. You can't survive a blast at this range."

She grabbed his wrist and squeezed it. "I don't care. I won't let them die."

"No," Emanuel said, shaking his head. "I won't do it."

The Spiders shrieked at the sound of Emanuel's voice.

Diego took a step back, shouldering his rifle. "We have to move, guys. Pronto."

Emanuel could see him saying something into his mini mike, but couldn't make out the words.

"Command isn't responding," Diego replied. "Get down!" he yelled, raising his rifle and firing.

Sophie held Emanuel's gaze as Diego emptied his magazine into the mass of aliens. The pulse rounds infuriated the hungry group.

Scratch, scrape, scratch, scrape.

Emanuel pulled his wrist free from her grasp and reached for the straps securing the RVAMP to his back. With trepidation he unfastened the device and laid it in front of them.

"Sophie. Please don't do this," he said. Tears flowed freely down his face.

"They're coming!" Diego shouted between shots. "If you're going to do something, you better do it fast!"

She managed a smile. "I love you, Emanuel." Then she dropped the .45 onto the ground and pulled the RVAMP between them. His fingers intertwined with hers.

She forced their fingers down on the green button together. An invisible blast of electromagnetic energy exploded from the device. Pain raced through her system, lighting her nerves on fire. She twisted, jerked, and twitched uncontrollably. And then it was over. She felt her body slump into Emanuel's arms and heard his screams as darkness overtook her.

———————

The sun glimmered high in the afternoon sky. On the horizon, dark clouds of dust moved away from the base. The carcasses of several armored vehicles rested in the storm's wake, their fading paint reflecting the abuse inflicted on them over the past few months.

Flanked by Kirt and Ort, the captain stood with his arms crossed, staring out over the tarmac. He watched Howard and Riordan climb into the cockpits of the X-90s. His team had maneuvered the jets and the drones around the wreckage and cleared a path for their takeoff.

Both pilots gave a thumbs-up as soon as the glass windshields locked into place above them. Then, with a ground-shaking roar they flared up the engines. Flames burst from their cylinder exhaust tubes.

Noble smiled and, in sync with Ort and Kirt, saluted the two pilots. They returned the gesture. The concrete rumbled a second later as the jets lurched forward.

The captain shielded his face from the heat and a powerful wind gust, watching through a fort of fingers as the jets raced down the tarmac and lifted into the air. With the planes clear, Andy launched the drones, controlling them manually from the command center.

Within a minute the sky was filled with the most beautiful sight Noble had seen in months—human air power.

The X-90s screamed across the skyline, streaking northwest, three drones following in their exhaust trails. And then they were just black specks. The other six drones peeled off in different directions.

Noble nodded, watching the final blip disappear on the horizon. With a deep breath he turned back to the hangar. Their first target, Mount McKinley, was a little over 2,600 miles away. With jets capable of speeds up to 2,200 miles per hour, the pilots would make it there in a little over an hour. That would give them at least thirty minutes to take down the pole before the Surge reconnected. Now all he had to do was wait.

Operation Redemption was officially underway.

When the rumble from the jets had completely vanished, Noble heard a distant voice. He spun to see a soldier running across the tarmac.

It was Diego, and he was screaming.

CHAPTER 26

THE ceiling had stopped rattling a few minutes before. The rumble from the X-90s and drones had waned away. Noble's men had successfully launched, just narrowly avoiding the blast from the RVAMP, but Emanuel didn't care. He held Sophie's limp body in his arms, sobbing as he watched her life force drain away. He shook her softly, mumbling her name over and over.

She twitched, her chest heaving and torso jerking, just involuntary muscle spasms. Her frozen pupils stared in different directions, a result of the electrical current the nanobots had released when they were destroyed.

In the end, it was the device he had made that killed her. He would live with that guilt for the rest of his life.

He glanced up, tears cascading off his face and plopping onto the concrete. They were surrounded by a blue field of alien bodies; twisted and mangled from the RVAMP's blast.

Beyond their corpses, the four floating orbs had crashed to the ground, their translucent skin melting around the child imprisoned inside.

Setting Sophie softly on the ground, Emanuel stood and raced over to them. As he approached he heard several stifled whimpers. But the sound wasn't coming from the children. He stepped over the Spiders and found Holly and Bouma lying in the shadows of the hangar doors. They had been so close to escaping, the marine's hands just feet away.

"Help the kids," Holly choked. Emanuel quickly scanned her body. A large gash decorated her upper arm, but she would live. Bouma, on the other hand, was a wreck. He was unconscious, and when Emanuel saw his injuries he could see why. The Spiders had pierced his right thigh and upper left chest. His uniform was soaked in scarlet.

Holly dragged herself across the floor and applied pressure to Bouma's leg. She glanced up at Emanuel, a curtain of bloody blond hair hanging from her face. "Go, Emanuel!"

He nodded and ran to the children. Jeff and David lay just feet away from each other, their eyes closed. Emanuel crouched down and felt David's neck for a pulse. He found one—weak, but he was alive.

Then he moved to Jamie and Owen. Their small bodies were covered in blue goo. He pulled Jamie from the fluid first, removing the gunk from her mouth and face. Then he put her softly on the concrete and worked on Owen. They were both breathing, but their heartbeats felt weak.

He couldn't wrap his mind around what had happened. Adrenaline kept him moving. *Save the living,* he thought. *You can't do anything for Sophie now.* His eyes welled up again as he cleaned the children of alien slime.

It was hard to imagine that he and Holly were the only original members of the Biosphere team left. What had started out as a mission to save the world had turned into World War III, and he was the only one left unscathed.

Grinding metal rang out at the other end of the chamber, startling Emanuel. He glanced over his shoulder as Diego waved a squad of NTC soldiers into the room. They spread out under the *Sunspot*, their sleek black armor glimmering in the withering blue light.

"We need medical attention!" Emanuel shouted.

He looked up at the ship looming above them, his eyes focusing on the open door, and then suddenly he remembered. Why hadn't he thought of it before?

The ship had a full medical facility, just like the Biosphere at

Cheyenne Mountain. And inside there were a dozen or more cryo chambers, all designed for extended space travel. If he could get the children into them, he could basically freeze them until they reached Mars. Surely Dr. Hoffman and his team could save them. Maybe they could even save . . .

He looked back at Sophie's limp body. A soldier leaned over her, his headlamp illuminating her pale face. Emanuel knew it was a long shot, but maybe she could be brought back.

Shocked into motion, Emanuel stood and snapped his fingers. "Diego," he shouted. "I need your men to get these kids and Sophie into the cryo chambers inside the ship."

"On it," the soldier said.

"We need a medic, too," Holly yelled. She pumped Bouma's chest frantically. "He's not breathing!"

One of the soldiers sprinted over to them and, dropping to a knee, opened a small black medical kit. He shooed Holly aside and began working on the marine.

Above them, the bank of red lights surrounding the door to the *Sunspot* blinked. The NTC soldiers rushed back and forth.

Emanuel's vision blurred. He could hear someone yelling his name, but the words were indecipherable.

They were so fucking close! So close to leaving the damned planet and all the death behind. And now Sophie, his beloved Sophie . . . He couldn't bear to watch the NTC soldier carry her body up the ramp into the *Sunspot*. His only hope rested with the cryo chambers.

Moving aside, Emanuel watched the other men scoop up Jamie and Owen. Their arms hung loosely over armored shoulders, their eyes detached, staring at nothing. Sucking in a long, measured breath he closed his eyes and then followed the group into the belly of the spaceship.

———

The mission clock on Captain Noble's HUD read 1705.

Almost there, he thought.

He paced nervously behind Kirt's monitor, his gaze shifting from the display to the hangar doors every few seconds. He still hadn't heard back from Diego. The man had come tearing across the tarmac, screaming about Spiders that had attacked the Biosphere team. He'd deployed all but three of his men to help.

The wait for their return was eating him alive. He turned back to the monitors, anticipation building in his gut as he watched Howard's and Riordan's jets inch across the display. Marked Red 9 and Green 6, the two X-90s were now a finger's length away from their target.

Thanks to Lolo, they had secured an encrypted feed with both pilots. The video streaming from the cockpits fed straight to Noble's command center at Offutt. He saw what they saw. It was like being behind the wheel, without having to drive.

A coward's game, he thought, wishing again he could be there himself.

Crackling white noise filled his earpiece. He flinched, waiting for the transmission. He hoped desperately for good news, but a long wave of static washed over the channel.

He didn't have time for this. He reached up and tapped his helmet with an armored finger, as if it would help the weak com feed.

"Captain, this is Diego. Do you copy?" Diego repeated the message, his voice shaky and unsure.

"Yes. Yes. I'm here," Noble replied. "Give me a full report."

"Sir, there have been casualties. Doctor Sophie Winston appears to be . . ." he paused. "She appears to be dead, sir. The children are all severely injured. Doctor Rodriguez thinks they might be able to save them if we put them in the cryo chambers to preserve their bodies until they can find proper medical care."

"My god," Noble said, choking on his words.

"It's bad, sir. And that's not all. Doctor Brown and Corporal Bouma were injured. They should both live, but the other marine, Kiel, was killed inside the *Sunspot*. They woke up a fucking nest of aliens."

Noble hammered his fist down, stopping just short of the table. He should have used the rover to scan the *Sunspot*, but after discovering the drones he'd simply left to plan the rest of the mission.

Once again he'd failed, and lives, precious lives, had been lost due to his negligence.

"Sir, they're almost to Mount McKinley," Kirt said.

Noble shook his thoughts away. He needed to focus. He couldn't lose it now, not when Howard and Riordan were so close to their target.

"Diego, do what you can for the team. Have your men help them prepare the ship for launch and then get back here."

"Roger."

Noble filled his lungs with a deep breath, relieving some of the built-up anxiety. A bead of sweat trickled down his nose and landed on the stubble growing where his mustache had filled his face weeks earlier. He wanted desperately to run his finger across his face. It had always calmed him. Instead he moved to the seat next to Kirt. Crossing his arms, Noble said, "Get me the feed inside Red 9."

Kirt reached to his left and swiped the screen. The monitor flickered and the view from Howard's cockpit emerged. Clocking 2,200 miles per hour, the jet screamed through the air. The skyline was a blur of orange light. A black speck glimmered on the horizon.

"That's Riordan," Kirt said, pointing at the dot.

Noble nodded. "How are our drones doing?" He turned to Andy, who sat a few feet away, his eyes plastered to a set of dual monitors.

"They're flying on autopilot, for now," Andy replied.

"Once they reach their targets, we'll switch them back to manual. That's where I come in," Kirt said.

Data scrolling across the bottom of Howard's monitor showed the pilot's X-90 was at terminal velocity.

"Be advised, target incoming," Riordan said.

Kirt keyed a series of codes into the holo interface and said, "Advise reducing speed in T minus thirty seconds."

The red and green dots on the radar screen blinked as Howard and Riordan acknowledged the request. In the bottom right corner of the display, Noble saw their speeds slowly reducing.

As Howard's jet descended, the feed cleared. For the first time during the flight, Noble could see the landscape below.

Closing his eyes he pictured the great Alaskan frontier before the Organics had invaded: thousands of square miles of grass, crystal-clear streams snaking through the fields, herds of wildlife grazing freely, and snow-tipped mountain peaks.

All reduced to ash.

When his eyes snapped open he saw the grave truth. The gray mountains were approaching fast, their jagged peaks devoid of snow, their ridgelines filled with petrified trees. A wildfire burned a section of forest for hundreds of square miles in the distance, filling the horizon with dark smoke.

"Check your weapons systems; prepare to attack," Noble said.

"Roger that, Offutt. Preparing weapons systems," Riordan replied. Howard responded with an "Aye aye," his Red 9 dot blinking green.

"Surge countdown is T minus forty-three minutes," Kirt said, looking up at Noble.

"Howard, Riordan. You have forty-three minutes to take this son of a bitch down," Noble said. He grunted when he saw the majestic peak of Mount McKinley rising out of the black smoke cloud. "They're going to have to fly through that?"

A short nod from Kirt confirmed the captain's fear.

Static flickered over the com. "Offutt, are you seeing this? Please advise, over."

"We're seeing it," Kirt replied. "Proceed through the smoke. Target is just on the other side, over."

Noble watched the dots streaking across the radar. Red 9 blinked first, but Green 6 hesitated before acknowledging. He moved back to Howard's display. Flares of exhaust trailed Riordan's jet as it streaked toward the cloud. And then it was gone, swallowed by the smoke.

The radio crackled a moment later.

Riordan's voice sounded distressed. "Captain, we're picking up a strong magnetic disturbance. Please advise, over."

Kirt glanced up at Noble, his forehead lined with wrinkles.

"Tell them to hold course for now," Noble replied.

"Aye aye," Kirt replied with a short hesitation.

Noble checked the radar. Both dots looked like they were on top of Mount McKinley. That couldn't be right, could it?

Holding his breath, he counted down the seconds. Just as he reached seven, Howard's X-90 exploded out of the smoke. A chorus of warning sensors chirped over the channel. Emergency lights flickered across the dashboard.

"Be advised, impact imminent," came an automated voice inside the cockpit. "Take immediate evasive measures."

Before Noble had a chance to respond, he saw it.

Mount McKinley towered above both jets. They were coming in too fast. Seven hundred fifty miles per hour too fast. He didn't need Kirt to tell him what had happened. The magnetic disturbance had disrupted their navigation equipment and the smoke had rendered them blind.

Screaming, Riordan yanked hard on the control stick. The jet pitched upward, and rays of sunlight washed over the cockpit.

Intense light filled the display, forcing Noble to look away. He waited for an explosion as Riordan's and Howard's jets smashed into the gray mountain.

But the sound never came. When he turned back to the monitor he saw clear skies and the black dot of Riordan's X-90.

Relief washed over Noble.

"Circling," Howard said. His voice faded as an explosion rang out. "What the fuck was that?" the pilot said. He twisted in his seat, his camera showing two of the drones trailing him. The other had smashed into the side of Mount McKinley, flames licking the sky where the craft had blown to bits.

"We lost Drone 3," Kirt said, pointing to the radar.

Noble grunted. "I can see that." He shifted his gaze from the radar to the feed from Howard's X-90.

"My god," the pilot suddenly said.

Noble instantly saw why.

The alien tower Lolo had discovered rose out of the south side of the mountain into the sky. The metallic sides pulsated, a blue light moving up and down the shaft in intermittent bursts.

"That's it," Noble said, locking eyes with Kirt. "Take that fucking thing down."

"Engaging," the pilot said. He swiped the screen, deactivating the autopilot on the two remaining drones. Andy sat up straighter and grabbed the joystick as his drone came online.

"Riordan, Howard. Protect the drones," Noble said.

"No sign of contacts," Howard replied.

A lump formed in the captain's throat. He'd expected resistance. Major resistance. But the skies appeared clear, the pole seemingly unprotected.

He focused on the strange Organic architecture. It throbbed with life. The pulsing of the alien light gave the impression of breathing.

As Howard maneuvered around the tower the light suddenly changed rhythm. The entire pole became solid blue. Seconds later it changed again. This time hundreds of miniature lights flickered. And one by one they pulled away from the construct. Countless cylinder-shaped objects peeled off the tower.

Noble's stomach sank when he realized what they were. Shocked into motion he stood and leaned over Kirt. "Hurry—use the RVAMP while we still can."

Kirt navigated through the minefield of alien drones. The sky was filled with them, like blue fireflies they were everywhere.

"There's too *many!*" Andy yelled. Noble saw the feed from his drone flicker and fade as it detonated into a thousand pieces.

"Fuck," he said, cupping his head in his hands.

Noble moved back to Kirt's monitor. The expert pilot zigzagged around the alien ships. With a quick jerk to the right he pulled them away from the mountain. Then with another swift movement he changed course, this time straight up toward the sun.

"Firing," Howard said.

The captain's eyes darted back to the X-90 feed as a volley of rockets launched at the sky that was now choking with tiny blue dots. Explosions burst across the display, several of the missiles sending the aliens into fiery poofs. But there were so many.

"Bogies on my tail," Riordan said.

Howard cried out over the channel. "They're everywhere!"

"Keep them off Kirt's drone," Noble replied. "He has to get closer."

Both of the pilots acknowledged, their dots blinking green on the radar. When Noble looked back at Howard's video, he saw impossible odds.

The same odds humanity had faced all along.

For a moment Noble couldn't move; he couldn't even speak. He watched a wall of alien drones moving along a collision course with the X-90. They would do anything to stop the pilots from taking out their life source, even if it meant sacrificing themselves in the process.

Howard screamed and jerked his plane to the right, but it was too late. Fire filled the display as the X-90 exploded in a cloud of debris.

The monitor panned to Riordan's feed just as his jet exploded as well.

Anger pulled Noble from his trance. "Use the fucking RVAMP, Kirt. Now!"

The pilot shot him a glance, his brown eyes pleading behind his visor. "But we aren't close enough."

"You have to do it now! While we still can."

Kirt nodded and tugged the control stick to the left, angling the drone back toward the mountain. The tower, now just a speck on the mountain, blinked as if it was tempting them.

"Just a little closer," he muttered.

Kirt's fingers hovered over the RVAMP button. Hovered too long. And in a fit of rage, the captain leaned forward and reached for it himself. He punched the button and waited for the invisible electromagnetic magic to work.

Kirt, gasping in surprise, turned back to his interface and keyed in several commands.

"The drone's gone, sir," the pilot choked.

"Did it work?" Noble glanced down at him with bated breath.

The pilot shoved the monitor away, sending the display crashing to the floor.

Noble felt his heart sink. He knew, like Kirt, that Operation Redemption had failed.

The planet . . .

Lost.

CHAPTER 27

Emanuel removed his glasses and, using his shirt, cleaned the smears of blood off the lenses. When he put them back on, Sonya's hologram had emerged above the AI interface. The bridge, crowded with NTC soldiers, reminded him of a beehive. The armored men moved from station to station, activating the life support systems.

Within minutes the room flared to life, holo displays spreading their warm light over the cold metal floor. Diego's team had already removed Kiel's body, and those of the ship's previous crew—what was left of them. The smell of rotting flesh, however, still lingered.

"Doctor Rodriguez, all systems are now online," Sonya said.

"How are the children?" he asked. "How is—"

"Their vitals are all unchanged," Sonya replied. "Doctor Winston has entered a completely frozen state. Her body is technically alive, but her brain activity is minimal."

The words hit Emanuel like a belt to the face. He flinched and closed his eyes. Deep down he knew before Sonya answered that Sophie was beyond saving. That she had died in his arms. But science and technology gave him hope, as it always did. He still held on to that hope. Without it, he had nothing.

He felt a hand on his shoulder and turned to see Diego standing next to him. Emanuel caught his gaze, finding strength there. "I'm sorry, Doctor. I really am."

Emanuel nodded.

"Listen, I don't mean to detract from your loss, but there's something I think you should see."

Taking a deep breath, Emanuel attempted to pull himself together.

"Follow me," Diego said.

The soldier led him away from the bridge and through a passage that connected to Biome 1. At the end of the hall, two of his men held black garbage bags.

"What's left of the crew," Diego said, gesturing toward the gore-soaked walls.

A partially raised metal blast door covered the glass entrance to Biome 1. Holding his nose, Emanuel looked over at the lieutenant, not quite understanding why he'd brought him here. He ducked under the door.

The chamber looked different from the one at Cheyenne Mountain. Instead of the curved ceiling that defined their old Biome, this one was low. A bank of glowing lights extended from the panels illuminating the room. The dirt looked unscathed. The space completely undisturbed.

It was then that he understood.

Diego smiled when Emanuel nodded.

"These brave men and women made their last stand in this hallway to prevent the aliens from getting inside," Diego said. "They sealed off the rest of the *Sunspot* to protect the water supply and the other Biomes."

Emanuel didn't know how to respond.

Diego put a hand on Emanuel's shoulder. "They saved the *Sunspot* so that someone else could take it to the stars."

Emanuel managed to move his lips, but the words wouldn't come out.

"Hold on," Diego said. "I'm getting a transmission from Captain Noble now."

Emanuel turned back to the Biome, scanning the perfectly level dirt and clean white walls. Despite everything that had happened, he couldn't deny the hint of hope growing inside him. The hope that maybe they could still get to Mars and save Sophie.

"Captain Noble's on his way here," Diego said. "He wants to see you before you take off."

"Me?" Emanuel asked, finally finding his voice again.

"You're in charge now, aren't you?"

With a nod, Emanuel said, "I suppose I am."

Captain Noble stepped into the fleeting sunlight and looked up at the sky. Mars was out there, somewhere, and so was Dr. Hoffman's magical colony.

Crossing the tarmac with Kirt and Andy on his heels, Noble thought of the old scientist. The mile-long walk to the hangar provided him with ample time to consider everything that had happened. It dawned on him that Hoffman had known all along that the aliens couldn't be defeated. He had been right after all. It was Noble who was wrong. From the beginning, the bastard had realized that no amount of human military muscle could keep the Organics from what they desired—the most important resource of all.

The Biospheres and the colony on Mars were the only options left for the human race. And it finally all made sense. Why jump ship from a dying planet to an already dead one?

The answer had never been so clear.

Mars was free of the monsters. And with the terraformers and NTC technology, the Red Planet would soon be habitable for humanity.

There were still the Biospheres, though. Why had Hoffman even bothered with them?

Perhaps it was a fail-safe, one of many in the old bastard's delusional plan to save humankind. Maybe he thought they could survive the invasion and, if the colony failed, the species could find a way to survive.

Noble shook his head. He could talk himself in circles trying to figure out the scientist's master plan, but what did it matter? Redemption had failed. He had failed.

There was only one thing left to do: make sure Dr. Rodriguez and his remaining teammates made it into space.

As he walked he thought of his own crew back on the GOA. Surely they knew the mission's fate by now. They had access to Lolo and would have tracked the battle from beneath the surface.

"Sir, with all due respect, what are we going to do now?" Andy asked as they crossed the concrete.

Noble felt his heart sink. He had known the question would come, and that he would have to answer his men. They were out of options. They could always take the *Sea Serpent* back to the GOA and try to survive until the Organics drained the oceans.

But that seemed like too much of a risk. The gunship was already in rough condition, and he doubted it could make the journey back to the GOA. For the first time in months he had no plan.

"I'm not sure—" Noble began to say as a supersonic boom thundered overhead. The sound sent a shockwave barreling down on the base. Noble cupped his ears.

The alien cavalry had arrived.

He looked up at the skyline, expecting to see a drone racing toward them. Instead, the outline of one of their black mother ships descended over the south part of Offutt.

"Run!" he yelled.

Dust swirled around the three men as they raced across the tarmac. Noble risked a glance over his shoulder and saw the oval craft hovering over the ruined structures at the opposite end of the base. It moved slowly, scanning for life.

Hunting.

"We have to launch the *Sunspot*!" Noble shouted. He bumped his com to open the channel to his men.

"Diego, do you copy?"

"What the fuck was that?"

"Get those doors open. You need to launch the *Sunspot. ASAP!*"

"On it!"

Kirt ran past Noble at a dead sprint for the hangar. They were close, maybe two hundred yards away now. One of the soldiers peeked through the open door and waved the men forward.

The ground rumbled and Noble pushed harder, running as fast as he could.

Bursting through the door, he slid to a halt. His team surrounded him, their anxious looks pleading for information.

"Redemption was a failure," he said, shaking his head. "I don't have time to explain, we need to get Doctor Rodriguez and his team in the air. If any of you want to go with them, you have my blessing, but you have only seconds to decide."

He scanned each man's dusty visor. They all stood quietly. Not a single soldier moved.

"Then let's buy them some time!" Noble shouted. "Grab your weapons and let's show these motherfuckers there are still some humans left to fight."

Cheers roared behind him. He turned to move back outside when he felt a hand on his shoulder. "Captain," Emanuel said. "Thank you for everything."

Noble smiled and said, "Go. And good luck!" Then he followed his men out onto the concrete.

"Diego, get your ass over here," he shouted as he ran.

"Here, sir."

Watching his men fan out and form a perimeter around the hangar, Noble said, "Find Ort. I want you two to go with Doctor Rodriguez."

"But sir," the man began to protest.

Noble craned his helmet and found the terrified man's gaze. "They're going to need your help. And Ort's, too. Do this. For me," Noble pleaded.

The hum from the alien ship's engines forced Noble to look away. The vessel hovered over the hangar where he'd set up the forward operating base.

"Go," Noble shouted. He turned and ran, listening for Diego's footsteps. They came seconds later. Satisfied, Noble took up a position behind Ramirez.

"Give me your electromagnetic grenades," he ordered.

The soldier plucked two from his belt and handed them to Noble. Chinning his com he said, "When that thing gets close enough, use your grenades. We'll bring down the shields and then concentrate all our fire on the underbelly." Noble remembered Colorado Springs, when the *Sea Serpent* had torn a hole in the other ship.

Behind them, the *Sunspot's* engines roared to life. Noble knew this was it. No more time for memories or for revenge. Only one thing left to do: clear a path for the Biosphere team.

Pressing the buttons on both grenades, he coiled his arm and launched them toward the ship. They detonated in midair, sending the alien shield pulsing. A half dozen more of the devices sailed through the dust, bursting into blue ripples along the ship's surface.

When a tremor shook the shield, Noble yelled, "Open fire."

Pulse rounds streaked into the sky, finding their targets and exploding across the sleek black surface. Noble grunted, the detonations filling him with satisfaction.

His earpiece suddenly came to life and the sound of Diego's voice emerged over the channel.

"Captain, the Organics are blocking our exit."

"Not for long," Noble replied. He aimed his rifle at the ship's undercarriage and concentrated his fire. The other soldiers mimicked his action. Fire burst through the hull, ballooning around the ship. It jerked and pulled away from the tarmac.

"Now's your chance," Noble said. "Get out of here!"

"It's been an honor, sir," Diego replied.

The captain and the other men moved aside as the *Sunspot* maneuvered out of the hangar and pulled onto the tarmac. With a lurch, the ship jolted forward and took off screaming. A cloud of exhaust trailed the spaceship, the heat scalding Noble's armor. He watched the last hope for humanity tear into the sky.

And then it was gone, nothing but a speck on the horizon.

Noble took a deep breath and looked for the alien ship. With fire bursting from its underbelly, it didn't engage in a chase. Instead it hovered beside the runway, as if the alien pilots were trying to decide what to do next.

The hum emanating from the ship grew louder and its muffled explosions grew closer. Noble crouched on the pavement and waited for what came next.

The captain had accepted his fate. In the end, he'd failed Earth, but their sacrifice would allow the survivors of Cheyenne Mountain to reach Dr. Hoffman's colony. He could only hope there actually was a colony to reach.

A powerful electric current surrounded him. Paralyzed, he listened to the buzzing of the advanced alien engines.

His men's muffled, panic-streaked voices filled his earpiece. Their shouts of terror grew louder as the current pulled them toward the ship. The blinding blue light burned his retinas. He and the others were being pulled into a halo of blue surrounding a circular door. He kicked in protest, earning himself a painful jolt from an electric current. Defeated, Noble embraced the tractor beam and let it take him.

———

Emanuel ignored the lingering smell of death in the hallway leading from the bridge to Biome 1. He already knew that on the other side of the glass separating him from the garden he'd find the same clean, artificial environment they'd first experienced at Cheyenne Mountain.

When the glass panels hissed open, the crisp air filled his lungs. For a moment he forgot where he was headed.

A sudden tremor shook the floor below him and the whine of equipment under the metal platform kicked on. Startled, he reminded himself that all systems were functioning at 100 percent. Sonya had reassured him of this before he'd left the bridge, shortly after she'd activated the autopilot system and coded in the coordinates to Dr. Hoffman's colony on Mars.

The platform shook again.

Somewhere, deep in the hull of the *Sunspot*, the artificial gravity generator rumbled. His sour stomach felt better already.

He didn't linger to enjoy the moment. He waited impatiently for the AI to open the next set of doors. Cocking his head, he looked at the camera and said, "Sonya, will you open these, please?"

The glass parted and he moved into the next corridor. As with the Biosphere at Cheyenne Mountain, the biomes were all connected by a single set of passages. In a sense, they reminded Emanuel of arteries connecting to a central heart, in this case, the mess hall.

Navigating his way quickly through the other hallways, he finally came to the last door. A sign hung above the window.

Sunspot: Medical Ward.

He stood there, staring through the glass, scanning the row of cryo chambers on the far end of the room. Exhaling his anxiety, he entered, closing the door behind him, careful not to wake Bouma or Holly, who slept quietly in beds on the right side of the room. Their bio-monitors chirped, illuminating their bodies with a faint green glow. Emanuel checked their vitals. Both were stable. Satisfied, he walked to the cryo chambers.

He rubbed the glass surface of the first tube. Inside, he saw David's body was curled up in the fetal position. A quick glance at the other chambers revealed the same thing. The kids all rested peacefully, so it appeared, in cryo sleep.

Leaning closer, he checked the wall of monitors above the row of tubes. All systems looked normal. He walked to the final active cryo cylinder.

Biting his inner lip, he reached out and cleaned the glass surface.

His heart jumped when he saw her eyes, the pupils still angled in different directions. Emanuel rested his head against the glass of Sophie's coffin. He wanted so desperately to hold her again.

Lifting his head off the metallic surface, he saw his own reflection for the first time in days. His black beard hid his emaciated cheeks and his sunken dimples. He looked past the reflection and reached forward to check Sophie's biomonitor.

Her brain activity was weak, hardly existent, but there was something still there—something still working inside her brain. He kissed the glass lid and backed away from the chamber. "You're going to Mars, Sophie. You're finally going to Mars."

Captain Noble awoke to blue light. His first attempt to move earned him the same jolt of electricity he'd felt just before being pulled into the alien ship. The pain felt distant, and so did his body.

He blinked his eyes, the one movement he still had control of. His blurred vision revealed nothing but the same blue glow. Beyond that he couldn't see anything.

Over and over he blinked, his vision slowly clearing each time. He waited, patiently.

And then he saw his prison.

A translucent skin surrounded him on all sides. He glanced down, finding his naked body suspended in some sort of liquid.

Terror gripped him.

An orb.

He was inside a fucking orb.

His body was shot with another surge of electricity as he struggled to move. Beyond his cage he could see thousands of the blue floating balls all throughout the ship. They sparkled, the jail cells encasing the poor souls of countless other victims.

He was in some sort of warehouse, filled to the brim with the blue balls.

He vaguely recalled the black ship Dr. Winston had claimed she'd boarded back at Colorado Springs. She'd described it as a modern-day alien Noah's ark, built to entomb the races of other species the Organics had destroyed throughout the universe.

If she was right, then Noble was one of them.

Fueled with rage, he finally managed to tilt his head to the side. Through the skin of the orb he saw Kirt. The young man stared back at him from his own prison, his eyes wide with fear. And then, by some miracle, the man reached forward, his hand pressing against the translucent wall of his coffin. His lips moved, but Noble couldn't hear the young pilot's screams.

Misery.

A human term, and a feeling that I have experienced in the past twenty-four hours. I take no pleasure in writing this entry. I find no joy in being right about the end of the human species on Earth.

With Operation Redemption a failure, the last of the survivors will likely perish in the coming weeks. Even those who have somehow managed to hide beneath the surface will die from the extreme heat and lack of water. My sensors indicate the average temperature has risen to 105 degrees Fahrenheit, with the highest temperature documented by Lolo at 125 degrees Fahrenheit. The satellite scans reveal the ocean levels are currently at 53 percent of what they were preinvasion. With forests around the world dying or already dead the oxygen levels, too, are diminishing.

Soon the only life left on the planet will be the Organics.

But there may still be hope for the human race in the most unlikely of places. Another dead planet, Mars, may hold the key to their survival. Many would question why the human race would leave Earth for an environment even more desolate.

I have known all along. The secret, hidden inside my hard drive, was never meant for the Biosphere team to know. However, with the Biosphere mission a failure, I find this is the perfect time to reveal that secret.

Dr. Hoffman's vision for Mars was never just to build a colony. It was to build a second Earth. NTC developed and installed terraformers there secretly in 2059. Without data to support my claim I can only conclude that after two years the devices are already producing a semi-atmosphere. By the time the *Sunspot* reaches the colony the planet will already be yielding a hospitable environment.

That's not all. The most striking fact is the significance of the planet in the Organics' history. Dr. Winston believed the Red Planet was their home, that they had left it after consuming their most important resource—water.

Dr. Hoffman knew this long ago. He gambled on the idea that they would never return. That humanity would be safe there. That Mars could become the new home of the human race.

Only time will tell whether he was right.

A sensor alerts me to an incoming transmission from Lolo's communication channel. The *Sunspot* is attempting contact.

When I open the feed I'm surprised to see Dr. Rodriguez. He's flanked by two men I don't recognize, both of them wearing armored NTC suits.

"Good morning, Alexia," he says.

"And to you, Doctor," I reply.

"As you probably already know, Operation Redemption failed."

"Yes," I say.

"Then you probably also know that most of the team was severely injured and that Kiel was killed."

"Their sacrifices will never be forgotten," I finally say. Empathy is not one of my strong suits, and I find myself struggling to find a better, more human response.

Emanuel nods and wipes something from his eye. Then he glances up and in a confident voice says, "We're on our way to Mars, Alexia. Before we lose radio contact, there's something I want you to do." He pauses. "There's something I *need* you to do."

I wait patiently for him to continue.

"Do what we couldn't. What our species couldn't."

Again I wait.

"Survive, Alexia. For the sake of history. The great cities of man won't last long. They will crumble into dust, into ash, like the rest of the world. But you," he shakes his finger at the camera, "you can outlast the Organics. Your hard drive is the most in-depth history book the human race has left behind. All of our discoveries are inside *you*."

Dr. Rodriguez understands why I wanted to stay behind. I remember what Irene said to me days earlier: The future of the human race rests on Mars.

She was right.

Humanity's time on Earth has come to an end.

"Doctor," I say with a pause as I consider my words. "Take care of the others. Save the human race. Good luck and Godspeed."

He nods, and as his face fades from view, I see a hint of raw human emotion.

Fear.

End Entry.

THE END

ABOUT THE AUTHOR

NICHOLAS SANSBURY SMITH is the bestselling author of the Orbs and Extinction Cycle series. He worked for Iowa Homeland Security and Emergency Management in disaster mitigation before switching careers to focus on his one true passion—writing. Smith is a three-time Kindle All-Star, and several of his titles have reached the top 50 on the overall Kindle bestseller list and as high as #1 in the Audible store. *Hell Divers*, the first book in his new trilogy, will release in July 2016. When he isn't writing or daydreaming about the apocalypse, he's training for triathlons or traveling the world. He lives in Des Moines, Iowa, with his dog and a house full of books.

Discover the bestselling ORBS series

ORBS

NICHOLAS SANSBURY SMITH

ORBS STRANDED

NICHOLAS SANSBURY SMITH

ORBS REDEMPTION

NICHOLAS SANSBURY SMITH

NOW AVAILABLE IN TRADE PAPERBACK